Burning Karma

Davíð Rafn Kristjánsson

WILD PRESSED BOOKS

Published by Wild Pressed Books: March 2016

First Edition

This is a work of fiction. Names, characters and incidents are the product of the author's imagination. Any resemblance to actual events or persons, living or dead, is entirely coincidental. The publisher has no control over, and is not responsible for, any third party websites or their contents.

Contact the author through their website:

http://burningkarma.net/

Chief Editor: Tracey Scott-Townsend

Cover design by: Jane Dixon-Smith

Paperback ISBN: 978-0-9933740-0-5

eBook ISBN: 978-0-9933740-1-2

Print edition

Printed in the United Kingdom

Wild Pressed Books Ltd, UK

Company registration number 09550738

http://www.wildpressedbooks.com

Dedication

I dedicate this book to anyone who has suffered abuse of any kind.

Acknowledgements

Countless people have influenced this book in various different countries such as China, Thailand, Cambodia, USA, England, Iceland and more. It's impossible to name all the great people I've met in my life that influenced and helped this story come alive, it would take an extra book to cover all that but I want to name a few.

First and foremost I'd like to thank my darling Dagný for all the help, patience and encouragement. I love you.

Also I'd like to express my gratitude to my best friend, my dad and his wife Erna for their love and support.

My three spiritual teachers for helping me and opening my mind and heart. Greetings to Baba Dai in India. Jai Ma! Vimala (Chris) in Myanmar. My dear Kalyan Mitra, teacher and a friend. Thank you for everything and always beware of the goat! And to my first spiritual teacher in the USA "Om Namah Shivaya". You know who you are. I'm so blessed to have met you all!

I began to write this story in Beijing when I was surrounded by people who believed in me (when I didn't) and encouraged me day in and day out to experiment with things and work on my creativity. The Beijing crew like Ana Sofie, Theresa, Walter, Tim, Rich, Diana, Rob, Eric, Svenni, Charlie and Flo, Will and Anita, Norma Bisbal and all the others I'm forgetting to mention. Thank you for the support and showing me that there's another way!

Guillaume Ravineau and Sylvain Montagnon. I'll never forgot you two and the magic of couch surfing!

The story continued to evolve in Cambodia and all my friends over there influenced and helped me in various ways; Steinunn, Emil, the Aussie Gang, the Golden Gekko Gang, Milan, Nik, Guilia, Qing, and many more. Thanks! Special thanks to Romi Grossberg for helping me out with the book and teaching me the epic mantra "I just can't be bothered".

My dear Sangha in India. Sati, Prasad and Renuka. Thanks for the whole ashram experience. Jai Ma!

All my dear friends and family in Iceland. You know who you are. Special thanks to Maggi, Svenni and Reynar Kári for always believing in this book.

Urður Gunnarsdottir, for all the support and the Sunday brunches.

Tracey and Phil at Wild Pressed Books for an incredible

support and always being open to listen to my crazy talk and willingness to move this book forward.

All the people in 12 step programs in various countries.

Hilmar for showing me what's important in life. RIP

BURNING KARMA

Kafli 1 - Kunming, China, 2011.

The Hospital

MY MOUTH TASTED like a dirty pavement, my head pounded as if demolition was happening inside it and my body ached all over. What the hell had happened to me? More to the point, I didn't even know where I was.

I called out, managing to mumble something in Chinese. At least I was able to remember that I was in China. With the tread of quiet shoes a nurse appeared, looming over me.

Oh, so I am in hospital.

"How do you feel?"

"I'm good" I mumbled haltingly. But my face must have been telling a different story.

As I scratched my head I felt the rough surface of a bandage under my fingertips. I also noticed some bruises on my hip. I saw that my foot was hanging out of the bed, too. What clothes

I was wearing were filthy: thin black socks, underwear and a ripped stained t-shirt that used to be white.

A thorny, dry throat made it hard to swallow.

"Please," I said to the nurse. "Can I have some water?"

"Give me a minute."

Why the fuck is she laughing? Wasn't that against some kind of nurse-patient agreement? *How dare she laugh at me?*

I tried desperately to remember what had happened, why I was at the hospital, but I couldn't and my head hurt even more by trying.

"Where is my wallet?"

"You didn't have any wallet yesterday," the nurse replied. She was still laughing, her face contorted with it. Or was it my fucked-up brain making me think that?

I watched the nurse tidying an empty bed while I tried to recall the previous night.

Absolute blank.

Damn, I needed to get out of this place, whatever hospital I was in.

She must have sensed my restlessness because the nurse paused in her duties and came over to me again. She asked if I needed more water. I nodded, watching her closely, hoping she wouldn't laugh anymore.

As she left I looked around the room, afraid that people might hear my thoughts, they were so noisy.

Three beds in the room. On my left side an empty bed, the one just made up by the nurse. On my right was an occupied one. I couldn't see the other patient's face because it was hidden behind the curtain between us. I only saw feet. It looked like a woman's feet; they were small. They were also dirty and yellowish. No movement. I wondered if she was already dead. The thinking made my head spin, so I tried to stop but that was impossible.

Where's my phone? I have to get out of this place. What time is it? But I didn't really want to know what time it was. I just wanted to sleep and wake up somewhere else where my life was a bit more manageable. I wished I had my cell phone so I could call someone to pick me up. My flatmate would do. Anyone.

I tilted my head back, closed my eyes for a rest.

Kafli 2 - Iceland, 1993.

House in the country

THERE WAS A clear river not far from my grandmother's house. It was peaceful standing alone on the riverbank seeing the water flow endlessly with the mountains in the background. The river seemed so big in the eyes of a seven-year-old boy.

Alongside the riverbank in the valley you could see four houses. These houses belonged to my grandmother and one of them was her home. Next to it was a garage, which looked like it was under construction but it had been the same for many years. A big half-painted barn was a bit further away and a small house stood next to it, used for hay storage and machines.

When I looked at this scene I only saw the garage, everything else was a blur. I was terrified of this garage but at the same time I was curious to know what was inside it. There was a family joke I heard often and didn't understand until later in life. It was that if they would ever clean out the stuff in my grandmother's garage they would probably find the bodies from the Geirfinnur case.

I used to tease my grandmother that I was going to peek inside the garage, but in reality I was too scared. I was also afraid of Grandma's husband. His name was Reynir. He was a big man who didn't like to talk and he rarely said a word to Grandma except when he was asking her to do things. Sometimes he talked to my brother and me in the evenings though, while drinking from the bottle he hid behind the couch. He also talked to us when he wanted us to do some work at the farm; picking up eggs or cleaning the floor in the barn. Reynir trusted my brother to do more than me, he was even allowed to milk the cows. I was too young.

My brother, Palli was fourteen at that time. He was my hero, the one I looked to for comfort when things got scary. His face, just turning into that of a young man, was my safety haven and I put all my trust in him. He was tall for his age and slim, but I knew he was strong because we wrestled in Grandma's garden for hours. My brother was my only friend at the farm. He took care of me and was good to me except when he was in a bad mood. Then he would order me to leave him alone.

I was often scared at nights. I cried in my brother's room when I heard Reynir and Grandma fighting. During those incidents Palli calmed me down. He allowed me to crawl into bed with him. Then I felt safe and knew that if I stuck with him everything would be all right.

We had stayed at my grandmother's farm for almost three months. Seven or eight times I heard bottles being broken, heavy things thrown at the walls and my grandmother screaming out for help, and all the while we brothers hid behind a closed door, feeling powerless and wretched.

But even during the scary times at the farm I knew they would pass and things would go back to normal. They always did. It was like living in two worlds. One world was scary, dark, filled with tears and wishing Grandma would stop screaming. In the other world it was bright. We had breakfast while listening to the news on the radio, all laughing and chatting before it was time to milk the cows, although a couple of times I noticed my grandmother wearing sunglasses inside and I sensed something was wrong, but was too afraid to ask. It was just easier to forget and get back to work, or even better, play by the river. The river was the place where problems didn't exist. It was like a third dimension, where everything was peaceful. Entering that world made the other worlds fade away.

It was the last day on the farm and my mother was coming

to pick us up. I was looking through the kitchen window when I heard a car. It sounded distinctive like our old family car, a yellow Lada Sport; there were not many of those around. I jumped out of the chair, got my boots on and ran outside. My brother was working down at the barn and I felt bad for him to miss out on this moment of seeing our mom, but I had to be there.

Mom parked the car and stepped outside. The wind blew her blonde hair up in the air, slightly obscuring what I knew as her beautiful face. She stood for a moment, shielding the wind from her eyes. Mom was still wearing her work fleece jacket, blue jeans and worn-out brown leather boots that my dad gave her years ago.

"Mom!" I was smiling, waving my hands in the air.

"Hi, Böddi," She gave me a small grin, coming towards me purposefully.

But my world collapsed as she walked by, offering me only a small pat on the head. After all this time without seeing her.

The feeling of emptiness in my chest grew bigger. She went to talk to Grandma in the kitchen while I waited outside. I sat down on a small chair next to the door, feeling like one of the pieces of wood stacked up in front of me. The ones not good enough to build with. Footsteps stomped out of the house after only a short time inside.

"Böddi, go get your brother, we are leaving," Mom ordered me in a tone I knew all too well.

She's angry again.

"Okay, Mom." I tried to express my disappointment without showing her the true depths of what I was feeling because that would only make her more mad and guilty.

I ran to the barn where Palli and Reynir were fixing some machinery and told my brother that Mom had arrived. As we walked back towards Grandma's house he put his arm around me and whispered in my ear.

"Böddi, we have to stick together, always."

"Yes, of course."

I didn't want to ask what he meant by this, it sounded worrying.

I wondered how he knew Mom was angry without having seen her.

I hate being kept out of things.

When we came to the house, Mom and Grandma were fighting loudly outside.

"Get in the car, boys." Mom pushed hair off her face. She looked even more upset than when I left her.

I couldn't understand why or what they were fighting about, but I got the feeling they were arguing over me and my brother. That we were a burden nobody wanted to bear, being tossed between the city and the countryside. I wondered where

Dad was and if he would be at home. Most of all I wished Palli and I could just take care of ourselves.

Mom was quiet now and busy lighting a cigarette. She started the car, pulling smoke into her lungs. As she drove away from my grandmother's house I plucked up the courage to ask her,

"Mom, why doesn't Grandma let me see inside the garage?"

There was a long pause. She took a shuddering breath before answering.

"Because it's where your grandfather died."

There was silence in the car. My brother looked at me protectively. Later I found out that my grandfather had taken his own life in the garage. Drunk.

Kafli 3 - Kunming, 2011.

Painkillers

IT WAS ALMOST two o'clock and the sun was shining through the window. The best thing about living in Kunming was the weather, it was almost always warm. For that reason the Chinese call Kunming 'The Spring City'.

But today the sunlight only increased my headache. I called for the nurse to get me some painkillers. I was proud that I knew how to say painkillers in Chinese after only four months in China, but then again I took countless painkillers for my regular hangovers. When I was hungover I drank a big glass of water, took some vitamin C and ate painkillers. Most of the time I forgot the vitamin C.

The nurse gave me some painkillers. This time she wasn't laughing, and perversely that pissed me off, she could at least try to cheer me up. Everything about that nurse irritated me.

Questions about her swarmed my brain.

Why isn't she fit like ninety-nine per cent of other Chinese girls?

Do they teach laughing at other people's misery in Chinese medical schools?

Has she ever been to a dentist?

The nurse grunted and left the room, probably sensing my hostility.

I had a horrendous anxious feeling and an urgent compulsion to get out of bed. I wanted to see if I could walk, maybe I could just walk right out of the hospital. But as I tried to sit up, slowly, dizziness overwhelmed me. I was about to vomit.

Fuck.

I closed my eyes, took a deep breath.

When I could open them again I moved my head so I could see the 'dead woman' on the next bed. She was in the exact same position as before. Her immobile feet were a chilling sight so I pulled my gaze away.

There was a drawer next to my bed and I checked to see if there was anything in it. I was hoping to find money, drugs or some of the things that usually make me feel better. Surprisingly, my phone was there. I looked at the screen. There were no missed calls.

Dragging myself off the bed, I stumbled towards the door. It turned out that the dead woman was in fact an old man.

He really looked dead.

Fuck.

His face was pale, he was probably around eighty-five years old. He was fully dressed in typical Chinese migrant-worker's attire. He looked like Chairman Mao in one of these old posters you see hanging in Chinese living rooms.

Shaking, I peeked through the door before venturing a walk down the hallway, paranoid that someone would catch me and strap me back down on the bed. The hospital was dirty and there were quite a few people sitting in chairs that were lined up against the wall. No smiles. Everybody looked even more miserable than I was, and strangely that was somewhat comforting.

I walked down the corridor, not knowing where I was heading. Then I noticed a hospital guard smoking a cigarette. He stood beyond a propped-open doorway into the stairwell. It was even filthier in that small space than in the corridor and smelled much worse. I hesitated before approaching the guard, but when I plucked up the courage, I asked him for a cigarette. He was only about eighteen, this guard, skinny and wearing an over sized uniform. He looked at me as if he'd seen a ghost, which was not far from the truth. But after some muttering he handed me a cigarette with a sour expression on his face, a brand I'd never seen before. I could hardly stand up.

Shit, I think I'm going to pass out. Still, the need for the cigarette was strong. I lit it while bending down towards his lighter and took one drag. That's when it happened. I grabbed my stomach, leaning forward, and vomited all over the floor. The vomit saturated the guard's unpolished shoes and my own socks. *Oh, shit.* I straightened and sneaked a look at his face, a foul taste in my mouth.

The guard stood very still with his lips hanging open. It was probably his first encounter with a foreigner, certainly not what he might have expected, not by a long chalk. He started to stutter some words in a local dialect that I couldn't understand, his voice getting louder by the minute. But I couldn't hear properly anyway. Sweat prickled on my forehead.

I definitely think I'm about to faint..

Despite my shame at the abominable decoration of his shoes I struggled through the language barriers to ask the guard to help me back to my room, using a mix of hand gestures and broken Chinese. The guard glanced nervously around. I sensed he wanted to complete this mission without fuss, drawing as limited amount of attention as possible. He walked with me, holding my arm, his nose in the air. With my spare arm clutched around my middle, it felt like the longest thirty metres of my life.

As I passed the 'dead man' again I averted my eyes, feeling even more ill than I did before. By the time I crawled into my bed I thought I might be dying too.

***

No missed calls, I thought, checking repeatedly. I was bored, now. Had I done something terrible last night? Maybe my friends in Kunming didn't care about me enough to even check up on me. I'd only known most of them a few months...

The world outside the hospital ward seemed like nothing more than a vast desert filled with disappointment and failure. The bad shit always happened to me. Always me.

The Incident: it had to be the reason my life was so crap.

Thinking about it fueled me with hate and violence. Hate propelled itself through my weak body. I continued to dwell on the horrific image in my mind as I observed the sun's rays moving across the ward and a door slowly closing, apparently by itself.

It's only the wind coming from the window.

All the feelings of that time had come back.

I wished I was the dead guy in the bed next door.

Kafli 4 - Iceland, 1998.

The Incident

THE WHOLE SUMMER had been about football. If I was not at football practice, I was playing outside on the school playground or watching the English leagues on TV at the weekends. I was a big Arsenal fan. My father was an Arsenal fan too and that was probably the only thing I shared with him. It was all we ever talked about, except when we argued about the importance of education.

Dad bought me my first Arsenal T- shirt at the age of three, his proudest moment. Since then football had been a big part of my life. It was the one hobby of mine that had remained constant. I'd tried a lot of things from a young age but never managed to stick with anything. I used to play the piano, then I took up karate, swimming, skateboarding and even did a few months of archery. There was a pattern in these constant changes of hobbies. I began something with enthusiasm and was very good at it for a while, often better than the people around me, but then I reached the point of quitting. It was always the times I felt stuck. I had no patience, but I was good at blaming my mother for not being supportive enough with things I wanted to do.

I knew that was not really the reason I quit. The truth was that I was raising my standard faster than my ability to keep up with it. I saw someone better than I was and instead of letting that inspire me to get better, I just began trying to do something new.

By this time I was living with my mother in Breiðholt, a suburban neighbourhood in the city of Reykjavík. I was twelve years old and we lived in a twelve-floor apartment block. Our apartment had three bedrooms. My stepfather lived with us, but in my mind I was living alone with my mom, because my interactions with that man were almost non-existent. My mother was a carer; working night shifts at a place for disabled people and the years of unstable sleep patterns had made her continuously exhausted. My stepfather was a fisherman, so he would go away for a month or so for work, but then he had long periods of vacation where he stayed at home. His hobbies were his obsession with Jeeps, and drinking beer. He spent his free time fixing up and maintaining Jeeps with his only friend, Bjarni Óskarsson. They would buy them at auctions and keep them at a garage outside the city limits in Heiðmörk. The two of them spent months preparing for what usually turned out to be a single one-week Jeep trip every year.

I hated the times when my stepdad was home. The whole house was contaminated by his oppressing presence. Mom and me talked and behaved differently when he was around. There was always some mental preparation to get through before he got home from the sea, it was never talked about, we just knew.

I liked it best when it was just the two of us, my mom and me. I felt like the man of the house when her husband wasn't there. When he was gone I felt I had more to say and I definitely had more power. I could easily manipulate Mom in allowing me to do things, like staying outside longer to play football or play computer games during the night.

My mom was drinking occasionally and when she was hungover I felt like an adult because I could do whatever I wanted. When she was lying in bed all day after a night of drinking, filled with guilt and remorse, that was the time for me to ask for things. She would grant all my wishes then.

I came home from football practice on a Friday night one time in July. My stepfather and Mom were out at a dinner party. This meant they'd be drinking and come home late. I always felt anxiety when they went out in the evenings, because it meant they would come home drunk, and that caused its own problems. I always woke up when they got home late at night. Even though it pissed me off, I didn't dare to go talk to them. I was too scared of my stepfather.

I really enjoyed being home alone on a Friday night. When I got back to my apartment I called my friend Lárus to come over. We could hang out and play computer games in my room. I had one of the larger bedrooms in the apartment, which was reserved for me when we moved in. My mother fought with my stepfather to get me that room instead of turning it into an office for him. It was my good luck and I was forever grateful for Mom's intervention. I liked my room even though the bed under the window was a bit small; I was growing faster than Mom realised. My room was the space where I could escape to and I felt anxious if the adults interrupted my privacy.

Lárus lived in the same apartment building and he'd been my friend for a long time. He was not the coolest kid in the neighbourhood, but he was a good friend, happy-go-lucky, and our relationship was simple. We never argued. We played computer games together for hours on end, almost with no verbal communication. If we interacted, it was usually related to the mission we had to finish. We rarely competed in our gaming, our bond was about completing any mission together that the game had to offer. In between we ate whatever was in the fridge, usually experimenting with different sandwiches and finishing off with a bowl of *Skyr*. We were highly creative (and competitive) when it came to making sandwiches.

Lárus went home around eleven PM, because his parents didn't allow him to stay out any longer. He wasn't even permitted to be home alone in the evenings, like I was.

After Lárus left the house I watched a movie in my room. I always watched films, listened to music or played computer games to help me fall asleep otherwise my mind would keep me awake. On that night I watched some crappy sci-fi movie before nodding off...

Thousands of cars were stuck in traffic in front of me. It was so noisy; cars honking their horns and everybody in a hurry. The sky was purple and lit by three huge suns. It was also pouring with rain. There were skyscrapers all around, high enough to touch the clouds. Everything was grey; buildings, cars, the pavement, the streets and even people's clothes. Everybody had the same face, the same evil-looking, grey face.

I was standing on the only green spot in the whole city. It was about six metres of beautifully green grass. I was wearing only my underwear.

It was not raining on my spot. I knew it was the only safe place in this mad world in front of me. A beam of light cast brightness on me and it was coming from one of the three suns.

I had to lie down; the loud noises from the cars were overwhelming. I covered my ears but the sound didn't go away. I lay there in the grass, starting to feel very uncomfortable. People from the cars were watching me, meaning me harm but I knew they couldn't enter into the beaming light that surrounded the grass.

I started to feel even more uncomfortable. The people in the cars were touching me with their eyes. They were touching me with their horrible gazes. I tried to kick them. I couldn't kick.

I was frozen. Frozen with fear. Something was touching my leg. I wanted to scream but my voice was trapped in my throat.

As opened my eyes I understood that there was really someone stroking my leg and I was frozen, just like in the dream. My eyes stayed open in shock for a moment before I stuck my eyelids together again. *No.* I had my back turned to the person who was tracing my thighs from behind. I felt myself stiffening, inch by inch from my toes to the top of my head but carried on pretending to be asleep. Otherwise I would have to face it - the person - who was doing this to me. And I couldn't. There was loud, heavy breathing. It was a man. A stinking animal of a man who was touching me. Gusts of alcohol-breath blew on the back of my neck and washed over my scrunched-up face.

My eyes squeezed even more tightly shut, *please let this be a dream.* But it went on. I wanted to say stop, but I was too scared. I wanted to kick him but my body was rigid. There was only that crazy mayhem going on in my head. I thought about what things were around me that I might be able to hit him with. I was facing the wall, so there was no weapon

I could reach for.

Please, let it stop. Then he touched me more, really touched me. Pushed his hand between my thighs. I wanted to resist but if I did I would have to let him know that I knew. *Pretend I'm not here. Pretend it isn't happening.* Slowly I let go of myself and the conscious part of me seemed to slide off to one side as I felt my legs opening. He kept on touching my private places with his rough hands while I hovered away somewhere. *This can't be happening.*

After about ten minutes, maybe, or it could have been five or even one, but it felt so long, it felt like forever; the touching stopped. The hand had withdrawn. I opened my eyes a tiny crack and in the gap of window between the curtains there was a reflection. A face. A monster face. Quick, I pasted my eyes closed again. The bed creaked, rolling me back slightly and the monster had risen from the mattress and lumbered out of my room. His footsteps reverberated through the floor, through the bed, through the walls and through my brain. I was shaking so much I could hardly stand, but half-walking and half-crawling I managed to get over to the door so that I could lock it.

My room smelled of alcohol but worse, it also smelled of my shame.

I could hear music from the living room and muffled voices. Was The Face in there with my mom and stepdad, acting as though nothing had happened? The time was six twenty-five AM. My shaky knees lowered me onto the bed, boiling with anger and hurt. Now the questions came. *Why didn't I kick him? Why didn't I hit him with something? What's wrong with me? Am I such a chicken I can't even protect myself?*

I crawled back into my bed and stared at the ceiling, hating myself so much. Angrily I jerked the curtain across the narrow strip of glass that had shown me The Face.

I was angrier with myself than with the owner of that face.

I tried to comfort myself with the thought that whoever did that was probably too drunk to remember the next day, so he would not tell anyone. And I promised that I would never tell anyone about it, ever.

I also promised myself that I would find the person who did this and kill him one day.

Kafli 5 - Kunming, 2011.

The Experience

IT WAS DARK but the light from the hallway shone through the half-open door of the hospital ward. Afraid and confused, not knowing if it was night or day, I closed my eyes and tried to go back to sleep.

Eventually I gave up and rolled over to check my phone. It was two AM: still no missed calls. Lying back again, I twisted my head to see around the ward. The 'dead man' was gone and the bed on the left was still empty. I was all alone in the ward, the hospital, the world. Maybe I'd just imagined myself and didn't really exist. Then, hey, what was it? Something was weird and different about the room.

Probably it just looks different in the dark.

As I lay in the silence, all my muscles relaxed and I was strangely peaceful. My mind was finally at ease. The room looked perfect somehow, the furniture in the right places, the lighting poetic and the most bizarre thing of all, I felt I was in the right place. I couldn't understand why everything was now so peaceful. I tried not to over-think it because I wanted this feeling to last. The peacefulness and my still mind. I hadn't felt like this for a long time, if ever.

After a while changes began happening in my body. There were vibrations in my left side. Something coming from the bed on the left side of me. *What?* I was still at peace but now my mind started to wander.

Am I mad?

Where does this overwhelming sense of peace come from?

As soon as I put the physical sensations into mental words, the feeling of 'me' coming back to myself took over. The peacefulness was drifting away. I tried to focus and recapture the peace but it was like sand pulled by a receding tide. Desperately, I closed my eyes and put my hand on my heart.

Please come back. Please.

I was shaking again. The force on my left side had control of me. The shaking permeated my bones, my veins, my blood; all my organs.

Then suddenly a most wonderful feeling swamped me. I was subsumed by it, yet still thinking with clarity and focus, observing the situation as if my mind and body were separated from each other.

What's going on? Is this really happening?

Perhaps I had been given some medicine, or maybe it was something to do with the dead guy.

But really I knew, deep in my heart, that it was something in the bed next to me causing this unexpected feeling of, like *nothing and everything* at the same time. The word 'bliss' came to me. I lay shaking and filled with a kind of energy I had never experienced before. Something way bigger than me, a totally foreign experience but it was like I'd always had it in me and I was just coming home to it, or it to me.

As if I was detached from myself, I watched thoughts wandering around my head while I was shaking in a trance. Suddenly I could understand how lost human beings are in the world. Lost in thoughts. Thoughts that are uncertain and unclear and therefore *people* are uncertain and unclear.

Like a flow of water, awareness poured into me. People base their way of life on *thoughts*. How limited and impure most thoughts are. That was why there was so much suffering. That was why *I* had suffered.

Totally at home now in the pulsing vibrations, it was overwhelming to be flooded with this new understanding. How messy and sick I was. How messy and sick the world is.

The shaking suddenly stopped, as if someone had pressed a button. I had lost all track of time but I leaned over to check my phone. It was two thirty-five AM. So little time had passed yet it felt like the experience had lasted much longer.

An awareness of emptiness; the energy had gone. I ached with loss and it came to me that it hadn't felt good to be me for a long time. I wanted the energy to come back but somehow I knew it wouldn't return. Still, I felt immense gratitude for this experience and now I craved it again, at any cost. It was comforting to think that there was some force out there in the universe that wanted me to feel better.

I was exhausted, tried to go to sleep, knowing something was different. I still felt bad but something was different. I had this feeling of having time. Yes, I had time. *Time to do what?* But I couldn't answer my own question. I tried again to relax and go to sleep. My head was quietening just as it hit me.

Time is hope. Hope is time.

I have hope.

Kafli 6 - Kunming.

Watching the Trees

IT TOOK ME a few moments to work out what day it was. Monday. I was feeling better and wanted to get out of the hospital as quickly as possible. Since no-one had bothered to find out about me, I finally called my roommate Jeff and asked him to pick me up. Jeff was from London, he was a stylish hipster-type, neatly dressed; usually wearing his black Buddy Holly glasses.

I'd woken Jeff up when I called. He agreed to come pick me up and also to pay for the hospital stay, since I'd lost my wallet on that mysterious night and I still couldn't remember what had happened. I got myself ready to leave and hoped Jeff had the answers to all my questions about what had happened to me.

I'd known Jeff for four months. Like me he loved to drink

but he was the kind of guy I would only have hung out with in a place like China. I couldn't see myself being friends with him back home in Iceland; he wouldn't be from a place like Breiðholt, he'd be too much of a yuppie for me with his interest in indie music and wine bars.

I waited for Jeff outside the hospital in front of the big sign for Kunming Tongren Hospital. I was quickly reminded by the rushing cars and pollution that the city was a busy hub whether or not I was participating in it. While I lounged against the sign I thought about The Experience, the shaking, the energy and 'the dead guy' and wondered if they were all part of the same thing. I couldn't pinpoint what was different about me now. It was embarrassing to think about that strange experience. If people could hear my thoughts they'd lock me up in a different kind of hospital.

Jeff arrived, the loud scooter engine chugging to a stop in front of me.

"Hey, buddy," he grinned. "I had no idea you were at the hospital."

"What?" I was genuinely surprised to hear this.

"No, really, why didn't you call?" Jeff felt in his pockets for cigarettes.

"I was busy."

Busy. But I wasn't going to admit I was wallowing in self-pity over having no missed calls.

"What happened on Saturday night, mate?" Jeff asked with his thick British accent. He struck a second match because the first one had gone out. He lit up.

"I was hoping you would tell me what happened, I have no clue. I just woke up in the hospital."

"You disappeared from the club, mate. Me and Martin had no idea that you ended up in the hospital! We thought you might have hooked up with some girl or something." He grinned.

"I wish." I tried to smile back.

"Are you okay?"

"Yeah, I guess. Thanks for asking."

Cigarette in the side of his mouth, Jeff gave me a funny look. Then he grabbed hold of the scooter and turned it round.

"Jump on, mate, want one?" He patted his pocket.

"No thanks, man. Let's just go home."

I noticed something was different when I was sitting on the back of the scooter. As the wind blew in my face, I noticed the trees around me. They seemed greener than ever. I felt lighter. I didn't know what to think of it. Maybe it had something to do with what had happened at the hospital. I was also surprised that I'd said no to Jeff when he offered me a cigarette. I just didn't feel like smoking.

I mulled over my newfound hope. From the bike the world moved fast around me. I considered patience in relation to time. It took Jeff around twenty-five minutes to get from the hospital in South Kunming to WenLin Street, the popular foreigner's area in which we lived. But I was in no hurry. I felt the urge to just watch the trees, the city, the people and other things around me. It was about patience. Yeah. Being patient equates to the absence of time. I'd never been patient in my life. I'd always taken quick decisions and jumped from one thing to another. I never really enjoyed the moment I was in.

In the hospital I'd experienced a timeless state. The more I forgot about time the more patient I was. When looking at the trees around me, without thinking about them moving, without thinking about me moving and without thinking about the twenty-five minutes it took to drive home, I could just observe the trees. I wasn't looking, I was observing, without time. *The trees are timeless. They are beautiful.* Watching the trees made my mind become stiller and calmer. All of a sudden it came to me, as if it was whispered in my ear by a voice behind my thoughts: *One of the biggest aspects of maturity is patience.*

My mind-set had changed. What was going on? Jeff's scooter puttered to a stop. I disembarked and looked up at our apartment building, a typical eighties construction with its fifteen floors and utilitarian appearance. There were hundreds of air-conditioning boxes hanging outside of its neglected grey exterior and it looked like it had been in use for centuries. China is a country that prides itself on harmony and togetherness of the people but they seem to have a hard time getting things like Residents Committees together.

"Okay, man, I have to go to work." Jeff brought me right back to the present.

"Okay, well, thanks for picking me up." I still felt resentful that he hadn't tried to look for me when I was gone.

"Are you sure everything's all right?" he asked.

"Yeah, I'm fine. Feel a little stupid with this bandage around my head, though."

"You look fine, mate. Paddy's tonight?"

Paddy's was an Irish bar we went to almost every night.

"No I don't think so. But maybe..."I wanted him to insist that I came.

He gave me another funny look.

"See you there, mate, no bullshit." Jeff looked me over again before riding away.

Kafli 7 - Iceland 2004.

Crisis at 18

"YOU ARE GOING to end up like your brother." Mom's voice cracked like she was about to burst into tears.

"Mom, you are crazy." I made a rude gesture in the air instead of in her face like I really wanted to.

"What are you going to do if you quit? What's the next thing you are going to come up with? What is the next solution to your problems?" She was yelling in her usual way and grabbed the back of the kitchen chair, like she was holding it down and trying to push into the floor. Her shoulders tightened up, making her neck disappear. Her eyebrows became like the letter V.

Our kitchen was small but messy, and I'd already pinpointed my escape route.

"Well if I had any support," I yelled back, "I might not quit things so easily. You're my mother and mothers are supposed to support their kids."

"How dare you, Böðvar." She glared straight into my eyes when she said that. She only used my real name when she was really angry.

I was trembling, but managed to take two steps backwards towards my room before exploding.

"You all think you're so fucking supportive of me. Dad wants me to be a doctor like him, you want me to be successful like Uncle Hjörtur. My brother wants me to be a pro football player and my teachers think this and that about me, all different things. Everybody thinks they know what's best for me but nobody asks me what I want. It's like everybody is trying to relive his or her failed dreams through me. I can't do everything for everybody at the same time."

Tears were squeezing out of my eyes. Mom hesitated before taking a deep breath and lowering her voice.

"So, this is the reason to quit college? This is not about other people, Böddi, this is about you. These people don't force you to drink every weekend, and surely I'm not supportive of that either? These people don't force you to hang out with the crowd you're hanging out with. You are only eighteen years old. Of course people are trying to give you suggestions for your life."

"You're the one to talk about drinking," I said sullenly. That was her weak spot.

"You are not going to turn this on me, Böddi. It's your life. You can do whatever you want." She seemed calmer now, but you could never tell what she might do next.

"Okay, then," I tried to calm myself. "Why are you angry at me for quitting school? I'll figure something out. I'll be working at the pizza place until I find something better."

I pictured myself at forty years old, still putting pepperoni onto pizza bread.

Mom lit a cigarette and held it between trembling fingers as she looked me in the eyes again.

"You'd better find something else because you will have to pay rent from now on. I'm not supporting a working man with free food and shelter, that's for sure."

There was a moment of silence.

"Your father called," she put in. "He asked if you were going to his place today. You can tell him about this great decision of yours over the game. He will be thrilled, I'm sure. Maybe you could go live with him, it's about time he took some responsibility for you."

When she left the kitchen she slammed the door harder than usual.

I hadn't made a decision to quit college; I'd simply failed to meet the attendance requirements. I'd tried to negotiate with the teachers but they wouldn't let me go through again this time. I had played all my cards. I told them I was depressed, that I was taking care of a sick mother, and a few other lies to try to not be expelled. This time it didn't work.

It was Sunday morning and the Arsenal game started in a few hours. I was not in the mood to see my father today, especially not when I was as hungover as I was. But I knew I had to fix this mess about quitting college so I decided to do it right away and get it over with. I sneaked out of my room and didn't say goodbye to my mother. I didn't have any money after the previous night's partying, so before I went out the door I looked into my mom's jacket for bus money. I was not going to ask her for money, she'd only throw the request back in my face. As I took the elevator down from the apartment I couldn't stop blaming my mom that I quit school, even though I knew it wasn't really her fault.

The bus was full of older people, a group of disabled people with their carers; and teenagers. In my opinion the teenagers were too loud, the old people were smelly and the disabled people would all be drooling and doing their thing; I wasn't planning on looking at them. I didn't belong in this bus and hated the fact I didn't have a car, like some of my friends. I spent the next thirty minutes judging every person in the bus to avoid thinking about my meeting with Dad.

I always had the same feeling of shame as I walked into my father's house. He owned a big white villa in Kópavogur, a nice suburban neighbourhood. Kópavogur is Iceland's second most populated town and is in the greater Reykjavík area. The house had three floors and a large garden, filled with toys for his kids. He had five kids altogether: my brother and me with our mom, and three others with his current wife. My step-siblings were my two brothers aged eleven and seven, and one little sister aged three. Everything seemed perfect on the outside when entering their home, but I knew better. I always felt like an outsider. There was nothing about this place that made me feel welcome or at home. Every time I came here I was a stranger in this house.

The younger two were playing in the living room and the eleven year old was downstairs playing computer games. Dad's wife was making lunch for the family and Dad was already on the sofa preparing to watch the game.

I greeted my stepmom with, "Hello," as I entered the front door. She replied in kind and that was the longest conversation we'd had in a while. Occasionally she came to talk to me and we shared a few minutes of superficial chat about this and that. But I didn't know this woman at all, even though it had been ten years since my parents divorced. I was eight years old when they parted and I still remembered the feeling of relief. Their parting meant the war was finally over.

My father was a well-known doctor, also a politician and a respected man in Reykjavík society. He'd been elected for the independent party in local government a few years back and was slowly moving more into national politics. He was still doing work at the hospital and was on several political committees. When he had any free time he played golf. My stepmom and my dad had been arguing about him playing too much golf for a decade. I often thought that the glue in their relationship must be that they never talked to or even saw much of each other.

"Hi, Böddi, sit down. The game starts in twenty minutes." My father was opening a Carlsberg beer.

"Hi, Dad, how are you? Have you seen the starting line-up for Arsenal? Who are we playing?" I wanted to keep the conversation strictly about football.

"Well, I feel better than you, I guess." Dad threw me a glance as he placed his beer on the coffee table. "It looks like you had fun last night. Are you still hanging out with those crazy friends of yours?" He gave me a more direct stare, then added, "We are playing Stoke, at home."

I avoided eye contact, shuffling my feet.

"I just had a bit of a drink last night, nothing serious."

My stomach was upside down. I wondered when I should tell him the news about me quitting college. I was scared, trying to read the situation we were in. It was a positive thing that he was drinking beer because he was always more mellow after a few beers. If I broke the news before the game started he might get angry at me for ruining his favourite time of the week. I thought about doing it in half-time, hoping he would drink some more beer, that the conversation would only be for fifteen minutes and then we'd go back to watching the game. I finally decided to break the news *after* the game for two reasons: I just wanted to forget about this college talk for a while and also I wanted to enjoy next two hours of football.

Arsenal won. 3-2.

My dad was happy.

So.

"Dad?"

"Yeah."

"There is something I want to tell you."

"Okay, I'm here. Go ahead and tell me, Böddi."

"I quit college," I said quickly.

"Okay" He took a sip of beer number five.

"Okay? Is that all you have to say? You don't care that I just quit school?" I couldn't read the look on his face.

"Well, you are a grown-up now, eighteen years old already. So you can do whatever you want. As soon as you turned eighteen you were no longer my responsibility. This news doesn't surprise me at all considering how you are living your life. Drinking every weekend and probably doing drugs as well, just like your brother. If you want to ruin your life, it's your choice."

He was looking fixedly at a car commercial on the television. I couldn't figure out what he was thinking or what kind of parent game he was playing.

There was a long silence. My feelings had totally shifted from being scared, on the brink of a panic attack at telling him, to this boiling anger that was like electricity running through me. I didn't know how to react. I wanted to take the empty beer bottle on the table and smash it on my dad's head.

I thought about what Mom had said about staying with my dad for a while. The anger kept rising inside me, up to my throat. I couldn't ask if I could stay at his place. My mom was right; he had never taken any responsibility for me. It didn't matter if I was eighteen or not, he had never done anything to support me. I had to say something. My teeth were grinding. I felt a burst of adrenaline. My body was overtaken by rage. I stood up, walked towards where he was sitting in his favourite leather LayZ-Boy sofa.

"So if it's not about Arsenal or playing golf, you don't care. You are an asshole! You are a fucking asshole!" I could hear how unnaturally high my voice had become, but I couldn't stop. "You are nothing. It's all fake, this whole family is just fucking fake. Fuck you and your stupid bitch!"

Oh, shit. What have I done?

"What did you say to me?" He grabbed the handle to roll down the chair and stood up.

I was scared, determined to stand my ground. But I couldn't believe the words that had just come out of my mouth. These were not the words I had planned to say. I recognised the feeling in this moment. It was the same feeling as the two seconds after someone tackled you badly in football. I had got into trouble before, when I acted on those feelings during football matches. I once almost got expelled from the football club when I attacked a kid on the football pitch after a bad tackle. Now I was too scared to do anything.

My father stood up. He waited, with his lips pressed together, the muscles on his face twitching. He was breathing heavily. I couldn't go back and make excuses now. I'd let the beast out. But I lowered my voice and tried to look him in the eyes.

"You don't care about me and you never did. You just care about your new kids and that stupid bitch. I wish people in society really knew what kind of father you are."

The anger was already subsiding and remorse starting to creep in even as I finished saying it.

My dad's face turned into something I had never seen before. I could see that he felt tackled, hard, from behind.

Rushing towards me, he grabbed my sweater at the chest and started shaking me. He put his face an inch away from mine.

"You. Ungrateful. Little. Fuck." His hand moved to my neck. He was pushing me back, shoving me against the wall.

I saw red. I lost it. I started throwing punches at him and one hit his ear. Ouch! My knuckles hurt. But the pain felt good.

"And you even lay hands on your own kids, you fucking asshole."

He'd let go of me and was holding his ear with one hand. Again, a feeling of remorse crept in. But I had no time to think about it.

"You just made a big mistake, boy."

Dad pushed me as hard as he could, my knee hitting the corner of his fancy coffee-table. As I turned my back on him he grabbed my hood, twisted me around and slapped me on the face. I could feel my body go into shock, while he dragged me towards the front door, the sweater tightened against my neck.

I had given up the fight. I just wanted to get out of there. As we reached the door I saw my eleven-year-old stepbrother Svenni standing in the hallway, watching it all.

"Svenni, go to your room. You don't want to watch this." Dad shoved me out the house.

***

The door slammed, the second door that had slammed on my face that day: disowned by both of my parents. I stood shaking outside the house, breathing heavily and looking around me in case anyone had seen what had happened.

Shit. My shoes were still inside the house but I couldn't go back in there.

I knew that there was a pair of canvas shoes in a large wooden box in the garden where they kept their gardening tools, so I sneaked around the side of the house. The grass was still wet from yesterday's rain. Luckily, nobody saw me running around wearing only my socks.

My hands trembled and I was full of adrenaline. I had a burning sensation in my chest as I rushed back to the street, now wearing the lightweight shoes over my wet socks. Seeing my father's black Range Rover, I considered breaking a window or smashing the wing mirror, but before that thought even manifested properly I only wanted to get home. I had to walk since I didn't have any money for a bus. It would take me about two hours. I walked fast alongside the road and wanted to hit every car I walked past. Instead I hit a tree branch that was hanging above me from a garden next to the road, it gave me a tiny cut on my knuckles but the stinging felt good. Even though I wanted to smash every car I saw, the consequences would be more trouble than they were worth, so I carried on walking and waited for the next tree branch to smash.

After walking for twenty minutes, turning everything over in my mind, I had calmed down. I went over the fight, wondering why my father didn't care about me, replaying the scene when I entered his home, how I had hoped he wouldn't get angry. Why did I snap after he didn't get angry? I was confused by my own behaviour.

I hated my father and his life, except for my younger brothers and sister. They were too young to blame for my misery.

There were times my father had said to me that he hoped I would become a doctor, like so many members of his wider family. In my mind now I wanted to go straight to medical school, just to show the bastard I could do it. There must be a way, surely there must - even though I'd just quit college.

About an hour into my walk I crossed through a small valley called Elliðárdalur, which is a natural free zone within the city of Reykjavík. It's placed in the middle of the city and there's a river running through it. I rested on a bench by the river and watched families walking with their children and men fishing at the river's edge. There was a couple sitting on the bench next to mine, they seemed to be in love. The atmosphere was tranquil, in total opposition to my state of mind.

Everything around me seemed alive but inside I was empty. I couldn't feel anything. I was just numb and totally disconnected from my surroundings.

A kid ran along the riverbank and his mom was shouting not to go near the water. That's when I started to cry. I had fought with both my parents on the same day. I had no money, I'd just quit college and the future seemed darker than ever. My mind started its usual escape route, like a record playing

on a loop. I have to fix this, over and over again. I couldn't
understand how my parents could treat me like they did. I was
drowning in my usual self-pity.

Why don't they understand me?

Why don't they support me?

*Why do they not care about me, like that mom screaming after
her kid by the river?*

I remembered what my father had said; I was eighteen now
and not his responsibility. If I had enough money I'd get away
from them both and never talk to them again. It hurt that I
knew I wasn't able to support myself and live without them.

I continued to cry on that bench while the world went by,
ignoring me. In my powerlessness, my mind pulled me back to
the incident when I was twelve. I had only three or four times
thought about The Incident in my life since then. My whole
existence felt built on forgetting; I must deny and bury the
memory. But at times like this it felt the only logical reason
for my life being such a mess.

Eventually I raised my head. The couple in love were leaving
their bench, holding hands. I looked back to the river, feeling
drawn to it. I thought how easy it would be to jump in and end
this misery of mine. My stepfather had told me stories about
Icelandic fishermen that almost drowned and how he thought
it was the best way to die. These stories came back to me.
Many of the men had said that a blissful feeling in the process

of dying overtook them and that they even felt unhappy and disappointed when they were brought back to life.

I didn't jump in the river, it was probably not deep enough anyway and too many people were around to see. I didn't want to add a failed suicide attempt to my pathetic life.

I dried the tears from my face, stood up from the bench with a plan in my mind.

I would detach from my parents as soon as possible.

Kafli 8 - Kunming, 2011.

Party at Paddy's

AFTER I CAME home from the hospital in Kunming I was tired and weak. But I had already slept enough the last two days and couldn't sleep anymore however hard I tried, so I lay restlessly in bed watching movies, reading old magazines and staring at the ceiling. There was a large mirror in my room and I occasionally got up to have a look at my bruises, turning this way and that in front of my reflection. My rib cage was purple and my foot was swollen. I couldn't resist peeling away the bandage on my head as well and peeping underneath.

The doctor had sent me home with painkillers and some other unidentified pills. I was supposed to take six pills, four times a day, which seemed rather excessive. I decided to trust the doctor and follow his instructions. With Chinese drugs you were always given higher amounts than in the West, maybe because they were herbal. Finally by the afternoon I got tired of being tired and the urge to go outside kicked in. I had to do some job searching anyway, since I'd lost my English teaching job due to being late too often.

I got dressed in some clean clothes, and right before I went out of the apartment I grabbed a small notebook I'd bought a few days earlier. I thought I might as well go to a cafe to hunt for jobs and plan my future. Or I could pretend to be a writer if anyone asked.

It was good to walk, be outside of the apartment. I liked being part of the busy life of Kunming. I enjoyed strolling around watching people bringing their kids home from school and closing their shops. Older people were doing their afternoon exercises in the park. Nobody paid any attention to them but I had a few weird looks from people, most likely due to the bandage. It didn't bother me too much, one of the good things about living in China is that you just don't care about people looking at you, whereas in a small population like Iceland it is different, you are bound to meet someone you know while walking down the street and it might spark gossip. The next thing you know, the whole town of Reykjavík is talking behind your back.

I went to a small café near the backpacker's area (as we called it); sat down and ordered an Americano. The place was small, relatively clean by Chinese standards. I chose a seat in the corner with a picture of Frank Sinatra hanging above my head. It was a typical Chinese café, where they took whatever picture or furniture they could find that looked western and stuffed it in there to impress the foreigners. The effect was a strangely 1940s feel.

I sat down with my new, empty notebook in front of me, feeling anxious. It might be related to the fact that I didn't see anything positive coming up in my near future and it scared me to attempt making plans on paper. I sat there a while and stared at the empty page. This was not the first time I wanted to plan my life in a notebook. I had a history of buying them, writing on only one or two pages and then never looking at them again. I always bought new notebooks with the hope that this time it would be different but also to avoid the old ones because they were like failed plans of the past.

After a while of not having written anything I started to contemplate going to the Irish pub and try to find out what had happened last Saturday night. In fact it didn't matter so much now; I was more interested in investigating the meaning of The Experience in the hospital. But where could I start looking for answers?

Without even thinking about it I wrote the first word in my book.

ROUTINE.

I stared at the word for a while.

My life is a routine. I have a destructive routine.

Yes, I had a routine of starting and quitting things, also a one-page-notebook routine and a routine of smoking. It then hit me that I hadn't smoked since I puked over the poor guard's shoes in the hospital stairwell. Was I breaking my routine of smoking?

Now I started to crave a cigarette. A battle of past failures and a small light of hope from The Experience took place inside me. I decided to give hope a chance. It made me feel good. I would go to the Irish bar to meet my friends and find out the story of my disappearance. But I didn't want to end up having to pick up the pieces from another night of drinking. The word in my book summed up my repetitive behaviour.

✽✽✽

After sitting at the café the whole day, writing only one word in my book, I felt I'd accomplished something extraordinary. I phoned my buddy Sharif, a guy from Tunis, and we went to the bar together. He was a solid guy; one of the gang that hung out at Paddy's almost every night. He was the only one of us who didn't drink alcohol (because he was a Muslim) but he sure did smoke the hash, on a daily basis. In my narrow view that was a hypocritical way of doing things, but hey, he was still a good guy.

We arrived at the bar at nine and the rest of the usual group was there: Jeff, an American guy named Chris and his girlfriend, Cherry. Cherry was Chinese. As we walked towards the table, time slowed down, bringing to mind the movie *Groundhog Day* with Bill Murray, in which a guy wakes up and relives the same day over and over again. *Two bartenders standing behind the bar, two pool tables and flags and shirts hanging on the walls representing different countries, football or rugby clubs.*

"There's the missing link," Jeff chuckled, waving his hand at me.

"Oh my God, what happened, dude, is your head injured?" Cherry did a double-take.

"Yeah, it's fine, but I have no idea what happened. Do you guys know what happened, the other night?" I asked, looking around at them all.

"Know what?" Cherry piped in again.

I gave her an annoyed glance. "What happened to me on Saturday? I was in blackout, I barely remember the dinner we had." I stared at the floor for a few seconds, feeling irritated with everyone.

"Dude, we have no idea. Last time we saw you, you were wasted. You were talking to that girl," Chris said helpfully.

"What girl?" There were always a million girls.

Cherry took a sip of her beer. She said piercingly, "The Chinese one. She was Chinese."

"Thanks, Cherry, that narrows it down for me. Keep your voice down. Jesus."

"The one with long dark hair."

"Just keep on going, Cherry, it gets narrower."

"Oh my God, I'm just trying to help you." Cherry shook her head at me, looking to Chris for approval but he kept silent.

There was a heavy pause. I crossed my arms tightly and kept on studying the floor.

"Oh well, the past is the past, let's forget about it. Do you want a beer?" Laid-back Jeff tried to ease the tension in his usual way.

"No thanks."

Sharif grinned stupidly. I reckoned he was high as a kite. I didn't feel right around anyone. Nothing was right. It was like I didn't belong there anymore. Still, I sat down, called the waitress and ordered a glass of water to distract the awkward conversation I just knew was coming up.

Here we go.

"Water? You must have hit your head pretty bad, right?" Chris's nasal voice was even more annoying than his girlfriend's.

"I'll give him two hours and he'll be drinking a beer," Jeff added.

"What the fuck? Guys, can we talk about something else?"

"Easy, buddy. We just missed you, man," Chris said in a conciliatory way, with a fat, smug grin.

That reminded me of the *no missed calls* on my phone. I really wanted to throw their unconcern back in their faces but I couldn't risk losing my only friends in Kunming.

My hand gripped the water glass so tightly it was in danger of breaking.

I can't be here anymore.

I had no idea what was wrong with me, but I felt angry with everybody in the place. I looked around the bar and started thinking about the routine in my life, the strange energy I'd felt at the hospital and how everything was weird after The Experience. Everything was different, but at the same time everything was the same, I couldn't get my head around what was going on with me.

"Böddi."

I ignored Jeff.

"Böddi!" Jeff said it louder this time.

"Yeah, what's up?"

"Dude, snap out of it, for fuck's sake."

"And into this sad place?" The words seemed to come out of my mouth of their own accord. If I could have given myself the incredulous look Jeff did then I would have done.

"Never mind."

I couldn't blame them for the way they were all staring at me now. They must have thought I'd been abducted by an alien and replaced with a stiff-ass cloned copy. Jeff cleared his throat, glanced around the group. "Anyways, can you see that chick sitting over there near the pool table, the long-legged girl?"

Reluctantly I lifted my chin and followed his pointing finger with my eyes. "Yeah." I wasn't remotely interested though. Two guys were sitting at the table next to this girl Jeff was talking about. They looked like stereotypical truck drivers from Midwest USA, wearing over-sized jeans, caps and what seemed to be college football sweaters. They were both eating burgers and French fries, and drinking pints of beer. Looking at them eating beef burgers didn't feel right. Something was not right at all with this picture. *What's going on with me?* I thought again. Even I was finding myself weird.

"Go talk to her." Jeff seemed excited.

"What, who?"

"The blue giraffe behind the bar! What the fuck, man, the girl, of course."

"Oh yeah, she's nice." I was still uninterested. Jeff looked at me with his eyes wide open and throwing his hands up in the air like I was supposed to talk to his hands.

"Okay, then. She's mine, I warned you." Jeff had had

enough. Finally. He moved back to the group conversation and left me alone.

Picking up a local girl and getting laid was not on my mind at all. I now felt like an Icelandic alien in an Irish pub in China. I'd always been quite successful with girls, especially in China. If you wanted something to do to fill the void in the company you kept, it was chasing girls at bars and clubs. You took them home for a one-night stand and after that it was boring. For us it was a game, they were the trophies we won. That was what Jeff and I did. It had been my routine since I came to China, to chase girls.

I'd met Jeff for the first time at Paddy's. Jeff had this artistic look that girls were drawn to. And Chinese girls were also attracted to me; my white skin, brown hair and blue eyes.

"Dude, do you want a beer?" Chris asked, with one eyebrow raised.

"Are you deaf, mate?"

"What?"

"Exactly!"

"Dude, what's wrong with you?"

"Sorry, mate, just the third time you offered me a beer when I said no."

"Böddi," Chris said while Jeff shook his head, avoiding my eyes. "Just go home if you're not even going to drink, you're too boring this way."

The rejection hurt. Even though I'd probably asked for it. I got up, scraping the chair back. "Fine. Fuck you guys."

"Dude!"

But I wasn't listening anymore. I walked out of the bar in a fuzz, a sting in my stomach. *Why didn't I just drink with the guys like before?*

Because I didn't feel like drinking. It was my routine to drink and for the first time I really wanted to break that routine. The difference between now and my past promises of stopping was my new hope and trust in The Experience.

I walked home worrying that my friends were talking behind my back. I stopped when I came to a park that was on the way home and sat down on a bench. I put my hands over my face and began the routine of my usual inward rant when hitting rock bottom.

Why can't I be happy?

I can't fucking live like this.

I don't know what I want.

There is a hole inside me that causes all my pain.

After a load more of these crazy thought processes I closed my eyes, tilted my head backwards and leaned it on the bench, using the bandage as a pillow.

Everything was quiet, no people, which was unusual for Kunming at this hour. Trying to recreate The Experience I began to understand the battle inside me; unlike before, it was

Böddi vs. Böddi. I could visualise this battle. I pictured it as a boxing ring. No audiences, just two boxers in the ring. They were two extremes.

One boxer was wearing white shorts and he represented The Experience, some kind of divine space. The other boxer, wearing black shorts, represented my habits, my routines, my past behaviour, my thoughts, my life, my pain and how I perceived myself. Before the hospital experience I had only been living as the black-clad boxer, not knowing that I was capable of anything else. I watched these two guys fight in my mind. Now I seriously worried that I was crazy.

My mind was a roller coaster, riding between my destructive habits and this newly discovered space.

After a while I stood up and headed out of the park. Another group of older people were doing Tai Chi by the gate. After stopping to watch for a while I began walking home between the high buildings of modern Kunming. You could see the contrast everywhere of old versus new China. Fancy cars next to cycles, high-end shops next to street-food stalls. I felt a bit calmer by now, but the anxiety knot in my stomach was still there. Once inside our apartment I decided to go to bed early. As I was lying on my bed I thought about my behaviour at the bar. I'd done thousands of stupid things in bars throughout my life but nothing had made me feel as bad as I did that evening, and I hadn't even been drunk.

I tried to calm my mind so I could sleep, and thought about the boxers again. I saw that I had three options.

The first was to wait and see, let go of control, observe the fight and see which boxer would win. (Deep down in my heart I knew that if I did this, the boxer with the black shorts would destroy the boxer in white within a matter of days and I'd be back to my old routine.)

The second option was to knock out the black-shorted boxer, eliminate him totally; go down a different path than I had been doing. But I had no idea what that meant or how I would do it. I didn't know how to not be *myself*.

The third option was to do what I'd always done, say "fuck it" and go to Paddy's for a beer tomorrow. I would then probably keep struggling and living in pain for the rest of my life. It was a tough decision because to take real action would be a hard thing to do.

Have I got the strength?

Going over my options repeatedly, I eventually fell asleep.

Kafli 9 - Kunming.

Meeting Henry and Pau

WHEN I WOKE up my brain was going full-on, the thumping headache I had was like waking up in a bunker in a battlefield. There wasn't even room for thinking about The Experience. I had slept for ten hours. I really wanted a cigarette now, for the first time since the hospital. I hadn't smoked for a few days but now I needed a cigarette. I must have one. I looked in every trouser and jacket pocket and every drawer in my room. No luck.

Maybe Jeff has some.

I walked to Jeff's room and pushed at the door. It would barely open due to all the pirate DVD's lying around. It was like a vertical Blockbuster store. How can someone collect so much junk after only five months in Kunming? Jeff was lying with one eye open. He looked as hungover as usual.

"Hey, Jeff."

"Yeah?"

"Do you have a .."

"Yes I have." Jeff knew by the look of me what I was after.

"Well, can I have one?"

"So now we're friends, just because you want a cigarette?" he mumbled, due to part of his pillow being in his mouth.

I stood with my right hand on the door. "Hey, I wasn't angry at you yesterday, I'm sorry."

"Okay, whatever." He wasn't convinced. "You coming tonight?"

"Hmmm yeah, probably, what's going on?" Really I just wanted to find a cigarette. That was all.

"Poker night," Jeff reminded me.

"Yeah I'll be there." But I was already thinking of excuses not to go.

"The cigarettes are in my jacket."

Jeff stuffed his face back into the pillow and I stepped inside and reached into the jacket. Jeff wasn't looking so I withdrew two cigarettes. But then I thought about the word in my notebook, the one that was supposed to change my life.

ROUTINE.

Seeing Jeff all hungover again; poker night; cigarette craving; me waking up in a bad mood: they were all routines in my life. In slow motion I returned the jacket and started walking backwards.

"No thanks, man, I'm good."

"What?" My friend resurfaced, his half-open eyes sitting in violet hollows. He squinted at me. "You came in to pester me for cigarettes, mate, just take one."

"Well, now I don't want one."

There was an uncomfortable silence as I moved backwards to close the door.

"Mate, c'mon." Jeff was barely controlling his annoyance. "You're playing games with me now. You should check that head of yours again, you've been weird after the hospital."

"I know, I know. But I'll be fine," I said. "Don't worry. See you tonight. Peace."

"Huh? Well, fuck you, mate." Jeff stuck a finger in the air and screwed his head further into the pillow.

"Yeah, you too, sleeping beauty." I dragged the door behind me over the debris on the carpet.

I walked back to my room still craving a cigarette. I must fulfil that craving with something. Breaking routines was hard and I tried to think of things to do that were not destructive. The only healthy thing I could think of was getting some food into my damaged body. Once I tried to stop one addiction, another would take over, I knew it. I pictured myself as an octopus, each tentacle as one addiction. I could withdraw one of them but the others would go out, always on the move. I stop smoking, I start eating food. I stop eating, I start watching porn. I stop watching porn, I start chasing girls. I stop chasing girls, I start smoking weed. And so on.

I decided to cycle to the same café as the day before for some brunch and a cup of coffee. I took the notebook with me. The café was empty when I arrived and I chose the same seat as last time, right in the corner under the picture of Frank Sinatra.

"Ni hao." The waitress came over and smiled, not always the habit of Chinese service workers.

"Ni hao," I smiled back at her.

I felt excited when I sat down in my little corner under the picture of Frank Sinatra, it was like he was watching over me. I took the small notebook with the striped purple cover out of my pocket while I waited for my coffee. I put the book on the table and ran my fingers over it. It didn't make sense the way I felt scared of a notebook, since I had only written one word in it. Maybe this book was my ticket to a happier and more successful life; maybe this book represented a small hope for my future. *Or maybe it is just a regular notebook.*

I wasn't even sure what I wanted from life. When my mind wandered off to the future, a cocktail of negative feelings blustered in like a tornado.

I closed my eyes, took a deep breath and thought about The Experience. After taking a sip of my coffee, I opened my notebook. Just like last time, without thinking about it, I wrote down one word.

DESIRE.

Desire?

I drank more coffee, looked at this one word and my mind took off.

What is my desire?

What does this mean?

Is desire something that is constant or something that comes and goes?

Are some desires good and some bad?

I was not raised in a religious environment but I had learned that most religious and spiritual leaders asked their devotees to suppress their worldly desires in order to get closer to God. It felt natural to strive towards worldly things. I couldn't grasp what 'desire' meant when I was looking at the word in my notebook, or why I had written it. But something told me I *didn't* want these worldly things anymore. There had to be something more important than the need to possess. My routine of constant moving from one place to another; having a girlfriend to not having a girlfriend; having a car to not having a car; having money to not having money; had no effect on how happy I was but still I strived for these things in the belief they would make me happy. I was a living and breathing black hole that swallowed everything but I could never be filled up, only numbed for a limited amount of time.

I continued to sip my coffee, allowing my thoughts to float free. *It's normal to desire a drink of coffee, surely. To desire things like education, healthy family relationships, clothes or money; those desires must be all valid. But some desires and wanting must be unhealthy too, those that result in pain and suffering. Desiring money for necessities; that should be acceptable, but desiring excessive wealth is not.*

I snapped my notebook closed, then reopened it, smoothing out the pages with my fingers. While touching the book I thought about touching, and how we experience life as humans. I considered our five senses. We can touch, hear, smell, see and taste. *In my past I have touched women, heard great music, inhaled the scent of roses, seen beautiful pieces of art and tasted gourmet food but nothing of this has ever filled me up with love like The Experience did. The Experience was above the pleasure of all my senses.*

I tapped my coffee spoon on the edge of the cup, determined to pursue this line of thinking further. All of our senses are constantly desiring. The eyes desire to see, the nose desires to smell, the taste desires satisfaction. The ears desire to hear, the mind desires to think. I leaned back in the chair, propping up my chin with my right hand. *I have lived my whole life by avoiding pain and chasing pleasure. My daily struggles; my disappointments, anxiety and other negative feelings are a result of me chasing my wants and desires.*

It was all an illusion. The Experience had taught me that. But without The Experience I would never have known because nothing had ever moved me that way before.

In my mind I saw a rainbow where each colour represented my wants and desires, and I had been chasing the rainbow. But I still hadn't found any gold.

That ride home from the hospital, when I sat on the motorbike watching the trees; I had suddenly seen how beautiful they were. I had felt no desire, only enjoyment. I didn't need the trees to do anything for me; I didn't need more trees or anything else. I was just enjoying the trees. *There must be something inside me. Something childlike that wants to be free; spontaneous and playful.* I tapped my pencil on the cover of the notebook and smiled at the waitress who was now cleaning the table in front of me, her arm moving quickly backwards and forwards across the wood. She smiled back.

"Wǒ kěyǐ yǒu yīgè kāfēi?" I asked.

"Hao," the waitress responded. She awarded me another smile.

A few minutes later she brought the coffee. It was something about her smile that made me wonder if people were always smiling at me but I just hadn't noticed before. Now I had a desire to smile more and the new desire of getting rid of all my old desires.

I was so caught up in my tangled thoughts that I didn't even notice I was no longer alone. A guy with a French accent had approached me.

"Excuse me?"

"Hello." I gave him the new smile I was practicing.

"Hello," he said. "Nice to meet you, my name is Henry and this is my friend Pau." He gestured just behind him. "We need some help. Do you live in Kunming?"

I was not a big fan of French people, a prejudice passed on to me by my father, he hated the French national football team and anyone he associated with them. I was especially down on people from Paris; I had heard they represented all the negative clichès about the French. But what I liked about them was their funny English accents.

You could recognise most of the backpackers in Kunming by the way they dressed. Most were either going to or coming from Laos or Thailand. Usually they dressed in the new-age hippie style; everybody trying to be so different that they ended up being the same. These two French guys standing over my table were different from the people who were *trying* to be different. They looked like they'd come straight from a jungle.

Henry had a full beard. He wore sunglasses and an Indiana Jones-style hat; with a ripped white shirt and shorts, he looked like something from a teenage movie in 1982. Pau was dressed even worse. He had a long beard as well, and was shirtless and not only wearing the ugliest boots I'd ever seen but also the tightest shorts, allowing me to see parts of his body I really didn't want to see.

"Yeah, I live in Kunming, where are you guys from?" I said once I'd taken in their appearance, as if I hadn't guessed.

"France," Henry said.

"Paris," Pau added.

"I love Paris," I said. "But I have never been. So, where have you guys been? What jungle have you come from?"

I laughed self-consciously, intensely aware I was seeking approval but not knowing why.

Henry sat down in front of me while Pau stood to one side. "Well we have been travelling for sixteen months. We started our trip in Africa and we've been in Asia for almost a year now. We are planning to work our way through China and up to Mongolia. We are staying in Kunming for some days before heading north."

"Yeah, we just wanted to check if you knew any good places to stay around here? We are on a tight budget now, so if you know about some cheap hostel or something like that, it would be great," Pau added.

"Yeah, no problem, I have one in mind. Are you guys hungry? You want to sit down with me for lunch?"

They looked at each other.

"Yeah, brother, why not?" Henry smiled through his beard.

Pau sat down next to Henry and in front of me. I'd surprised myself by offering them a seat. First of all because they looked like they were from another planet, secondly because they talked funny and thirdly because they were French. There was something about these guys though I couldn't pinpoint what it was.

Do I think I might get drugs from them?

Yet they were different from the people I usually hung out with. They were smiley. But they seemed way too careless and free-spirited to *not* be drug users. I decided to talk to them for some minutes and then go quickly so I would not end up smoking a joint with them and destroy the few days I'd had without alcohol, drugs or cigarettes.

"So how's the food here?" asked Henry.

"It's pretty solid by Chinese standards," I assured him. "The chicken sandwich is good." I had it in mind that I already knew they would not like the food. *After all, they're French and their national sport is complaining.*

"Okay. But we are vegetarians, so maybe we go for the salad and rice?"

"Are you serious?" I asked, raising my eyebrows.

"Yes. We are both vegetarians." Pau was laughing.

"Really?" I felt awkward now.

"Yes. Really."

"How long have you been vegetarians?" I couldn't imagine a diet without meat.

Pau leaned on the table. His eyes studied me.

"I have been a vegetarian since I was seventeen and I'm twenty-eight now, so, eleven years."

"Me only three years," Henry added.

The waitress came to take the orders and I helped the guys decide on a couple of veggie dishes and some rice. It was weird that these two guys were vegetarians; I'd always thought vegetarians were either middle-aged women who were obsessed with health, or movie stars, or gay people.

"So what do you do here in Kunming?" Henry asked when the waitress had gone back to the kitchen.

"Well, I'm teaching, or I was. Teaching English. But I'm doing nothing basically, now," I said. I didn't want to think about my career plans at this moment.

"What happened to your head?" That was Pau.

"I was playing football." I wanted to change the subject because I felt they could see straight through me. "So tell me, why are you guys vegetarians?"

Pau answered, "I was working in a slaughterhouse right outside Paris. After that I just didn't want to eat meat anymore. Couldn't face it. When you see that treatment of animals every day from nine to five you become numb and don't see the pain that's going on. That frightened me."

"So what made you quit? Surely you must like the taste of meat. Must be some serious reasons?"

"I like animals, that's my only reason. Animals can be sad, they feel pain and suffer like humans do. Animals can feel love as well, you know. How we treat our animals for profit is just disgusting. I don't want to be a part of that."

"Feel love?" I had never thought about that before. It was hard to believe a fish might be in love with another fish.

"Yes, they can feel the energy of love." Pau was apparently reading my thoughts. "It's a bit different from how we humans experience it, it's not the feeling of being 'in love', I wouldn't say."

I was sceptical but still curious. I couldn't help picturing my friends at the bar as animals, suddenly I perceived it as animalistic behaviour, the way we chased girls every weekend. I even started thinking about when people danced at bars, and that reminded me of a BBC wildlife documentary in which a certain kind of bird attracts females by flapping his wings and dancing. *So we are all animals, really.*

The food arrived, the waitress smiling at the French guys, making me slightly jealous. Henry and Pau attacked their food like they hadn't eaten for days. Henry poured us all water and Pau offered me some of his salad. I declined and started dabbling my fork into the chicken sandwich on my plate. It was my routine to play it safe when it comes to food.

"Okay. I'm interested to know more. What about animals who are not nearly as intelligent as humans, why can't you eat them?"

"Listen," said Pau, as Henry looked on, nodding his head slightly. "If aliens would arrive on earth who were more intelligent than us, does that mean they should eat us? Just because they are smarter than us?"

He has a point.

"And you, Henry, same reasons?"

"Yeah kind of, I suppose," Henry said. "I had a spiritual experience when I was in an ashram, in France."

Hearing this, I wanted to tell him about The Experience. Maybe I could talk to them about it. This tingle arose in my stomach, the same feeling I got before I talked to cute girls. I slowly lifted my head and looked them in the eyes. I had a feeling of déjà vu, zoned right out of the conversation for a few seconds. It was not like a normal déjà vu where you feel that something has happened before, this felt more like a memory from the future. Everything was weird, it was like them being here at this café was a part of some process that had already been decided, like a script, a play in which every character has its role. It had perfect lighting as the sun moved around the room, in the set that was the café.

"What's an ashram?"

A feeling of snapping back into my mind.

"It's a spiritual centre," Henry explained. "A place where you can do yoga, meditation and stuff like that."

"What happened to you there?"

Henry smiled at me. "Well I had been slowly getting rid of all my bad habits, like drinking, smoking, using drugs and stuff like that. I smoked a lot of weed when I was younger, almost every day. But I was getting more and more depressed. So I started to search for some answers. I started to meditate. That's when I went to stay in an ashram with a teacher for one month. It's actually where Pau and I met. After that experience, everything changed for me. I don't eat meat for many reasons. They include ethical, health, environmental .. the list goes on."

He said, after that experience.

He had an experience, too.

I felt like a child learning lessons. And I had more questions to ask.

"Okay. So. Do you guys eat fish?"

"No."

"And both of you don't use drugs or drink alcohol?"

"No, we don't." They spoke almost at the same time.

"Do you?" Pau asked.

Huh yeah..

As I was about to explain it all the waitress came and asked if we'd finished eating. I said in Chinese that we were just about to finish. I told the guys that asking someone in China if he'd already eaten was a greeting in Chinese. They laughed and seemed fascinated but I admitted my use of the language was quite basic and limited to 'restaurant Chinese'. I called the waitress back just to show off and she came to clean up the table. I wanted to keep the guys there a bit longer though.

"So would I need to find a teacher or someone like that to learn how to be a vegetarian?"

Henry looked at me in a more focussed way.

"Teachers or heroes are not the way to find out if you want to be a vegetarian or not. Find out *why* you eat meat, *why* you drink, *why* you smoke, first. If you do this, then change will occur."

They must be recovering alcoholics, I thought. If you don't drink in Iceland it's very likely that you have been in rehab or you are doing some programme in one of the institutions for people struggling with alcoholism. I was fascinated and confused about these guys. I couldn't figure out if I had changed because of The Experience, or if they were just interesting.

I had never thought about vegetarianism, not even for a few seconds, and when they talked about being a vegetarian it seemed such a big deal. The way I felt when I saw those two American guys eating burgers at Paddy's. Had that something to do with them eating meat? Was this a sign? *Or am I crazy?*

We talked for an hour and a half more, having ordered

more coffee. Their travelling stories of people they met, places they'd seen and situations they'd got themselves into kept me engaged. I liked the way these guys seemed so happy. When they smiled, they meant it. When they laughed they meant it. They seemed real. I felt good around them. I decide to follow my instinct as they got up to leave the restaurant.

"How long are you staying in Kunming?"

"We are leaving tomorrow morning," Henry said.

"Do you guys want to stay for free at my place?"

There, I said it.

"Thanks." Henry glanced at Pau. "That would be good."

"Are you sure, Henry? Shouldn't we look around first?" Pau was more pragmatic.

"First choice is always the best one, well, sometimes." Henry nodded towards me.

"Oh, you and your contradictions." But Pau was laughing.

"Okay then," I said, relieved. "That's settled. Meet you guys here around nine tonight and you can come back to mine."

Kafli 10 - Iceland, December 2007.

Drugs and Money

I'D BEEN WAITING outside in the freezing cold for almost an hour. The heater didn't work in my car, a bashed-up '91 Nissan Sunny that had somehow managed to dodge the police and not get thrown into a car cemetery. I was parked outside an apartment building in Grafarvogur, a suburb of Reykjavík, Iceland, my arms wrapped around myself.

It was a Monday night in December. Sparkling lights lit up banks of snow on windowsills. There had been a constant snowfall for the last two days, already it was piling up on the bonnet of my car and obscuring my view through the windscreen. If only the wipers worked properly.

It didn't surprise me to have to wait for my brother, but an hour was kind of stretching it. I knew if I called him it would make no difference, he'd just get angry.

Palli had said it was urgent so I wasn't going to leave, but I was losing my patience, not to mention any physical sensations because of the cold. Finally I heard the muffled thud of a door banging and my brother came running out of the building wearing one of those big black snowboarding jackets. Through the filthy side window I watched him come closer, his face was as pale as the snowy pavement. He slipped as he got in the car, cursing and rubbing his shin.

"It's freezing out there."

"Wow, I really feel sorry for you."

He glanced at me sideways. "Sorry for taking so long, man, it's a madhouse in there."

"Man," I said. "You look like shit, are you okay?"

His pupils were tiny like specks of sand. His lips were chapped and his jaw was jerking from left to right.

"I'm fine. I've just been partying since Friday, it's been a long weekend. I've also been busy with other stuff." He hunched his shoulders, his hands jammed into his pockets, maybe to keep them still. "I haven't slept since Thursday night."

He pulled a hand out of a pocket and drummed one knee with his fingers. I knew the signs. *What's he going to ask me?*

"Bro, I need you to do me a favour. I need you to exchange some money for me. Krónur into Euros."

"What for? Why don't you do it?" I asked. "Are you going on holiday or something?"

I knew he wasn't going anywhere on holiday, especially in that awful state and not just before Christmas.

"Don't ask questions bro. It's for a friend." His jaw was still working in that disturbing way. "It's complicated. You just need to go to three or four banks and get me some Euros. It's easy. Just do me this favour, bro. You know I love you." I hated it when he gave me that look which made me unable to refuse him.

"Three or four banks? Is this dangerous?"

He didn't answer.

"How much is it?" I went on. "Why don't you do it?"

I had million other questions, but, "It's not dangerous," he interrupted. "I would never put you in any danger. You can even ask some of your friends to help you. We'll reward you."

"Reward me with what?"

"I'll give you three grams of cocaine and a few ecstasy pills. Okay? It's the easiest thing in the world. It'll take you two hours, maximum. This guy I'm supposed to meet is on his way so let's just wait a few minutes."

A few minutes had its own meaning in my brother's world. I hoped it wasn't too long. In my mind I had already decided to do this for my brother. How hard could it be? What was wrong with exchanging some money into Euros?

Palli took a bag of white powder out of his pocket and grabbed one of my CD cases to make lines. I watched him snort the lines one by one. It didn't tempt me at that moment, too many other things to worry about. And he was no advert for cocaine in the state he was in. At the same time it was exciting knowing I would get cocaine and ecstasy for a couple of hours' work. Cocaine is expensive on the streets in Iceland. I could sell it. But I loved cocaine. I knew I would take it myself even if I meant to resist.

"Do you want the last line?"

"No, not now, it's Monday, man, got work tomorrow."

He shrugged and snorted it himself.

"Ah, here he comes."

Palli stuck his hand through the window and waved into the cold. My brother's friend saw us, stopped beside the car, looked through the side window and opened the back door. He was a big guy in his forties. He was neatly dressed in a leather jacket, blue jeans and sparkly white sneakers. I watched him covertly as he handed my brother a thick envelope through the gap between the seats. He was in the car for only one or two minutes. They muttered a few words to each other and then the guy took off.

Palli told me how to do the currency exchange at the bank and gave me the envelope. It felt heavy. I was tempted to look into it, but I decided to wait and listen to my brother explain the process. Also my hands were too cold to get the flap open.

"Don't fuck this up."

Palli got out of the car. I watched him disappearing into the thick flakes of snow.

My heart was pumping fast, partly because of nervousness and partly excitement. This was the first time I'd ever held a wad of money this thick, let alone three grams of cocaine and six ecstasy pills in my pocket.

***

It was Friday, the day I had been waiting for all week.

I had exchanged the money my brother gave me and I hadn't touched the drugs the whole week. It was tempting but I wanted to give Palli the money before I went out partying. I was glad I hadn't done anything stupid. My paranoid brother called a few times every day to check up on the money. I told him I had gone to four different banks over three days to exchange it, reasoning that if a twenty-one year old exchanged roughly three hundred and twenty-two thousand Icelandic Krónur in each bank at a time into Euros it wouldn't make the bank suspicious. It seemed to have gone all right.

The money was meant for drug smuggling. I knew my brother was involved with a crowd of criminals but I'd always pretended he didn't get into things like that. I liked to think of him as the party boy. But it didn't take a rocket scientist to see that my brother was in the drug world. He'd been to rehab more than six times but he never got to more than a few months of sobriety. My brother was the reason nobody messed with me all through high school and even today at the age of twenty-one, people wouldn't dare to touch me. Palli was well known in the Reykjavík nightlife and his friends were people you didn't want to rub the wrong way.

My brother had been so smart when he was young and I still hoped he would one day stop this nonsense and use his intelligence to do something useful. He'd always had grand ideas about starting a business. He said he wanted to work for himself but there were no signs that he would begin anytime soon, at least not a legit one.

At four PM Palli called and said we needed to get rid of the money. He asked me to meet him at a bar in downtown Reykjavík. I was used to getting these instructions on short notice.

At this time I was living with a friend in Skerjafjorður, next to the domestic airport which is about twenty-five minutes' walk from downtown. I put on my warmest jacket, gloves and hat in preparation for if I had to wait for my brother in the car with a broken air conditioner. It was snowing, dark already and the one-minute walk to the car was on packed-down snow with thick ridges that could trip you up. I couldn't wait to hand the money back. It had seemed a long week.

The drive to the bar downtown took a while in the snow, since I could barely see a few metres in front of me. Luckily I was unlikely to hit anyone, since there was nobody outside at this time, in this weather.

As I entered the bar, I scanned the place. I saw a family on one table and a lonely drinker at the other end of the room. Palli was sitting in a corner with his best friend, a wimpy-looking guy known for his hardcore drug use. I never liked him and I'd always thought he was a bad influence on my brother.

"Do you have the money?" Palli asked as soon as I sat down, still looking to see if there was anyone near us. He sounded paranoid.

"Yeah, and hey, thanks for thanking me."

"You got your rewards, so shut up." Palli had a sour look on his face, snatching the now tattered envelope and shoving it into his jacket without checking.

While I contemplated the bar, wondering if it was too early to have a beer, my brother brought out his phone and called some guy to come pick up the money. I felt very relieved now I'd handed Palli nine thousand Euros. It was the end of a stressful week for me.

I kept glancing at my watch and scanning the bar, until Palli's friend made a loud sound of exasperation.

"Go get a beer, you seem nervous."

Who is he to order me around? But he was right.

I walked to the bar and ordered a pint of beer. I had a gut feeling that this weekend was going to get crazy. There were three grams of cocaine and six pills in my pocket. The moment had arrived. I'd planned to go and see my friends after this meeting.

When I sat down next to my brother I finished the beer so fast it surprised even his junkie friend. I stood up. It was time to have some refreshment in the bathroom. I deserved it after this stressful week.

***

"Call an ambulance, he's not breathing. Do something, goddamn it, do something!" a girl was shouting.

It was Monday morning. The sun was up. I was in an apartment in downtown Reykjavík with some people I didn't know at all. I had finished all my stash and was in the process of getting some more drugs from a scary-looking guy at the party. There were around a dozen people in the apartment, all well-known in the underworld as criminals, drug addicts and people who lived for weekends like this. Everybody was fucked up, including myself.

"We can't call the police, no way. Don't fucking do it." A

guy who looked like a member of a motorcycle gang shoved the girl who was getting her phone out.

"What the fuck! Are you fucking crazy? He's dying! Let me call a fucking ambulance, you fucking idiot." The girl was hysterical.

I stood close by, immobile with shock, watching two strangers fighting over whether they should help the guy lying on the floor. He was becoming paler by the minute, white stuff drooling from his mouth. His body twitched every five seconds. I looked around for my brother. I hadn't seen him for who knows how many hours.

This is madness.

What the hell am I doing here?

The only idea I could come up with was to get out of there. Patting my phone and wallet in my pockets, I ran to the front door.

The sun hit my eyes as I reached the outside. It was freezing. I was wide awake from all the drugs I had taken.

I was satisfied that I'd had the sense to get my ass out of that apartment, despite my fucked-up state. It was none of my business. I ran down the stone stairs wondering where I'd go at this hour. But something stopped me in my tracks. I saw a street sign. I turned my head, registering the number of the house.

Walking slowly away from the building I took out my

phone and as chills were running through me I dialled the emergency line...

"I'm on Brávallagata. There's a guy dying in the apartment." When I was sure they had got the address, I pressed End Call.

As I walked home, coming down from the drugs, I felt like a vampire having to block the sunlight with my hands. I passed normal people who were going to work or couples taking their kids to school. I hadn't stopped drinking and drugging since early Friday evening when I had my first beer with my brother.

Just another weekend.

I started to feel sorry for myself, trying to remember how much money I'd spent and that it was Monday, my least favourite weekday.

Later I found out that the guy at the party had died.

Kafli 11 - Kunming, 2011.

Sharing with Henry and Pau

I SPENT THE afternoon alone in my apartment. After meeting the French guys that morning I was experiencing extreme swings of emotion. I went from wanting to be the president of the world to filling up with self-doubt. It was like a roller coaster. I had glimpses when riding the positive emotions that I was on some kind of track, some path. I had a gut feeling that I wouldn't have met the French guys if it weren't for The Experience.

Then I questioned my decision to invite the French guys to stay at my place because Jeff didn't know about it. But I decided not to listen to my fear.

I walked to the café again to pick up Henry and Pau. I didn't see them when I walked in. It was quarter to nine in the evening, so I sat down outside to watch the city, and ordered an orange juice.

The area was lively and almost all the seats were taken. It was an international crowd, having drinks in a perfect Kunming summer. I watched the people around me, those on the street passing by and those sitting near me at the café, and I couldn't help but notice that everybody seemed to have companionship. People were chatting with their friends and enjoying life. I was alone and felt out of place.

Kunming was a fascinating place, full of people who came here for different reasons. It was full of expats, travellers, students, NGO workers, artists and business people. I didn't fit into any of those categories.

What am I doing waiting for some weirdo vegetarians who don't even drink?

What am I doing in Kunming at all?

I felt frustration rising and started to crave a beer, but I held myself back, decided I would give this new process of mine a bit more time.

I could spot Henry and Pau miles away. They stood out from the crowd; maybe that was the reason I was drawn to them. They had big smiles on their faces. I wondered if they'd had those smiles for the whole day or if I was the one making them happy.

"Sorry we are late." Henry's voice sounded loud, even a few metres away from the table.

"No worries, do you guys need help with the bags?" I squeezed out a smile. It felt good to see them, like meeting old friends.

"Yeah, thanks. Maybe you can grab the small one? We are so tired after walking around the whole day looking for cowboy boots."

"What? You just bought these boots you are wearing, Pau?" My mouth curved up of its own accord.

"Yeah. We are going to ride a 'orse when we go to Mongolia, so I decided to buy good boots." Pau's big proud smile lit up the street.

"An 'orse?"

"Yeah, 'orse, you know, 'orse riding." Henry said and started jumping up and down, swinging his hands. People at the café were laughing at this weird jungle guy imitating a person riding some animal called 'orse'.

"What the fuck is an 'orse? Do you mean an ox? Do they have oxen in Mongolia?"

"H, Böddi, H." Pau was trying to explain in his French accent. "'Orse with an 'H'."

I finally understood, remembering that French people have trouble pronouncing the letter H. We laughed a bit more and grabbed the bags to go home. Walking home we laughed and chatted. I'd made the right choice asking them to stay. There was at least less chance I would get into trouble staying with non-drinking vegetarians. I was breaking my routine. This could be happening for a reason.

❊❊❊

As the three of us arrived home Jeff was just about to go to Paddy's. His eyes grew big as two light bulbs when he saw the French guys. I said they were staying and he seemed cool with it, but as he said goodbye Jeff gave me a: *you must have gone mad*, kind of look. I didn't care. I just regretted the time I'd spent worrying what he might say or think.

"Put your bags over there, guys," I told Henry and Pau.

They were only staying for one night and I wanted to know so much that I didn't know where to begin.

While Henry was unpacking some stuff he answered my questions about the countries they had been to in the last sixteen months.

"We've been to Egypt, Israel, and Jordan. We spent about three months each in these countries. Then we flew to India: Mumbai. We worked our way to south India, all the way to Sri Lanka. We spent seven months in India all together. It's a crazy place." He straightened up, stroking his beard. In his eyes was a depth that was hard to comprehend. "It's a different world out there."

"Wow, seven months. It sounds more like you lived there instead of just travelling. And then what?"

"We then flew to Thailand. We have been doing the classic circle of countries in East Asia, like Cambodia, Vietnam and Laos. We just came from Laos on a bus to Kunming, just to meet you."

He made a silly face.

I settled into a corner of the sofa, folding my legs under me.

"So. You were in Egypt, Jordan, India and now in China. You'll be able to see four of the wonders of the world in this trip, that's awesome."

Pau, sitting at the other end of the sofa, started laughing. I glanced at him, worrying that I'd got it wrong about the Seven Wonders of the World.

Pau interrupted his laughing to say, "We haven't seen any wonders of the world. The universe had something different planned for our trip. We were always going to see those places but then something happened. We met some people who took us to different places, or there was something more exciting to do."

I learned something new whenever Pau opened his mouth to speak. I'd never met anyone who constantly used words like the 'universe', 'divine' and the one word I was most interested in, 'energy'.

"More exciting things? Sounds pretty interesting to see the wonders of the world, right?"

Pau lifted his eyebrows and lowered them again a couple of times, a habit of his I was getting used to.

"Yeah, but we didn't plan our trip. We decided before the trip that we were going to follow our instincts and our instincts didn't take us to those places."

Henry reached across the table for a bottle of water and took a long sip. While swallowing he looked at me like he wanted to say something. "We did go to one of the Seven Wonders of the World but it's just not on the list." Pau started laughing again. My face must have been one big question mark as Henry went on. "We realised in Cambodia that we hadn't seen any of those wonders so we took a special trip to see the Angkor Watt temple. I was sure that it was on the list of the seven wonders and I convinced Pau to go. I just found out in Laos that it's not on the list. So I'll tell my grandchildren that I almost saw one wonder, in all my world travels."

"Cool. Wonders are wonders, whether they're on the list or not, right?" I said, reaching down next to sofa for a box of crackers that had been there a while. When I put it on the table, Pau's face lit up.

"There's a lot of poverty in those countries," I mused, watching crumbs fall onto Pau's chest as he munched on a cracker. "You jungle boys seem to be all right living in rough conditions, but didn't you think those countries were a bit sad with their poverty? Didn't you feel weird coming from a wealthy place like Paris?"

Henry looked serious. When he spoke the tone of his voice had changed. "Rich societies are much sadder than poor ones. If you go to Paris you see people who have everything they want but are still unhappy. I know when I go back to France I'll feel sad for the people there." He kept his head down while he seemed to be thinking. "What do you mean by wealth, Böddi?"

My heart pumped faster. I wanted to answer this question correctly. "Well, I guess I mean, you know, *things*. Stuff. Nice apartments and cars."

"Interesting," said Henry. "I don't consider these things wealth. The world is pretty fucked up right now. We are eating up all our resources at a faster rate than ever. I look at wealth as clean water, fresh air and enough food to live. The other stuff is just one big illusion. The people in Kunming might be driving Range Rovers now and wearing French designer clothing but they are breathing air that will kill them in the end. The concept of global warming is so big for the individual that it's easier to deny it. It's hard to change the way you think about huge problems like climate crisis, pollution, and water shortage and so on, so people are in total denial over all the problems in the world. Denial is the easy way."

I was ashamed. These guys had something I didn't and I was shocked to be acknowledging that. Before, I would have just labelled them as hippies; dreamers or just stupid, because they didn't go with my conservative world view. Pau was nodding his head. It was like they were connected on some profound level of friendship. I felt distant from it but I was open to discovering a deeper truth than my shallow, acquired views. That was new to me. Realizing I was brought up to have opinions, not just to listen.

"The key word in what Henry said is *illusion*. In general, people seem to search for the meaning of life in worldly ambitions such as wealth, in the common understanding of the word. And then the other illusions like prestige and success. But chasing these things limits your ability to raise your consciousness. It's impossible to see the reality of life with that mind-set. People locked in this illusion will never be free."

Although I found Pau's choice of language difficult to understand, from this I got the main idea. Chasing these things resulted in an unhappy and unfulfilled life. That made sense to me, especially in light of past few days. And the words in my notebook. I drew my knees up to my chest, bursting with new questions.

"You guys are something else. So are you religious? What made you want to go down that path in life?" I used the word 'path' because I wanted to talk like them. I was aware that this was one of my routines. If I met people I found interesting, I tried to be what I thought they wanted me to be.

I am a chameleon.

Henry looked at me without saying a word for a second or two. "You ask a lot of questions, that's a good thing. You are hungry like us. But wait a moment, I'm going to get some more water and then I'll tell you more."

I used the opportunity to take a bathroom break and digest what had been said. As I came back, Henry followed in my footsteps, returning from the kitchen. Pau was standing by the window in the living room and turned as we entered, waving a hand behind him. He told me how fascinated he was with the view. I'd never given it much attention, but he was right, those city buildings with their lights twinkling out into the dark looked quite spectacular. We all stood and admired the man-made vista for a few moments. I hoped the spell of our conversation hadn't been broken.

"Where shall we sleep?" Pau eventually asked.

So that's it, then. I was disappointed he wanted to settle down so early.

"Right here, in the living room. The sofa turns into a bed and we have a spare mattress in the walk-in cupboard, here."

Once we'd got everything arranged I turned to go, thinking they wanted to get some sleep in preparation for their early start the next morning. But Pau stopped me.

"Sit down with us a while longer, Böddi." He patted the sofa-bed next to him.

"Okay, thanks."

Henry grinned and took a pillow from the sofa-bed, laid it on the floor and sat down right opposite me with his long legs crossed.

"You asked an interesting question, Böddi. Are we religious or spiritual? Let me first tell you about our journey. When we began our travels we decided to be open to everything that came our way. We went on this journey to learn. When we arrived in Egypt we felt we must explore what Islam is all about. We met some amazing guys who opened our eyes to Muslim beliefs. From there we went to Israel where we met some very influential Jewish people. I remember this one guy who was practicing Kabbalah, which is the mystical aspect of Judaism; we felt that our journey had truly begun after spending time with him." He took a sip from his cup of water. "Then we went to India. We spent most of our time there in ashrams. In India we explored the world of Hinduism. Pau and I were meditating a lot and we both went through a huge transformation. Living in an ashram is hard, but the rewards were amazing. We met many different gurus and highly advanced spiritual beings. I can only speak for myself, but I'll never be the same again." He glanced at Pau, who nodded solemnly. "After that we went to South East Asia. We explored Buddhism and we continued to try to grow. It feels weird explaining this journey to you in so few words but to answer your question, from my perspective, on all my travels, meeting these amazing people, I discovered one thing."

I was all ears. The sofa bed made a creaking sound as I shifted on it in anticipation of what he would say.

"Now listen carefully. Not many spiritual individuals are religious and not many religious people are spiritual. There's a huge difference. Are you following me? Most of the spiritual beings we met are actually grounded people. Not what you might expect them to be, you know, not holy-seeming or anything."

After hearing the short version of Henry's travels I realised how little I knew. When he mentioned Kabbalah, my mind linked it to the pop singer Madonna, from what I had read in some tabloid paper. I associated Buddhism with monks living in caves in Tibet. I tied the mention of a guru in India to an image of a guy with a ridiculously long beard levitating above the ground. I'd only heard of Muslims in connection with news reports of someone building a home-made bomb to attack America. There was so much more than I knew regarding this stuff. Henry was right; I was hungry to know more.

"So, are you guys spiritual then?"

Henry laughed. "Yeah, if you want to put us in a box then yes, probably we are."

"Have you guys had, like, a spiritual experience?"

"Yes. Many of them, every day."

I had a feeling Pau would answer my next question and I was right.

"So how are spiritual experiences?"

Pau laid down the book he had taken from his rucksack. It had a picture of a guru-like person on the cover. As I was staring at the cover Pau said, "You cannot describe spiritual experiences with words. You can talk about divine energy, harmony, infinite bliss, inner peace or any other experience, but it's meaningless to anyone else until they have experienced them."

My stomach tightened. I knew he was not saying this to hurt me but that's the feeling I experienced. Maybe it was because I had a point to prove, that I was not any different from them.

"Well maybe I have."

"Awesome." Both Pau and Henry looked eager to hear my experience. "We have been babbling about us too much anyway. Please, tell us about it."

My face became hot, I was sure it was going red. "Well, it's very awkward. I'm not sure I should tell you."

Pau laid his hands flat on his book. "We've seen pretty much everything on our spiritual journey, I don't think you will shock us."

I still took a minute to prepare myself to open up. "Okay,"

I said. "Last Saturday I woke up in the hospital after a night out drinking. That's why I have this bandage around my head. Sorry for lying to you guys, I wasn't playing football. I don't remember anything from that night."

I couldn't tell them about The Experience, who was I kidding? As my words dried up I found myself zoning out. I scratched at the skin around my eye until it felt rubbed raw and then I looked down at the living room table, biting my lips. From the corner of my good eye I saw Pau and Henry glance at each other. It could have been an awkward moment, but I didn't feel rushed by them. There was some trust, some permission from them giving me space to be whatever I was at the moment.

Come on, I said to myself, *tell them.*

"In the hospital, something weird happened on Sunday night. I was lying in my bed and this 'energy' or something like that, was in the bed next to me. I felt this peace that I have never felt before. It was like I could understand things, suddenly. It was like my body was overtaken with this divine energy and the feeling was the best I've ever had in my life. I was shaking and vibrating. I'm probably just crazy, but after this experience my thinking has changed." I tried to slow down, pronounce everything clearly so they could keep up. "It's like my mind has realised some of its own limitations; not that I'm feeling superior or anything, just more humble and open after the experience. I am not feeling better as such but something has changed in me. I am constantly thinking that I must be crazy but I do know what I felt. I wasn't dreaming. Do I sound like a crazy person?"

Henry and Pau were both looking at me with dawning understanding. Henry glanced at Pau then back at me.

"It all makes sense now, why we met you."

"It just doesn't stop, does it?" said Pau. "Talk about flowing, this is unreal."

I didn't have a clue what was going on between them. Had they just listened to what I said?

"So, you guys think I'm crazy, or .. ?"

Pau got up. He picked up a cushion and moved over to sit next to Henry and it felt like they were now my audience.

"You are not crazy," he said. "Go with this. Listen to this. This happened for a reason. This is your experience and no-one can take it away from you. You have just rocked our world by sharing this, because it has been happening over and over again on our journey. We meet all kinds of people and we constantly feel we meet them for a reason. We were supposed to meet you."

Henry nodded. "Pau is right. Your ride is just beginning if you go with this."

I was confused but extremely excited at the same time. "How do I go with this?"

Pau took a quick look at Henry.

"Just trust this energy, just put all your trust in it. It's telling you something. Are the changes in you positive since you had this experience?"

"I somehow feel my mind is more open," I said, newly confident. "Difficult to explain it, but somehow I see things more clearly. And the weirdest part is that I haven't smoked or had a drink since this happened. I've had cravings for these things but something is keeping me back."

Pau looked straight into my eyes. "You have to go with this, man, seriously."

My chest expanded. I stood up and walked to the window of the living room again. There was complete silence within the room. I gazed at the skyscrapers and the city lights through the window and felt tears streaming down my face. I knew Henry and Pau were right. I had to follow this, however I would do it.

I wiped my face on the back of my hand. Henry was calling me.

"Dude, because this has been such an awesome night, I have to show you something."

He was going through his backpack on the floor.

"Check out this flute I bought in India. I bought it from a beggar. It's a magic flute. I want to play a song for you to celebrate our friendship. This is the friendship flute." He grinned while he put the wooden flute up to his mouth. Pau also gave me a cock-eyed smile and my muscles relaxed.

"I play the same song for all my friends with my friendship flute." Henry blew an experimental note before launching into a jaunty tune.

This is stupid.

No.

This is great.

Henry played 'The circle of life' from the Lion King over and over again, until my sides hurt from laughing with the two of them.

Later we talked more about their journey and our perceptions of spirituality. This had turned out to be one of the most interesting and enjoyable nights for me in a long time, with those two *jungle boys* from Paris.

Kafli 12 - Kunming.

Going to Laos

THE FRENCH GUYS were packing their bags outside my room at seven AM. I heard the toilet flush and taps running. They were talking in low voices and laughing softly, always laughing. But I stayed in bed, staring at the ceiling. The feeling of me was crawling all over my body, and I was sweating more than usual. It was probably because I hadn't had a cigarette for a few days.

Why have I quit smoking?

The craving was so strong. How could I possibly quit all my bad habits? Not mere habits but hobbies as well. Since I grew up my life had evolved around drinking, smoking and partying and now I was giving it all up. *Why the fuck?* It was too scary to contemplate.

A loud knock on my door, like someone was trying to make a song.

"Come in .."

Pau was standing behind Henry. The way they smiled I couldn't help smiling back.

I wished they would stay in my living room and not continue with their journey to Mongolia.

"We need to get off now, dude," Henry said in his funny French way. "Don't forget what we said, my friend." Pau nodded, smiling widely, his face squashed in the doorway next to Henry's. *If only I could shrink them both, clone them and have a pocket-version of Henry and Pau with me all the time.* I felt I'd known them much longer than a day or two.

"Do you want to have breakfast with me first, guys?"

They both shook their heads and said they'd already eaten breakfast.

"Departure time." Pau was doing that eyebrow dance of his. "C'mon over and say goodbye, Böddi. Hey and don't forget to give us your email address and we can keep in touch. We've written both of ours down for you." He handed me a sheet of paper when I got out of bed and I gave them each a hug before hurriedly scribbling my email address down for them on the back of a cinema ticket. Right before they went out the door Pau slipped me an envelope. I said thanks without knowing what was in it. Then off they went, pushing and joking with each other as they squeezed through the doorway with their bags. I stood for a few minutes in my room holding the envelope, reflecting on my time with the jungle boys.

I related to those guys on a level I had not experienced before and now I stood in my room lacking any plan for the day. I wanted to open the envelope in the right mood, and it wasn't now.

My body went into autopilot as I pulled on my clothes and started preparing to head off to the café I'd been eating at all week. But then I realised it was a bit early so I lay back down and watched a movie without really taking any of it in. My hand idled over the English teaching books, stacked on the cabinet next to my bed.

I kinda miss the kids.

Do they miss me?

At some point I'll have to return the books.

I pulled the comforter over me and kept staring at the books. The bandage on my head was itching. The reason for me working as a teacher had never been from a desire to educate Chinese kids, it was to get some money in my pocket and keep me away from the bar. I'd already spent half the small fortune I'd procured in Iceland (not entirely honestly) and had hoped to prolong my stay in Asia by working; in between drinking and the usual chaotic lifestyle.

When the crappy movie was over I stood up and looked in

the mirror, considering. Slowly, I started to remove the bandage. A big red lump blazed from my scalp, the size of a golf ball. My hair had been shaved off around it.

It looks horrible.

My hair can cover most of it.

Man, it's itchy.

***

I always took the same route to the café, but it felt different each time. I wondered if I was changing my perspective on a daily basis or if Kunming was so versatile that it could constantly surprise me. As I walked I even noticed new constructions that I'd never seen before. New buildings were rising at a rapid rate in Kunming but I doubted that even the Chinese could throw one up in two days.

I arrived at the café, the first customer of the day, and sat down in my usual seat under Frank Sinatra. I was aware for the first time since I met Henry and Pau of how sore the bruises on my ribs still were. If I leaned forward on the table they hurt, if I leaned back in my seat they hurt. I had to shift about until I could get comfortable. It was late morning and two waitresses were opening up the place, taking the chairs down off the tables. They greeted me with smiles. Maybe they had always smiled. I studied the menu; there were bacon sandwiches, chicken Panini, pepperoni pizzas and all kinds of meat dishes. I ordered a Greek salad (Chinese version) and an orange juice. It made me smile inwardly, because I was changing my routine. I didn't believe I would go on like this for long, but at least for one more day I would not eat meat.

I felt at home at this café, reflecting on the past week: The Experience; arguing at Paddy's; suffering in the park; the notebook and the letter from the French guys. I had the notebook and the letter with me. I wanted answers to my life, to my condition and my confusion. I missed Henry and Pau already. I regretted not thanking them enough when they'd left that morning and wished I'd joined them on their journey north to Mongolia.

I want to go on an adventure, seek the unknown.

I need to be free of my habits and my routine in Kunming.

I want to escape myself.

The salad arrived while I waded through the usual soup of questions in my head.

What do the French guys have that I don't?

Do I want them to save me from my misery?

Is there a reason I met them?

How can I possibly be so attached to these guys after knowing them for less than twenty-four hours?

Without giving it a thought I reached into my pocket for the notebook. Immediately I wrote down the third word.

ATTACHMENT.

I didn't know what 'attachment' meant. The word seemed negative to me.

What am I attached to?

The first image that popped into my mind was my father. I'd lived my life wishing to impress him and meet his exacting standards, failing every time. I was attached to my mother, but that was more about not wanting to disappoint her. I wasn't really attached to my brother anymore; I hadn't talked to him for a long time, since he moved to London in 2010.

There must be something more to this word 'attachment', otherwise why had I written it in my book? As I chewed mouthful after mouthful of food I became less hopeful of understanding it. My week had been crazy, maybe I was asking too much of myself. How many revelations could I actually have at this small café in Kunming?

I forced myself to look into every angle of the word 'attachment'. Nothing. I was stuck.

Finishing the salad, I ordered a cup of coffee. Time to read the letter from Henry and Pau. I opened it slowly, preparing myself to be disappointed.

Dear Böddi,

We are extremely thankful to you for letting us stay in your apartment. We really enjoyed being with you and meeting you was another wonderful experience in our journey. It is so obvious to me and Henry that we met you for a reason and therefore I wanted to say a few things to you before we head to Mongolia on an 'orse trip.

Böddi, it is your duty and responsibility as a member of this planet to evolve spiritually. You have a responsibility because you are the world and the world is you. After listening to your story yesterday, I can tell you that you will not grow spiritually if you live the way you did before. You are an amazing guy and we both see a beautiful human being behind your fears and insecurity.

That said, we think it's essential that you have to trust the Energy experience you told us about. Never doubt it, just go with it. Try to do the opposites of things you have been doing for the past years, trust that the Energy will lead the way. If you have always been looking for fulfilment in life and it has only caused you pain and suffering, then now is the time to look for emptiness so that the Energy can flow through you and fill you up.

Truth, simplicity and love
Henry and Pau

Something wet dribbled into the corner of my mouth. It tasted salty. Tears were trailing down my face. Something had broken inside me, my ego was cracked, I was naked to the world. Nobody had shown me this much love in a long time.

I'd seen it in their eyes, Henry's and Pau's, in how they talked and behaved. I dried my tears with the hem of my shirt and looked up from the table. I was in a public place and there were already two tables full of foreigners eating lunch and ready to start their day. I closed my eyes, hoping to reconnect to the Energy and get some answers, desperate to understand what this word 'attachment' meant.

There were now three words in the notebook:

ROUTINE

DESIRE

ATTACHMENT

The words were all linked; I could see the bigger picture.

First, Routines. My use of alcohol, cigarettes, drugs, women and food. My constant wanting: in the past it was to become a doctor, a famous football player, or even just be accepted by the people around me. Now there was my wanting to get rid of things: Fear and suffering, anxiety and greed.

Second, Desire: my chasing of pleasures was endless. I would never be completely satisfied. I would never arrive at any satisfaction of my desires.

I had never seen these things so clearly before. I took a deep breath and said out loud, but in a low voice so the other people wouldn't hear me,

"This is attachment."

An older man at the next table glanced up from his food

and met my eyes, I hadn't been as quiet as I had thought, so I continued my investigations in my head:

I'm attached to pleasure.

I'm attached to becoming something.

I'm attached to getting rid of things.

All the things I am attached to are limited and mortal and they can never be satisfying in themselves.

I felt short of breath with the effort of trying to discover. There was still a lot missing from the puzzle. I didn't know what further questions to ask or what to make of this new way of thinking. I must simply let go and trust that the energy would lead my way. Closing my eyes again, I tried to let it flow. *I am attached to pleasures. Sensual pleasures. Sensual pleasures that affect my seeing, hearing, touching, tasting, smelling and thinking. I am attached to likes and dislikes, to greed and aversion. If I could remove all these attachments, what would be left? Could I never eat a pizza again if I get rid of attachments? Could I never make love again without having an attachment?*

Again I saw the pattern of rising and falling. I was always trying to grasp pleasures on the rising but I would eventually come down from them. I drank, got hungover. I smoked, coughed my lungs out. I wanted, I got tired of. I suffered, I numbed it. I was in pain, until it healed.

I needed fresh air. Time to leave the café and take my sore body off for a walk. It would help me think. As I was putting my stuff away I noticed two overweight girls eating hamburgers. I didn't have judgemental thoughts about them like I would have done only the day before. I had recently read that one in every three Americans suffers from obesity. *If the mind is not healthy, if it isn't content and still, people have attachment to pleasures like eating which makes them gain weight.* On my way out I turned my head to have one more look at the fat girls eating their hamburgers. Hmm, perhaps it wasn't the act of eating a hamburger that was bad, only eating a hamburger just for the pleasure. *Maybe, it isn't about what you do, it's about how you do it, and why.*

I pointed myself in the direction of home. Now when I looked at all the people around me I could only see them chasing their desires. Rushing here, hurrying there, everybody chasing something. It was as if I had stopped and the merry-go-round was still spinning around me.

There has to be more to life than this.

What if this 'something' that people are constantly looking for is the Energy that I experienced?

What did the Jungle boys mean when they said I should do the opposite of everything I'd done? What I really wished was that I could go with them to Mongolia, I'd have loved to learn more from them. Then I remembered what they had stated in their letter: let the energy lead the way. *If I want to go north and I am supposed to do the opposite of my wanting, then I must go south.*

"South? What's south?" I glanced furtively around, realising that I'd again spoken out loud but no-one seemed to have noticed.

I wasn't a hundred per cent sure that this was the Energy directing me or if I was just seeking a way to escape my life in Kunming; the same way I had wanted to escape my life in Iceland. I took a deep breath as I walked along the warm pavement, feeling air go through me. I was intensely aware of the ground beneath my feet and the people around me, rushing and blurred. I looked up into the hot, blue sky. Yes. There was only one way to find out if the Energy was directing me or not.

"I'm going south," I was still speaking aloud, like a madman. "And the next country south of Kunming is Laos. I'm going to Laos."

Kafli 13 - Laos.

Arriving

I AM FINALLY here in the capital of Laos, Vientiane, after a thirteen-hour bus trip from Kunming. I did manage some sleep during the ride, but I had to position my head at an uncomfortable angle on the headrest to avoid the lump on the side of my skull. The Chinese tourist group on the bus with me was loud. Privacy in China has a different meaning than in the West; for example the Chinese guy sitting behind me didn't hesitate to wake me up to take photographs of him and his wife. But amazingly, I wasn't annoyed by them. Man, I really have changed. I am on a new adventure. Leaving Kunming is a certain relief.

It was chillier in Laos than I'd expected. I found the hostel, a small house in the middle of the city, not far from the bus depot. It looked rusty, dozens of bicycles parked outside. It had slogans like 'smile' and 'life is beautiful' written on its wall, graffiti-style. As I walked in, it became obvious that I was in a new country. There was definitely a different vibe in Vientiane than in fast-growing, fast-paced Kunming. I stood in the lobby observing the people around me. Backpackers and locals were all moving at a slower pace here and already I could see more smiles than I had done in China. I dumped my bags in the corner and checked in. The receptionist probably noticed how thirsty I was because he offered me beer but I asked for soda water instead.

I felt optimistic, all pumped up for this new adventure of mine, but at the same time I had no idea of my next move. Sitting at a table near the bar I observed my fellow travellers. Nobody seemed to be going anywhere in a hurry. People were just lying around on the floor, reading books, talking, sleeping, and checking emails at the hostel's computers.

A part of me envied them all, they seemed fully content in this moment. I also wanted to be *right here, right now* but I had this feeling that I had to do something or be somewhere else. My mind was busy in the future, creating scenarios about situations that might happen. I sensed that my worries were over-creative. If I could only channel all this creativity I wasted on worrying I'd probably be able to write bestselling novels with amazing plots and twists, instead of one word at a time, or silly thoughts in my notebook.

The French guys had told me to trust in the process, to go with the flow, not try to control. I decided to do something I would not have done before because this was a new adventure and I had to do things differently. I had to focus on opposites. For my experiment I picked out a group of six people at a table in the middle of the lobby. They were all of different ages, all dressed differently, so I guessed they were not a closed group of friends. I went over to them, feeling like the new kid at school.

"May I sit?" I asked, my face hot.

"Of course," answered a girl with red-coloured hair. She wore a hippy-style flowery dress and a nose ring. She budged up and I slid onto the end of the bench next to her. It surprised me how nervous I was in this obviously relaxed environment. These people all seemed well-travelled and adventurous. A guy near me, I guessed to be in his forties, had a camera around his neck and was drinking a beer. Craving a beer but not giving in, (I had only been in Laos about an hour) I felt insignificant amongst them.

While I sat silently, the group talked about surfing in Australia; discussed whether they liked the ending of the movie *Into the Wild*; one of them described full moon parties in Thailand and another spoke of how *The Beach* had inspired some of them to go to East Asia.

They spoke passionately, so much livelier than the regular barflies at Paddy's. Eventually I managed to squeeze in one or two comments of my own but they seemed to pop out of me at inappropriate moments. Why was I so shy?

Everybody at the table was searching for different kinds of answers. Perhaps a similar Experience to mine had pushed them on their journeys too. It was bittersweet to sit with them because it showed me that there must be millions of people doing exactly the same as me: travelling to discover themselves. It was somewhat of a blow to discover I was not unique.

"Hey, handsome." A British girl broke into my thoughts. She had light brown hair about the same colour as mine in a series of plaits and she wore a strappy orange top with a 'Peace' badge pinned on it. She sat opposite me at the table.

"Who, me?"

"Yeah, you with the ice-blue eyes. Are you going out tonight? And where are you from?"

"I'm from Iceland, living in China. Going where?"

"There's a party tonight in one of those bars close by. You should come."

"No, I can't. But thanks." I felt my lips smiling without any effort on my part. No need to be shy, after all.

"Why?" She scratched her head, between the rows of plaits.

"Well, because I don't drink; nor do I smoke. It's just not part of my lifestyle right now."

Was that me? I was not used to saying no when a girl asked me out, especially right after she called me handsome. It was good to say the words out loud. I was revelling my newly discovered identity, as unfamiliar to myself as to the people around me. They'd either just accept me, or not. Still, I couldn't completely shake off concern about what they might be thinking.

"Interesting," the guy next to 'Plaits' said.

I smiled at him. I could be whoever I wanted, create a whole new me during this trip. If I wanted I could reinvent myself as a spy, a porn actor or an astronaut, whatever. But something had told me to be real. To pierce through my shyness and discover the source of it.

"Cool. Are there any more things you don't do?"

"I don't eat meat." I spoke in a low voice, hoping they wouldn't ask me how long I'd been a vegetarian.

"Okay, cool. How long have you been veggie for?" the British girl asked.

"One week."

The whole table laughed. I laughed too. I felt better. My journey was really beginning. It was up to me how I handled myself from now on.

"So, why don't you drink alcohol or eat meat?" asked a blond Swedish guy.

I hadn't really thought about the answer to this, especially not to give a group of strangers.

"It just feels right. Why do you eat meat and why do you drink?"

Maybe I said it too sharply because I felt defensive. My ears buzzed as heat rose in my cheeks and I sensed a silence falling over the table like a cloth. Because I felt judged I guessed the meat-eaters felt judged by me; I was sure I'd offended them. As my hearing returned to normal someone was tapping his foot. The older guy with the camera broke the ice and asked if we should all head out to a bar. At that the others began standing up, collecting their belongings and shrugging on lightweight jackets. One by one they moved away from the table and left the hostel, trailing through the front lobby. I didn't move. The girl in the flowered dress threw a curious glance back at me, a frown between her eyes.

Part of me wanted to chase after those people and apologise for snapping at them, but if I was going to be real I must give up my old routines of trying to manipulate every situation I was in.

Have I ever been real in my life? If I've never been real, then have I ever experienced a truly deep relationship with another human being? Has my life so far been mostly fake?

I was seeing myself more and more objectively. I was no longer going to be shy. Even if it meant I'd spend a lot of time on my own from now on. Solitude frightened me but I had to do the opposite of what I'd done before, like Henry and Pau mentioned in the letter. I made my drink last as long as possible, wallowing in ideas of 'being real'. The lobby had emptied out. I felt alone in every sense of the word. A cold breeze coming from a fan close by gave me a tingling feeling. I must move, couldn't sit here all night.

Like an old man I pushed myself off the bench and crossed the deserted lobby. I climbed up to my room, reached via two flights of stairs in separate turrets with a long, windowless corridor in between. There was only one dim light bulb. The walls were dirty between patches of spray paint and spider webs hung in the joins between ceiling and walls. All the time I was thinking about what being lonely meant. I came to the conclusion it is to be uncomfortable with oneself.

The hostel had only two private rooms; I'd rented one of them. It was small, with one bed, a square table and a tiny bathroom with a bucket and a 'bum-gun'. There was nothing in the room except a notice pasted to the door saying check out at twelve.

I bet the dorms were lively. I bet they were happy places with people chatting away meeting new friends. I'd chosen to be private. Why did I?

I stuffed my bags in the corner and flopped onto the bed. I spent the whole evening trying to figure out what I would do next. The more anxious and lonely I got, alone in that room, the more I thought about women, or going to the bar to join those others after all, or buying some cigarettes. This turmoil resulted in me taking a nap, acknowledging that it was my routine method of avoiding loneliness.

But I couldn't sleep. Instead I lay on the bed looking at the clock. I was caught in a trap between knowing I couldn't return to my past behaviour and not knowing what to do in the future.

Cut yourself some slack, man. I had only been in Laos for half a day. I hadn't planned to isolate myself but it was better that I stayed in the room that night. Making a decision calmed me down. I had to learn to be with myself, only myself, without grasping my old routine pleasures to fill the black hole inside me. Loneliness, I needed to stop treating it as an enemy. That had been my plan in this trip after all; to free myself of attachments and listen to The Experience.

Hearing noises out in the corridor, I hoped no-one was about to try and enter the room, which was unlikely. What I really needed was to explore my deepest core right now. I held my body tense while the footsteps walked past my door, only relaxing when I heard another door being opened with a key in the lock. I listened to it slam closed and forced myself to close my eyes; hoping to reach that state of complete freedom and love again.

Pre-Experience, love was either represented by the fantasy of fairy-tales and films (with no foundation in reality whatsoever for me) but I also knew it meant pain. It meant disappointment, obsession and suffering. I'd never been in love before like in the songs and stories we were all brought up on: though a few times I thought I was. Now The Experience had convinced me that I'd never actually experienced love in any relationship with another human being. I didn't know what love was but I had to find out. Did the Energy want to show me love in Laos?

I was sure about one thing, where there's jealousy, hatred and fear there's no love. I needed to get rid of attachments to truly experience love.

Kafli 14 - Iceland, 2009.

Ex-Girlfriend

"I'M JUST NOT sure you love me."

I sat up in bed to light a cigarette, turning half-away from her.

"What do you mean?" Guðný sounded exasperated with me as usual. "Why do you keep saying that? I love you. I constantly say that I love you." She let out a loud breath and flung herself away from me, burrowing down into the pillow. As I exhaled I heard muffled words escaping from her.

"When will you get it into your head?"

"I just never feel it," I told her, after I'd smoked about half the cigarette. "I don't believe anyone could love me." My hand shook as I tapped ash into the glass ashtray on the bedside table. "I can't *feel* any love from you."

Even *I* could hear how pitiful I sounded. I changed girl-friends frequently enough to know it wasn't they who were the problem. It was me. *I'm incapable of feeling loved.* I wasn't sure what they should change about themselves for me to be able to feel love for them. At the start of each relationship I'd experience this blissful feeling of love but it faded like a battery running out. Reality soon sank in. "I love you" became mean-ingless. Evaporated into thin air, unable to move anything in-side me. I took another drag of my cigarette, looking at the snow outside the window.

It's always snowing. Just like it snows on the love in every re-lationship.

I knew I ought to put my hand out and touch her so we could make up the only way that ever worked for me. Or one of us needed to start a proper row, for the same reason.

"Böddi." Guðný now had a familiar harsh edge to her voice.

Now we're getting somewhere.

Break the ice.

She lifted her head from the pillow, sliding herself up in the bed. I glimpsed her frustrated expression from the corner of my eye, my head held rigid, gazing straight ahead.

"If I said those words five million times it wouldn't change anything for you. It's your destructive behaviour."

Her breathing became ragged. "I'm lying naked next to you, something I've been doing for the past two years, and frequently we have to discuss whether I love you or not. A stupid conversation we have over and over. Why do you think I'm here? Comfortable bed? Nice location? Think about it."

Finally I moved my head and saw that her fists were bunched on the sheets, her knuckles clenched and white.

Relief.

She carried on. "I'm here, look! But Böddi, these conversations suck all the life out of me. I start to lose hope in us."

"But I don't feel it," I continued to push, hearing her beginning to cry. We could make love soon and I could comfort her. That was a role I understood, being the caretaker. When she was crying it was like a drop of comfort for me in my ocean of wounds. I was needed, this created a little extra of the feeling *I* needed, which I called love. I leaned towards the ashtray and then slowly moved my hand onto her thigh, hoping her fingers would meet it.

No hand.

No reaction.

She was sobbing quietly to herself. I stayed, stuck in the moment of high tension and knowing it would either end in sex or in an explosive row. I moved to put my arms around her. She shrugged me off.

"It's too much Böddi. It's too frequent. It's just too hard to be with you." Her crying intensified.

"Come on, it will be all right."

Why doesn't she let me comfort her?

"How can you say these things?" Her face was blurred with snot and tears.

"What things?"

"That I don't love you. It makes me feel small. It makes me feel incapable. It hurts"

"It's not me making you feel anything."

Here it comes.. The explosion. She threw herself onto one elbow, her hair falling forward. She pushed it back angrily and glared at me.

"It's over, Böddi. It has to be."

There. Now it's time for my explosion.

"This just proves my fucking point, doesn't it? Why would you break up with me if you loved me?"

Shaking her head violently, Guðný swung her legs over the edge of the bed and stamped her feet onto the floor, hunching forward in another bout of raucous sobs. I stared impassively at the discs of her spine and thought how cleverly a human is put together. The staring started to make me hard. Guðný's sexy back caused me to forget all this arguing and want to cuddle. But she lashed out at my hand which was reaching across the rumpled sheet towards her and grabbed her pants off the edge of the bed, dressing quickly.

I kept my eyes hungrily on her flesh until it disappeared beneath her clothes; she was gone from me. I took another cigarette and lit up, mumbling to myself.

"Words. So many words. Relationships are just filled with fucking hurtful words. I hurt you. You hurt me. It's fucking words. Just fucking words."

I knew she was really leaving, she would actually go. When she said something, she stuck to her decision. This had happened one time before, when she left and it took me two months to get her back.

She had gathered a few possessions and stuffed them in her bag; the big one that she took away when we went on holiday. Still sniffing and occasionally hiccupping, she had put her shoes on and was out in the corridor now.

She's supposed to be letting me comfort her.

At the last minute I called her name but I left it too late. The front door had slammed.

Kafli 15 - Laos, 2011.

A New Day

IT'S TAKEN ME a few moments to remember I'm not in Kunming anymore. A blaze of sunlight from the small window near the bed makes me feel warm and comfortable on the outside, but inside I'm edgy. Today something has to happen, otherwise I will start losing faith in this trip. I haven't had any signs from The Experience since I came to Laos. Temptations will be everywhere: women, bars and drugs. Old habits die hard and I feel the boxer in the black shorts is getting stronger by the minute. He's punching his way through my defences and I need to stand strong against him.

I tucked my notebook away in the pocket of my backpack and pulled on my clothes. After a quick wash at the sink in the bathroom, I hurried down to the lobby for breakfast, feeling ravenous. Two girls were hanging out with the local guy on reception. They were both tall and skinny, wearing short skirts in contrasting colours. They stood by the front door, hoisting big backpacks. I guessed they were about to leave the hostel.

I watched with interest. From their appearance I guessed they were Scandinavian. I was compelled by an urge to talk to them. Without thinking I approached the less-attractive girl because I'd read an article about pick-up techniques that said it was an effective way to get the attention of the girl you actually wanted.

"Hi, ladies, could you help me with something?"

"Probably," the less attractive one said.

"I just arrived in Laos so ... uh, sorry, my name is Böddi." I offered my hand for a loose handshake. In Asia, people shake hands loosely; I wanted to show them I wasn't a novice.

"Hi, Böddi," she said. "I'm Lisa. This is my friend, Anita." Lisa shook my hand lightly in return while Anita gave me a shy smile. Anita was stunningly beautiful. My whole persona changed around beautiful girls and I could feel I was back in the game, like at Paddy's. I returned my gaze to Lisa.

"Nice to meet you, girls. I see you have your backpacks ready. Are you guys leaving Vientiane?"

"No, just changing hostels. We've got two more days in the city before we head off to the countryside for some hiking in nature."

Anita smiled wider. The brightness of it lit up the room.

Her brown eyes reminded me of a Persian cat and she had a body like a swimsuit model.

"Nice, where are you girls from?"

"We are from Holland." They both spoke at the same time. Anita laughed, opening her eyes wide. "So, weren't you asking for some help? What do you need?"

"Uh yeah, basically I just arrived in Laos. I was just checking if you guys know of anything cool to do in the city?"

"Hmm, well, we haven't done that much. You can join us when we go to see the Great Sacred Stupa if you want?"

Lisa looked at me like she wanted an immediate yes or no. I shifted from one foot to the other while some guys and girls in their twenties entered the lobby. The noise they made gave me a few seconds to think.

"Yeah, all right, sure." I blinked at Anita, like I knew what the Great Sacred Stupa was.

"Okay, cool. We are just going to drop our bags off at the other hostel, then we'll be ready to go."

"Sounds good."

I was so proud of myself for getting a day with two pretty girls at The Great Sacred Stupa.

***

I explored the Stupa with the girls all day. It was a large

construction covered in flashy gold pinnacles. Monks moved around in their robes in the midst of tourists taking pictures. It was strange seeing these monks wandering around and I wondered if they were actual monks or simply decorations for the place. I was interested in knowing more about Buddha and the religion but on that trip I only learned, from one of the signs by the entrance, that a stupa is a Buddhist monument traditionally containing relics of the Buddha. After all the walking, we sat down at a bench in the centre of Vientiane. That whole afternoon with the girls, I felt confident. I also sensed they were intrigued by the mysterious persona I had worked hard to convey.

"So, Böddi, what do you do when you are not travelling in South East Asia?"

"I've been living in China, working in Kunming."

"Doing what?"

The way Anita keeps looking at me with those beautiful eyes..

"Finance. I also own a company in Kunming, just a small business. Import export. Mainly from Europe."

I didn't even blink.

"Sounds interesting." Anita flicked her hair. Wasn't that a sign she was interested in me?

"Yeah, well." I lifted my shoulders like it was not that important.

"What do you plan to do in Laos?" Lisa shifted her glance between me and Anita.

"Nothing special. I've been busy with work so I decided to just kick back and relax."

"Lisa and I are going for a hiking trip to the mountains the day after tomorrow, for a few days," said Anita. "Do you want to join us? They say they have the best weed in Laos there. And they supposedly have magic-mushroom shakes there as well."

"Even magic-mushroom pizzas." Lisa mimed eating one.

"Hmmm yeah, I would totally be down, but ..."

"But what? You don't ..?"

"Of course I do drugs. I love weed. I want to go with you guys. You both seem cool. But ... I'll have to check something. Tell you what, I'll let you know if I can join you guys tomorrow."

I gave them my best flirty smile.

The three of us took a taxi back to the hostel. I kissed both girls goodbye. I showed a bit more affection to Anita by laying my hand on her shoulder for the first time since we'd been hanging out, another pick-up technique I had learned. I waved them off before running up to my room, going immediately to the bathroom to pee, while reflecting on our day. I wondered where all this bullshit about me being a businessman came from. I was happy that they wanted me to join them on the hiking trip but there was another feeling I had.

A brand-new feeling.

Guilt.

I had promised myself I'd be real, authentic and honest on this trip. What had happened? While I peed I looked at my reflection in the mirror next to the toilet, wondering what the girls' responses would have been if I'd showed up as 'the real' Böddi. I kept on looking in the mirror.

"I'm actually in a vulnerable space in my life right now," I could have said. "I really don't know who I am or what I am. I'm chasing an unknown Experience and I don't know what it means. I'm just trying to figure all that out. Bear with me, girls."

I flushed the toilet and moved to the sink to wash my hands.

"I am trying to find my path in this world," I continued, speaking into the smaller mirror above the sink. "How do I go about doing that? I find a lot of confusion and fear, both in me and in the world itself. I'm just trying to make sense of it all."

I turned off the tap and dried my hands. I was not used to looking in the mirror for longer than a few seconds at a time and I thought my eyes looked sad.

Tuning away, I moved back into the bedroom. Climbing into my bed I couldn't stop wondering why I'd not been authentic to Anita and Lisa. I'd felt good all day, but I was not being me.

Am I so uncomfortable just being me?

Am I just a flawed, scared and insecure human being who tries to control people's perceptions of me?

Am I so desperate for approval?

I lied. I exaggerated; I bent the truth in all my interactions with people. I constructed facts to lead people to a certain conclusion about me. That day I'd simply lied to their faces. I couldn't present one real thing about me that was good.

Fake self-marketing and never sharing the 'director's cut' version of myself was my routine, especially with girls. In the past I'd never been 'real' with any girl I had a relationship with. I painted a picture of a confident guy but slowly the game of hiding the core me inside the brashness got harder. I deceived them and as soon as I showed pieces of the real me, they were gone.

Come on, man. This was getting heavy. *Be positive.* I'd had a great day. The girls had even asked me to join them on a trip, so I shouldn't beat myself up too much. I hadn't found The Great Sacred Stupa that interesting but I had enjoyed spending time with the girls. They were cool; adventurous and free-spirited. My emotions shifted again. Yeah, at least I wasn't lonely like yesterday. Plenty of flirting went on between Anita and me, I'd even noticed Lisa getting frustrated. Yet another sign that my pick-up technique was working.

***

I found a local restaurant and ordered some fried noodles with eggs and a cold lemonade. A stack of old magazines was piled in a corner. I got up and sorted through them. There was one old newspaper, typeset in English. It was *The Vientiane Times* from 2nd April, 2007: four years ago. I opened it and began to read, for something to do. In the middle pages, the first article I saw caught my attention.

Life for an Australian caught smuggling Heroin at Vientiane airport.

An Australian citizen was sentenced to life imprisonment in Laos yesterday for attempting to smuggle heroin from the capital of Laos, Vientiane.

James Smith, 28, was found with bags containing 827g of heroin strapped to his body. He claimed that the masterminds of a smuggling ring threatened to kill him and his family if he refused to carry the drugs. The judges dismissed the claim by saying that there was no evidence of any force being used to influence the alleged crime.

Smith broke down in tears after the judge read the verdict. He is now one of many who have been caught attempting to smuggle heroin through Vientiane airport.

Man. Shakily, I pulled air into my lungs. My food was arriving. As I threw it down my throat, the article continued to affect me, but I couldn't pinpoint on what level. I felt bad for the poor guy, of course I did. Being in jail in Laos must be hell. I wondered if he was still there four years later. I'd often heard about people arrested for smuggling in South East Asia but this time it was different. Probably because I was now in the country I was reading about.

I pushed myself to my feet, folding the newspaper and leaving it on the table. Maybe someone would open it in another four years and start reading the same article as me. I shook my head, negotiating between the chairs.

Walking back towards the hostel I took in all the palm trees moving quietly in the breeze, occasionally a car passing by, as I planned a quiet night after a tiring yet successful day with the girls. I thought about the two of them, mainly Anita. There had definitely been attraction between us in the temple.

She's as hot as the sun. I imagined us making love under a palm tree somewhere in the jungle, far away from problems, worries and the rest of the world.

But Anita was not the only person on my mind while walking back to the hostel. James, from the article in the Vientiane Times, had also taken up residence. He was probably just a normal guy, my age, who made a stupid mistake. I'd been given a second chance when I woke up at the hospital. But though I *thought* all this I still couldn't really *feel* anything. Why was I so numbed to the pain of others? The fact that James was probably in a hellhole of a prison for life, didn't make me any more grateful for my own luck.

I arrived back at the hostel and climbed the stairs to my room. Lying on the bed I felt fully satisfied with the outcome of my day. I closed my eyes for a few moments.

When I opened them again anxiety rushed through me like electricity. I checked the clock; I'd only napped for two hours. It was eight PM. I wrapped my arms around my pillow and squeezed it. Anita came to my mind. If only she were here, the anxiety would go away. But it didn't. My pulse was racing. I sat up, feeling as if I couldn't breathe. The anxiety must be because I hadn't indulged my addictions. *My body is going through withdrawal.* That must be it. I distracted myself by inspecting the room: a bed, a chest of drawers, a lamp and curtains. That was it. I couldn't help thinking about James, wondering how he could live in a cell which was probably similar in dimensions to this hostel room but in much worse condition.

I would rather die than live in a place this size for the rest of my life.

How could I be so full of anxiety, fear and pain while I had all the freedom in the world? A glass pane between me and the gratitude I ought to feel when I compared myself to James, a guy I knew of only through a newspaper article.

Why do I have the feeling I know him? Was this the kind of feeling the Jungle Boys told me to trust? *Why am I thinking I should go to meet a convicted heroin smuggler and what should*

I say to him? Because I was thinking that. It was a crazy idea but I latched on to it. I paced my room in small circles. This was a sign from The Experience, I was sure. The Energy had spoken. It excited me, until I remembered the girls had invited me to join them on a trip.

This can't be happening. Must I really choose between a trip with the girls to the jungle or a search for a heroin smuggler?

I flumped back on the bed, arms behind my head. What should I do? I kicked one foot a few times at the empty room. "Fuck!" I said it loud enough to be heard in the lobby. Sadness swept over me, forced to accept I wasn't going on the trip with Anita. The powerful shift in my emotions was a sign that I had to go and search for James.

Trust yourself, the Jungle Boys had said. The Experience was testing me with my deadliest pleasure; girls. I was attached to girls. I had an opportunity to refuse my attachment but I was resisting it.

How could I contact James? This must be one of the craziest ideas I'd ever had but it was a mission to pursue. I had to follow the directing energy. The process of how, I couldn't even start to imagine.

Leaving my room, I jumped down the stairs two at a time to the hostel lobby. There I got myself onto the Internet, searching for information about James Smith. I discovered that he was jailed in Phonthong prison, also known as the 'Foreigners' Prison' in Vientiane. Now I had a mountain to climb, a mountain in a third world country. After about forty minutes of researching, I found out that the prisoners could apply for a fifteen-minute visit once a month. My task had to be impossible. First of all, I doubted that James would give me these fifteen minutes, considering we hadn't even met. Secondly, I didn't have any idea how I would go about getting an interview with James.

If The Experience had really spoken to me, there must be a way to contact James. I decided to write a letter even though I had not found an address for the jail. I had to trust that The Experience would take care of that. I took a pen, ripped a piece of paper out of my notebook and started writing.

Dear James

I read an article about you in a copy of The Vientiane Times from 2007. It may sound strange that I'm writing you this letter, but it is not any stranger than my life has been lately. A series of 'coincidences' have led me to write this letter. I have lived with fear, anxiety and depression most of my life. I am ungrateful and I don't know where to look for happiness. I had a spiritual experience some days ago and I turned my life around. Some people call it God, I guess, but I don't. I know that I have something for you or you have something for me. The Experience told me. I don't know what it is; I just know that we have to meet. Is it possible to meet?

Böddi

Kafli 16 - Laos.

Meeting Max

THE SUN IS shining through the curtains and the letter to James is lying on the floor next to a pile of clothes. It wasn't all a dream, then. I want to take a moment, close my eyes again and fantasize about Anita. Going through her morning routine, brushing her teeth and eating breakfast. If I could only spend time with her, do all the small, everyday things that couples do together.

Okay. That was more than a moment, I admit. The letter is still there. I need to complete my task, go to the post office and mail the letter to Phonthong prison. Part of me wants the mission to fail so I can go and join the girls on the trip. I want to manipulate the process The Experience has presented me with; trip it up along the way...

I entered the post office, surprisingly optimistic about finding the address of the prison. There were about ten people in there, only five of them waiting in line. The others were spread around the echoing room packing boxes and writing letters. As an older man with a beard approached the queue, I squeezed into it right before him, bumping his shoulder with mine. He made no complaint and I didn't say anything, I'd managed to save myself a few minutes that might have been wasted waiting for him to bumble through his business, otherwise. A tiny local woman in front of me had noticed the slight commotion though, glancing back at me with a disapproving look, shifting packages in her arms that were almost the size of herself.

I tapped my foot while her parcels were weighed and dealt with. When my turn came I grinned at the postal worker sitting behind the desk, a young Laotian guy in a green cap with Laos Postal Service sewn on in gold letters.

"Good morning. I need to find an address here in Vientiane and I was wondering if you could help me? I need to post a letter."

"Okay, sir, what address are you looking for?" The young guy sounded friendly enough.

"It's the Laos prison, the foreigners prison. Err, I mean the Phonthong prison. I want to send a letter to a man in there."

My heart was pumping so fast.

"Okay. You are indeed optimistic to ask such a thing but

it might be your lucky day. It's probably not my business or anything, but do you have a relative there?"

"No. Or yes, kind of. We are connected but not by blood. Why is it my lucky day?"

"Okay. It's not your family, but you are connected. Well, sir, this is the reason it might be your lucky day. The man standing behind you comes here every two weeks to pick up letters to take to the prison. You might want to ask him." He wore an expression like he was wondering if he was breaking some post office rules by pointing out one customer to another.

My heart thumped harder. I'd forgotten about the old man I'd rudely squeezed in front of in the waiting line. I turned to give him a sheepish look. He was tall and strong-looking, around seventy, maybe. He had a long white beard like a rough Santa Claus. He had some kind of slippers on his feet and was wearing beige-coloured shorts and a white shirt, open at the chest. For some reason he reminded me of Robinson Crusoe in a story my dad used to read to me when I was younger.

"Thanks a lot," I said to the guy behind the counter. "You have done the right thing, the energy will reward you today." My face split into a smile, my hand lifted towards him and he shook it loosely.

Then I took the two steps backwards towards the old man. Words came out of me in a rush.

"Hi, I met you for a reason. I have something for you, you

need to do me a favour." I felt confident because The Experience had taken control of the situation and it seemed out of my hands. "Please?" I finally remembered to add.

"You are here for a reason? Well, good for you. Now move away so I can talk to the young man behind the counter." The old man grasped my shoulder and gently pushed me away. Puzzled by his dismissal, I decided to sit down and wait while he picked up his letters. I found a metal bench along one wall and kept my eyes on him, trying to read his character and how to do this, tapping my feet on the floor in a frenzied rhythm like a member of Michael Flatley's *River Dance* troupe. When he finished his business the old man approached me. He gave me an assessing look from under thick eyebrows.

"So, you met me for a reason? Is that so? Now tell me about the reason." He was fully in charge.

I reminded myself to be real. Being real meant being honest. I let the ramifications of this sink in, they mostly involved vulnerability. "I had an Experience," I told him. "A powerful Experience. It directed me to write a letter to a guy who is doing time in the prison."

The man ran his hand over his white hair. His eyes were shiny, the light bounced off his suntanned face as he looked at me with a half-smile.

"Is that so? Well I'll give you a new experience, the answer is no. I'm certainly not going to do it for you." He waved a hand in my face and started walking away.

I wasn't expecting that; I'd pictured the conversation totally differently. *What the ... ?*

"But you have to take it!" My voice rang around the post office. A man who was sticking tape onto a box looked up and gave me a frown. In that part of the world shouting in public causes you to lose face.

The man I'd pinned my hopes on gave a little shake of his head, didn't turn back.

"Wait, I'll pay you," I said, desperately.

"I don't need your money." He continued walking towards the door.

"Hey, mister. I'll do anything!"

He stopped just outside the door; finally turned around and looked back in at me.

"Do you play piano?"

What?

"No."

"Then you won't do *anything*, will you?"

He started walking again. I couldn't believe he wouldn't take the letter.

"I'll learn how to play piano!"

His footsteps paused once more. I walked outside onto the pavement and right before I got close to him he moved to face me. And looked me in the eyes so intensely, I had to drop my gaze. It seemed way too long before he spoke.

"Come with me then. There is one thing you can do for me and if you'll do it, I'll take the letter to the prison for you. Deal?"

"Okay, deal."

What the hell have I just agreed to do? But I was one step closer to getting the letter to the prison. I would simply surrender to whatever The Experience was offering me.

"Let's go for a ride," he said. "There's my car, get in the front seat." The old guy pointed to a red pickup truck parked outside the building. A tiny hesitation.

"All right." I paused. "Why did you let me make a fool out of myself before you accepted that you would take the letter?"

The old man burst out laughing. He laid his hand on my back.

"I didn't force you to make fool out of yourself, that's all your doing. I knew you would come for this ride with me the whole time. I was just testing you, besides I haven't accepted that I will take the letter."

The car I got into was about fifteen years old. The engine was loud and it had a smell inside which reminded me of my grandmother's barn. The old man drove slowly down the road, in no hurry, humming a song I didn't know.

"What's your story with the prison?" I asked. "Do you know someone there? How come you pick up the letters? Do you work there?"

He glanced away from the road a moment, scrutinising me. "Yes, I know someone there, and no, I do not work there. This *is* your lucky day. Do you know that? Getting a letter to the prison is not an easy thing to do, I'm not sure it would have worked if you'd told the prison staff an Experience made you write a letter." He continued humming between his words.

"Have you been into the prison?"

"Yes, many times, but not as an inmate."

"How is it?" I knew nothing about third world prisons. My curiosity came from a place of wanting to understand what it is to be grateful.

The old man switched gear in slow motion. He glanced at me.

"It is not a nice place, my friend. It's as inhumane as you could possibly imagine. There are around six people in each cell and the cells are approximately four metres square. There's only one squatting toilet in the corner. It's a hell hole."

It somehow still didn't make me feel grateful for my life. But riding in the car with the old man brought up a good feeling. There was flow in our communication. I trusted The Experience to take care of this adventure and tried not to think too much. He must be part of this whole process, and I was sure he knew it too. I was silent for a while, watching the daily life of the Laotian people on the streets, through the dirty window of the truck.

"Where are we going?"

"To my home. Your assignment is waiting for you there."

Another lull in conversation.

"You don't have much to say, do you?"

"We'll have plenty of time to talk."

When he did speak, it was in a calming tone. I decided to just shut my mouth and go into the unknown with this stranger.

We were now heading outside of the city limits.

What if this man is dangerous?

What if he was an inmate before?

What's his story?

Why does he want to take me for a ride?

About twenty minutes down the highway we took a right turn into an old road. The road was bumpy and narrow, there were trees all around us. The landscape reminded me of Vietnam War movies. We eventually pulled up at an old wooden house that looked like something out of a Tolkien story. There were carved stones all around the house in a large garden. The stones were all of different sizes, artfully carved into shapes; not recognisable things or faces, just shapes.

The house was by the Mekong River, which flowed gracefully in perfect harmony with its surroundings. There was something special about this place. So simple. I wondered what it would be like to live here; it must be a straightforward life.

I followed the old man out of the car towards the front door, where he stopped and smiled at me.

"So, what do you think?"

"It's a beautiful home. It's simple but at the same time it's not. Who carved all these stones?"

"I did. Now, let's go inside and have some tea. Then I'll tell you what you can do for me."

Inside his home I had the same feelings as I used to get at my grandmother's farmhouse, it was plain; uncluttered and peaceful.

"You can have a seat wherever you want, just make yourself at home."

"Thanks."

I'd pictured the interior to be different, old-style cosy. Instead it was an open space with the kitchen and the living room in the same area, only a screen partition between them. No pictures on the walls, an old sofa and a small television in the living room. The place was raw. There were big pillows on the floor and that was probably the only thing that made the place somewhat cosy. I sat down on the sofa and observed my surroundings while I waited for the tea to arrive.

"Are you comfortable, Mr ...? Hmm, maybe it's time for introductions now."

He placed a tray onto a low table by the sofa and lifted a teapot off the tray.

"Böddi, my name is Böddi," I said. "I'm from Iceland."

He poured tea into my cup.

"Never been. Sounds like an interesting place to visit."

"Yeah, it's cool. And cold. What's your name?" I cradled the bowl of the cup he offered me in my hands.

"Call me Max."

"I am a little confused," I admitted. "May I know more about you, Max? What's your relationship with Phonthong prison?"

"I teach there."

"Teach what?"

"Meditation."

"Meditation? So what brought you to Laos to teach meditation in a prison?"

"A similar Experience to that which brought you here, I guess. It told me a long time ago to teach meditation at the prison. But this is a secret so I hope that can stay between us."

He sat himself crossed-legged on a cushion and peered at me with a smile. His eyes reminded me of the look I got from the Jungle Boys in Kunming. It was warm and trustworthy.

"Why is it a secret?" I asked after a few moments. Everything about this old man was mysterious. His home, his job, his smile and his whole presence.

"Phonthong prison isn't exactly a convenient place to set up a meditation retreat. This is a closed type of place. I'm not sure your letter would ever have arrived at the prison without me helping you. They deprive the inmates of food from their families, contact with embassies and other outside sources. For me to get in there was a long and hard battle. Now I'm respected and I can do my things there. But I follow strict rules and one of them is to not tell anyone about this. I hope you respect that."

"I do," I promised. "So how did you get into the prison?"

"By paying the right people, by proving what I was doing would have good effects on the inmates. The prisoners are calmer and behave better after meditation, so everybody wins. There is also another reason but I won't tell you about that, for now at least."

"Fair enough. How is it, teaching those people meditation?" I tried to organise the million questions in my head while each one was coming out of my mouth.

"Tough."

Max took a loud slurp of tea. Mirroring his actions, I raised my cup to my lips and drank deeply. It was refreshing. I was probably dehydrated from the heat.

"These are very sick people," Max said. "Many of them have been through torture. They are beaten, put into solitary confinement and forced to undergo sleep deprivation. That place kills your spirit, it tears your soul apart and weakens you in every sense. The prisoners are dealing with great trauma. Many of them are malnourished and have suicidal thoughts."

I couldn't think of a reply. When I was at the post office I'd had no idea what I was getting myself into. I realised how naive I was, how narrow-minded and very Icelandic. In Iceland, prison inmates would lose their PlayStation or DVD player for bad behaviour. I was in a different world now. The old man leaned forward and poured more tea into my cup.

"Do you know James Smith?"

I hoped it wasn't an inappropriate question.

Max opened his mouth in a childlike smile. "I can't believe you're taking the letter to James. Now it makes sense that you are here in my living room. I only have eight students but James is the most prominent one. He has the most potential of all of them to be free."

Max's face glowed.

"Can inmates get shorter sentences if they meditate?"

"No, no. He is getting free *inside* the prison walls. Freedom does not depend on outside circumstances, it all comes from within. I'm helping the inmates get rid of the *wanting* to be free, so that they *can* be free."

"So your aim is to set people free inside the prison walls?"

"Yes. That is exactly my aim, Böddi."

Here I was, sitting in a room with a guy named Max, who dedicated his life to setting inmates free inside their prison walls. A moment of silence. I interrupted it.

"I can't see any piano here, Max. What was it that you wanted me to do?"

I was trying to fill the blank space of quietness which I wasn't used to. In my friendship groups, you kept up the banter. It took Max a while to answer.

"See those carved stones out there?" He turned towards the window and I followed with my gaze.

"I want you to clean them. I want you to clean them with water. You can spend the afternoon cleaning the stones, then I'll give you a ride back to town before dinner."

What an odd thing to ask.

"Err, Okay. Can I ask what these stones are for?"

"They are a gift to a person very dear to me. Now go get ready to go out if you ever want this letter of yours to reach James."

Max and I walked onto the porch together in front of the house. He handed me a bucket and jammed a highly unfashionable cap on my head. He showed me where to fill the bucket with water and gave me a brush to scrub with and a cloth to wipe. Then he waved me off to clean the stones in the garden.

The sun was hot at noon. I was standing in a garden filled with carved stones ready to clean them. It seemed strange to me, to clean stones, but if it would enable me to get the letter to James.

First I walked around the garden, admiring the stones. They were beautiful. It was like pacing through a dreamland on magic mushrooms; it made me think of Alice in Wonderland. I was trying to see some pattern, some meaning or some signs in the stones. I found nothing. I sat down next to a middle-sized stone and started pouring water over it and scrubbing it. After five minutes of cleaning I came to the conclusion it was a stupid idea.

Who cleans stones?

They are not even dirty.

What's the point?

After about an hour of cleaning I was almost melting over the stones. The heat was killing me. It was burning hot and I was sweating like an Olympic athlete. I had poured as much water over myself as over the stones. My rubbing started to get slower. Every minute I could feel my mood getting worse. Thoughts were galloping through my mind.

I swore at the sun, at the stones, at Max and even at Laos.

As the day went by I got more frustrated. Max hadn't come out once to check up on me. I spent the final half hour hiding behind one of the big stones in the shade, counting the minutes until five o'clock.

I'm too hot.

I'm exhausted.

I feel anxious.

At four-thirty I finally heard someone calling.

"Böddi, I'll take you home now."

Thank God for that. I stood up and stumbled back to the house, carrying the bucket, brush and cloth. So relieved the job was finished.

"Okay, I'm finished."

I walked in off the veranda, entering the semi-dark of the living room.

"Who said you were finished? It's a two day job." The old man pushed himself up from a cushion. "You should come back tomorrow to finish the job. You didn't know I have a backyard, too, did you?" He chuckled to himself.

I was taken aback but determined to stick with the path.

"Okay. No problem. I'll come back tomorrow. But could you tell me why you carved all those stones?"

I took the hat off, laying it on the back of the sofa, running my hand over my head to remove the sweat. He didn't answer my question at first.

"You'd better bring your stuff with you from the hostel tomorrow. I have a feeling you might be staying here for a while."

Seriously?

Max slid his arm around my shoulder as we followed the crazy-paved walkway with grass growing high on each side, back to the car. I looked down at the cracks between the slabs, guessing Max had laid this path himself. It had the same feel as the carved stones.

"The stones," Max said just as I was thinking that. "They are a gift to my son."

Kafli 17 - Laos.

Moving to Max's

I WAITED WITH my bags outside the hostel. It was even hotter than the day before, at least I thought about the heat more since I was already dreading cleaning the stones. A gecko on the wall let everyone know it was a gecko with its chirp which went "gecko, gecko". I was picturing humans running around saying "human, human" when suddenly Anita came into my mind.

Why am I wasting my time cleaning stupid stones when I could be getting laid somewhere in the jungle?

Max arrived.

"Jump in." He kept the engine running.

I dumped my bags in the backseat and got into the car. As soon as I was sitting next to Max I felt calmer and reassured that I was doing the right thing. Max seemed in a meditative state while driving. He was untalkative, in the same way as the previous day. But I couldn't help asking questions.

"Where is your son?"

It took him a moment to answer. "He died many years ago."

"I'm sorry to hear that. What happened?" I thought it best to be direct. Max would surely see through me if I wasn't real.

"Don't be sorry," Max said. "He saved my life. He died in prison. Phonthong prison." He chatted like he was talking about something other than his son's death.

Pause. The noise of the engine preoccupied me for a while. But curiosity overcame my musings. "How?"

"He was serving a life sentence for drug smuggling. He got sick and due to lack of medical help he died. It could have been prevented but that's what happened."

I found myself picking his words apart for sorrow, but could find none. Putting the pieces together in my mind, it all started to make more sense. I didn't fully understand the whole picture but I had an idea about the carved stones, together with the meditation-teaching in the prison and why Max was in Laos.

"Did he do it? The smuggling?"

"I believe so." Max shifted gear as the truck bumped over stones.

"How did he save your life?"

"He turned me from ignorance to wisdom."

Did Max just give me a wink?

How can he seem so cheerful about this?

My arm resting in the open car window, I observed this exotic country named Laos. Occasionally farmers strolled along the edges of the road, wearing hats and carrying tools to work on the land. Every few hundred metres of driving there were houses and each one seemed to have a small road business, selling snacks and petrol in two-litre bottles. The closer we got to Max's house the fewer people we saw, it was fairly remote. The road got narrower with high trees on either side.

I even wondered if Max had built the road himself. It wouldn't have surprised me. It was like entering into a no-man's land where this mystical wooden house appeared out of nowhere. We arrived quite suddenly.

I got out of the passenger seat and stretched. We collected my bags from the back of the truck and stood for a moment looking at the house.

"Here we are," said Max. "Home."

As I climbed the steps to the porch, Max close behind me, I could feel his determination to throw me straight to work. My stalling tactics would not work here.

✳✳✳

I stood with the bucket in my right hand and a brush in my

left. The only thing different from yesterday was that now I was in the backyard and it had even more carved stones than the front. It was getting hotter. I could hide in the shade of a big stone until noon but I didn't because I felt bad that his son died and the stones were a gift to him.

Cleaning the stones now was even harder than yesterday and my thought processes took a similar direction.

The sun is too hot.

The stones are too many.

I'm too tired to do this.

Two and a half hours later, Max called me to come back inside for lunch. I sat down at his kitchen table on which he had placed a meal of tofu, grilled vegetables, bread and a big jug of water.

He put some food on his plate and then held his hands about three inches above it, closing his eyes.

"What are you doing?"

"I'm putting positive energy in my food."

"So you believe in Energy?" I selected items of food for my plate and set about eating.

"It's not about believing. It's not about knowing, either. It's about realizing. You are surrounded by Energy at this very moment. The Energy in the house is very high. It will affect you, you'll feel it the more you stay here."

"What is this Energy?"

"Everything is Energy, Böddi. The whole planet is Energy. Trees, flowers, animals, the food you are eating and you. You are Energy. Energy is alive and therefore everything is alive."

"Alive?"

Were the stones I just cleaned alive?

I was sceptical.

"Yes. Alive. Take a look at this jug of water." He moved a jug in front of me.

"Okay."

"The jug looks solid but it's not. Everything is made out of atoms. Atoms are mostly empty space. They are constantly vibrating. The nucleus of the atom is a hundred thousand times smaller than the atom but is almost all of its physical mass. The space in the atom is alive. It's a vibrating space where particles can appear and disappear for no reason. So this jug is mostly empty space."

I kept looking at the jug while Max talked. The only thing I saw was a jug. I had a hard time looking at the jug and thinking that the jug was mainly vibrating Energy. I glanced around the house and tried to look at everything as Energy. The only thing I saw was a simple house.

"Do you believe in God?" I asked next.

Max had stopped talking to chew his food.

"Hmmm, hang on," he managed. "Give me a minute while I swallow. God? It's a very contaminated word and again it's not about believing, it's not about knowing, it's about realizing. If you want to call it God then no, I don't believe."

"Can you call it Energy?"

"You can call it whatever you want."

"Why don't you have any pictures or symbols in your house? I can't see any altar or anything. How can you be spiritual when there is not even one picture of Jesus or Buddha?"

Max smiled at me while he poured more water into my cup.

"Böddi, what if we finish eating this delicious food and then I'll make some tea? In the meantime, you do the dishes and then we can move to the living room to talk."

I am asking too many questions. I just wanted to use my time well before I had to go back and clean stones. I wasn't thrilled at doing the dishes but it seemed fair, since he'd made lunch. We finished eating and I completed my chores, then we moved to the living room and sat down on the floor-pillows.

"Tea?"

"Yes, thank you. Why are the no pictures or anything on the walls? Why is everything so simple in the house when your garden is filled with carved stones?"

"First of all, Böddi, let's look at the word God. God is not in pictures on the wall, in statues on tables or on any altars. God is not in things. God is not in books. God is not even in churches or temples. Human beings have become slaves to symbols and images of gods. It's all man-made. Are you following me?"

"Kind of."

"Good. Then let's take a look at religion. Religions make followers. Followers of that particular religion seek comfort, security and other things in images. People have become worshippers of images instead of the truth. Life is not an image. Life is something that just is. Do you think it's possible to just live by facts? Just live with things as they are? To see things as they are? Just to be?"

"Uhm, not sure what you mean ..."

"Through centuries, God has been seen in mountains, the sun, in the moon, in trees and in stones. Today we build churches, temples, shrines, and we even build up people. Priests, gurus and other spiritual leaders are seen to represent God, that they are somewhat closer to God than other people. It's nonsense. It's nothing but mental tendencies in people to adore other people. Take a look at the Pope; he has millions of followers all around the world. People have forgotten the teaching he represents. The same goes with Buddhism, people adore Buddha without looking at what Buddha said, at the actual teachings. There's no difference between teenagers adoring a rock star on stage and hanging posters on their walls than an adult adoring the Pope or Buddha and having their pictures on the wall. It's the same mental tendency. This is all a way to distract us from the Truth. These are all images in our mind. It's a skewed view, which distracts us from the truth."

He watched me, holding his tea. His fingers around the cup were relaxed. Steam rose up into his beard.

"I'm confused," I admitted.

"That's all right, if you understood these things, you wouldn't be sitting here listening."

He took a sip of his tea. I pressed my hands around my cup.

"Now, listen carefully," Max continued. "Images are symbols, concepts, conclusions, or an ideal. The mind is constantly creating images. Like I said, life is not an image. Life is a constant conflict. Conflict is not an image. So if life is a constant conflict, which is not an image, then the image is an illusion."

"Could you give me an example?" I asked after a brief pause. I had a feeling like indigestion.

"Do you have a mom?" Max asked.

"Yes. Of course."

"Have you ever had conflicts with your mom?"

"Yes. Of course I have, who hasn't?"

"All right," Max said. "Let's go from there. What does the word 'mother' mean to you, in your mind?"

I looked at the ceiling and tried to think out an answer before speaking.

"It means someone who gave birth to me, obviously. It means that she has to take care of me, love me and nurture me. She has to be there for me when I need her?"

Max laughed loudly. "Why are you asking me? Look. The word 'mother' is an image. Behind this image are all these desires of yours: your greed and aversion. Can you see it? Your mother is not an image. She is a living, breathing human being. She is conflict. We choose to live in the image because it's easier to live in the image than to fully understand someone. That is much more difficult work. Your mind is seeking security in the image of your mom, but if she fails to live up to that image, you are in pain. If you live with images you are living in an illusion, which causes suffering. Right?"

"I guess."

"Well. If you live with mental images as your guide then you are a prisoner of those images. Do you think you can free your mind of images?"

"I don't know. I want to."

I *did* want to.

"Okay. So to answer your question about pictures on the walls; I live my life by the principle of non-accumulation, plus I live my life without images. But now I have an image in my head and that's tea." Max laughed again, holding up the empty pot. "Let me get us some more tea." He pushed himself up from the floor.

While he was busy behind the screen in the kitchen I looked around the empty walls. I wondered how our conversation could have gone from me asking him about no pictures on the wall to these revelations. I felt stunned.

"Max, where are you from?" I called.

"I'm from New Zealand, originally."

He walked back into the living room holding a tray of fresh tea. I awkwardly hurried to help but only got in the way. I sat down again while Max arranged the tray. The tea fragrance blended seamlessly with the moist jungle smell that was unavoidable in this house, since it was surrounded by trees. I liked the smell.

"When did your journey begin? Your spiritual journey?"

I was hoping to keep him talking the whole afternoon, to avoid going back to cleaning the stones.

"When my son was given life imprisonment, my life also changed. This was in 1981. I had been a bad father. I had lived my life as a selfish man. I was in a lot of pain. After my son was arrested I had daily suicidal thoughts and came close to committing the act more than once. I blamed myself for my son's imprisonment."

Our breathing sounded loud in the long pause that followed.

"I was back in New Zealand when I got the news. I spent two years here in Laos trying to do everything I could to save my son. Nothing worked. I lived to save his life but I didn't realise back then that it was my own life I was trying to save."

He stopped speaking for a few more moments. Resting his cheek on his hand, he then resumed, in a quiet voice.

"After failing again and again in trying to save my son, I became hopeless and finally gave up. Like many people have done before me I went to India to seek answers. Some people find their answers there, others don't. In that place I met a man who changed my life forever, a man who showed me a path to seeing things as they are. I stayed and served this man for a year. This was in 1983. He taught me that all holy men had sinful pasts and that all sinners have a possibility to become a holy man."

This is what I wanted to hear. "Please explain more."

"You don't have to look far," he said, "to see people throughout history turning from a sinner to an alleged saint."

"So, what more did this man teach you?"

"You won't stop asking, that's good." Max smiled, his face wrinkling. "There's no stupid question, only stupid answers. What he taught me, I can't explain over two cups of tea. What I will explain though is that this man taught me to seek truth, simplicity and love. Strive diligently and serve humanity, he repeatedly said to me. Give everything of yourself to others, he told me. There. With that said you should go out and clean the stones." Another peal of Max's childlike laughter made me feel positive as I stood up and stretched.

"Okay, Max. Thanks for the delicious lunch and for telling me this story. I'm going out to finish the stone washing."

I put on my shoes before descending the steps into the backyard again.

I collected my bucket and started pouring water in it. The words truth, simplicity and love, mentioned in Max's story, reminded me of something. I wondered if I was getting confused with the first three words in my notebook: Routine, Desire and Attachments.

The bucket was filled with water. I took the cloth and dipped it into the water and started splashing my face to cool off. It was refreshing. The words truth, simplicity and love were circulating in my mind. I suddenly remembered where these words came from; they were at the end of the letter from Henry and Pau. The exact words in the same order: Truth, Simplicity and Love.

I considered what Max had said about work and serving people. I was serving Max by cleaning the stones. This work now had a purpose. I was serving Max and I would get the letter delivered in return.

I rubbed the stones with more enthusiasm than before, but still constantly complained in my mind. The sun was still hot. The stones were still big. I was still tired. I was attached to the heat, to the sun and the stones. I couldn't distance myself from these attachments, instead I blamed them for my suffering. When reflecting on the external world of heat, sun and stones in relation to attachment I saw that maybe the sun was not causing my suffering. The stones were not causing it either. The tiredness was not causing suffering. My desire to want to change it was causing the suffering: the desire for coolness, for a cloud to block the sun and for time to relax. The suffering was its own entity. The environment was just an easy thing to blame.

At four-thirty PM I finished cleaning all the stones. I was proud of the job I'd done, even though the work didn't make any sense to me the whole time I was doing it. I was also proud of making the discovery that my desires caused the suffering, not the heat, the sun or the stones. I wondered if Max had ordered me to clean the stones so I would discover this.

I put the bucket where it belonged and went into the kitchen to wash the cloth. I noticed Max sitting on the sofa going through a pile of papers on a small side-table.

"Max."

"Yes." He took off his reading glasses and raised his head to me.

"Do you know what discovery I made while cleaning the stones?"

I was testing him to find out if he'd anticipated this.

"How should I know? I wasn't cleaning the stones. Tell me what you discovered."

I sat down next to him on the sofa and waited a few seconds while the speech prepared itself in my head. I remembered to be real and made sure to steady my breathing before I spoke.

"Honestly, I hated cleaning the stones. I hated every minute of it. It was hot outside. Burning hot. My thinking got more negative the longer I cleaned the stones. I was uncomfortable in the heat; exhausted, and the stones were too big. Then I made a discovery."

I paused, keeping my fingers busy, scratching the back of my hand and then my cheek. This discovery seemed so important a couple of minutes ago. The closer I came to conveying it to him it just seemed ridiculous.

"And?" Max raised his eyebrows.

"Uhm. I've always been suffering. All my life." Trying to re-frame the story, I watched the real me sliding further away. Into a place of fear.

"And? Was that the discovery you made?"

Truth. Simplicity. Love.

"No."

Breathe, Böddi.

"My discovery was that the sun was not causing the suffering in me. The stones were not causing my suffering. The work was not causing my suffering. The discovery I made was simply that I am suffering."

"Congratulations," said Max. "But you are wrong." He gave

his peal of laughter again and I instantly felt like a kid, an eight year old. I was ashamed. I'd wanted to impress him but he ended up laughing at me and telling me I was wrong.

"How am I wrong?"

"Böddi, it's all right," Max said. "Don't be sad. This was a big discovery for you and a part of the path you are trekking right now. But listen carefully, you are not suffering. There's only a presence of suffering, but you are not suffering. Do you understand the difference?"

I couldn't help the sadness that swept over me. At this moment, being real for me was feeling like an eight year old.

"No, I don't understand. If I'm not suffering then what am I?"

"Böddi. You are something great but a bunch of crap is wrapped around it."

Kafli 18 - Iceland, 2010.

Grandmother's Paintings

THE FATHER OF my girlfriend cut the meat like a butcher while his wife ran in and out of the kitchen placing food on the table. Their apartment was bright, with funky furniture and a lot of art around, everything from paintings on the wall to small sculptures on plinths or the floor. It was trashy but in a neat way. Fjóla and I sat next to each other, and her kid (a two-year-old boy) sat in his high chair chewing on some rubber toy.

How did I get myself into this situation?

I poured myself some more red wine and snatched a quick look at Fjóla, she didn't seem to mind how restless I was. Fjóla was a business student at the University of Iceland. She clearly meant to do the opposite of what her parents did: they were the hippie kind, the artsy people living in Vesturbær in Reykjavík. I'd heard about these people when I was growing up in the suburbs but now I was actually dining in one of those homes. They seemed to have money, from where, I didn't know.

"Which piece? Come on, Böddi, choose."

I stood up and stabbed my fork into a piece of lamb and as I dragged it onto my plate the fat leaked on the tablecloth.

"It's okay," Fjóla said with a cheeky smile. Finally, she'd noticed how nervous I was.

Fjóla and I had been dating for eight months. It had never been a serious relationship for me. The pros and cons of dating a single mother I weighed every single day. It was convenient. She lived next to the university in an apartment her parents paid for. She always seemed to have money and kept me away from drinking, too much at least. The sex was great and she didn't demand that I took care of her baby. In a way, it was perfect. But.

I always manage to bring myself to these situations. Always looking for the door.

Do they actually think that I will become some kind of father to this kid?

Her mom was the last one to sit down, and we all waited to see who was going to break the ice. Fjóla's dad broke it.

"So, Böddi. You are studying philosophy. I've been intrigued by philosophy since a young age. Mainly self-study though."

Oh no, please don't ask me anything about this topic. "Yes. It's my first semester. I wanted to become a doctor, but later I realised I want to study philosophy instead."

Please don't ask if I went to medical school. I took a sip of wine, almost emptying the glass in an effort to ease the knot in my stomach. I didn't have the grades to enter medical school from college and I had a feeling that might haunt me to the graveyard. I'd promised myself I was just going to play the philosopher card in situations like this.

"A year ago, we were in Greece. It was incredible to imagine that Plato, Aristotle and all these guys were there trying to figure out life. Have you been?"

"Böddi's only been to Denmark, Mom. Once."

I gave Fjóla a hard look, asking myself why she told them this. I liked the witty teasing part of her, but not while dining with her parents. Her mom continued.

"Oh, Denmark. We were there at a young age, studying. Oh, the people, galleries, museums and parties were great. Quite the time we had in Christiania as well. Right, my dear?"

Fjóla's dad nodded as he passed around the potatoes.

"It is way different now in Denmark. We had a wonderful time back then," Fjóla's mom said, with a dreamy face.

"Denmark is lovely. You liked it?" Fjóla's dad asked.

"Yes. It was Okay. I didn't visit many museums. More like a time of reflection......And uh, festivals."

What am I saying?

Was I reflecting with dope, beer, sex and hash?

"You stayed for long?"

"Just nine days."

Fjóla laughed. I took another sip of wine and started focusing on eating.

Please talk about something else.

The tactic worked. I managed to dodge uncomfortable conversations during the rest of the dinner. Fjóla parents were cool, worldly and relaxed. I wondered why Fjóla was such a stiff, coming from this home. This home was like a small gallery and Fjóla had never told me that her parents were into art. And rich.

Fjóla's mom and dad cleaned the table and offered us a coffee. I offered a helping hand, something I never did with my own family. They told me not to worry.

"Come, I want to show you something," Fjóla said.

Fjóla and I stood up from the dining table and walked around the apartment while her mom and dad were in the kitchen. I hated how Fjóla dressed and how she hid her nicely toned body. She was eagerly trying to look as business-like as possible, all in black and white. She dressed like a forty-year-old office lady at the age of twenty-two. Her body screamed sex at me all the time, but her clothes annoyed me. I loved handling her big boobs and often contemplated how amazing they must have looked before she gave birth.

Am I getting too involved with this girl?

"Do you like the art? You have any clue about art, Böddi?"

I strolled after her, looking pensive, trying to make sense of every piece she showed me.

"No not really. It's nice, I guess."

I took up one of the small stone sculptures in my hand. I tried to figure out what it was and to show that I had interest in her guided tour.

But I don't get it. What's so important about all this? Most of the stuff in here I feel like I can do myself.

"I wouldn't touch that," she warned. "Some of the things here are really expensive."

Now I am slightly more interested in this art thing...

"So how much are we talking about?"

"Let's just say that if you sold all the pieces in here you'd pretty much not have to work for the rest of your life."

Wow. Do they keep this place safe from burglars?

"For this?" I pointed at a wall with a few paintings on it.

"The coffee is ready."

Her dad called from the living room before she could answer. I continued thinking about what Fjóla had told me. Plans that could put me in jail were forming in my head. I tried to snap out of it.

After a couple of hours of chat and drinking, feeling a bit tipsy, we decided to leave before I could drink any more. I was driving, after all, and there was a kid. We put on our coats, boots and gloves, preparing to go into the cold weather outside. Her baby had to be put to bed soon.

Thoughts of the bar were pulling me away from her on this Thursday night, I'd checked my phone before leaving her parents and already a few texts in my inbox were informing me of gatherings here and there. She flirted in the car on the way home, using her dirty talk to keep me away from the bar. I gripped the wheel and stared fixedly at the almost-empty road. After ten minutes' drive we stopped outside her house.

The bar or sex? The bar or sex?

"Could you help me with Viktor?"

I unfastened Viktor from his car seat, he was already asleep. We both knew this scenario. It was hard to keep a tipsy Böddi away from the bar. With me reluctantly shouldering her sleeping child we entered her apartment. Clothes and toys lay on the floor everywhere.

The bar or sex? The bar or sex?

I carried the baby into his bedroom and held him up, his head lolling sleepily, while Fjóla gently dragged off his snowsuit. She took him off me and patted his bottom to check he wasn't too wet. When she had laid him in his cot with a kiss on his forehead, the two of us walked together into the living room.

"Fuck me," she ordered.

Sex, then.

I went for her right there in the living room, taking great pleasure in ripping her ugly clothes off one piece at a time, starting with the jacket, then the white cami top and her bra while she held her arms up and out for me. All the time I kissed, licked, and ran my fingers over her light brown skin. I pulled down her skirt and dragged it off together with her knickers which she stepped out of one leg at a time. She took off her glasses and threw them on the floor, tore the stretchy band out of her hair and shook it loose. She had totally surrendered, knowing I loved that. In bed, she always gave me all the power, letting me control what we did and when. We started on the sofa where I fingered her, making her all wet. Then I turned her around, pushed her stomach against the living room table and took her from behind. Fast. Hard. Swapped positions. Kept the pace. Sweat. Heat. Biting. Intense. Faster. Finished.

We lay on the floor, breathing heavily. She rolled around like she was still in her orgasm. I stood up and went to the bathroom for a pee. Looked in the mirror.

Sex and bar?

When I came out of the bathroom she'd already got up and

gone to bed, most likely expecting me to join her for some of the tenderness she liked after rough sex. Without saying goodbye, I sneaked out of the apartment and off to the bar.

It takes about fifteen minutes to walk downtown. It was cold but I kept my spirits up with thinking.

Could I make art and sell it?

Could I steal art?

Could I start to deal art?

The day after...

At lunchtime I had just sneaked out of another apartment and it wasn't Fjóla's. I was still downtown. I had skipped school and had an explosive headache.

Thank God it's Friday.

I'm hungry.

I walked to a small sandwich place on Ingólfstorg Square. Their food was known to cure hangovers, at least while you were eating it. They boasted of having a secret ingredient. I waited in line. In front of me were construction workers, speaking in foreign languages. When it was my turn I ordered my sandwich.

'Card denied'.

Fuck. It's only the 12th of October!

I sat down in that place looking over the square, watching

kids skateboarding and it made me think of my own skateboarding days in Breiðholt.

What can I tell Fjóla?

I can't lose the apartment she has. I can't lose the sex we have. I can't lose the money she has.

I need to come up with a story, and a good one.

But first, I took out my phone.

"Mom. Are you home?"

"Yes, Böddi. How are you? How's school?"

"Fine. Fine. Hey, I was wondering, do we still have those paintings in the storage?"

"What paintings?"

"The ones Grandmother left me and Palli."

"Yes, I think so, why?"

"Nothing. Just curious. I was at some dinner last night and we talked about art, and I just wondered if we still had those. Okay, Mom, I've got to go. Talk later, bye."

I hung up. Next I called my friend from uni to pick me up. Snorri arrived about half an hour later. We drove up to Breiðholt. When we got there my mom had gone out. I searched in the dresser drawers for the keys to the storage downstairs and eventually found them. Checking over my shoulder that no-one had come in while I was busy, I unlocked a door off the kitchen and flicked on a light switch at the top of the stairs. Then I went down into the dusty, windowless storage room and started looking through the piles of boxes for the paintings.

Yes! Three of them!

The frame of one painting was slightly broken after having been buried under boxes. I removed all three and wrapped them in a big black plastic bag from a roll I found on the floor behind a set of old board games.

Snorri was still waiting for me in the car. During my walk back to the street, the package tucked under my arm, I called Fjóla. The phone rang and rang. No answer. A couple of minutes later I got a text.

Fuck you Böddi. I know you were with a girl last night. Iceland is small you idiot. We're over.

I sighed heavily. *It's a shame, but...*

I got into the car. Snorri seemed relaxed as always.

"Do you have time for a little mission?"

Snorri nodded his head.

"Do you know any art dealers?"

Snorri shook his head.

"Let's find one then, yeah?"

Snorri gave me a grin and started the engine.

I need to get money to survive the rest of the month. Maybe even for some beers this weekend.

* * *

A few calls and some further investigation later, we parked outside a gallery that was known to buy art. As I walked in, a bell above the glass door rang and a man of about seventy looked up from behind a counter. He was impeccably dressed and wore a flashy gold watch that immediately had me wondering if it was real or fake. Paintings were stacked in the cramped space all around the counter and laid out along the walls, ready to be hung, I guessed.

"Can I help you?"

"I have a few paintings to sell. Or for you to have a look at, if you're interested?"

I stood with my legs slightly apart, hoping I came across as more confident than I felt. He nodded his lion's mane of white hair at me and I drew the landscape paintings carefully out of the bag, one after the other, and handed them to him. He examined the works methodically, moving a magnifying glass across the surface of each one.

"Where did you get these?"

"They are from my grandmother. She gave them to me when she passed away." I rubbed my hands together nervously. "It was in her will."

I'm not going to mention Palli. That might make things complicated.

The man spent some more time studying the paintings. He reached under the desk for a small tool and used it to remove the frames, then he turned each of the paintings over and examined their backs. Laying the paintings carefully on the counter, he moved over to a computer where he began tapping at the keyboard and rapidly scanning the screen. I shifted my feet, sweat prickling my armpits.

Finally he wrote something on a receipt form. He looked up at me.

"You can leave them here with me and I'll give you an estimated price tonight or tomorrow. Here's a receipt for each of the paintings. Give me your email address and I'll send you an email, letting you know my answer."

I wrote down my email thinking maybe the month was covered by what I would make, or at least the weekend.

Later that evening I hung out in Breiðholt. My mom was there. We didn't talk much, I was doing too much thinking.

I wonder if Fjóla will take me back?

She had some nice qualities.

How the fuck will I attend school living in Breiðholt, without a car.

At nine PM I checked my email, thinking it was pointless. I'd never get any money from the art dealer guy on a Friday evening. *Man, I'm stupid.*

There was mail in my inbox.

Sæll Böðvar.

We have taken a look at your paintings and the gallery would be happy to take them off your hands. The highest price we could offer is 1.4 million Icelandic Krónur. Please contact us on Monday if you wish to accept the offer.

Holy Shit!

Two weeks later.

"One coffee, please."

The waitress at the university cafeteria didn't smile back. I didn't blame her, it must be depressing to work there every day seeing students rushing by on their way to becoming doctors, lawyers and psychologists. Must make you wonder what you've done with your life. The cafeteria was packed, as always. Poor students, eating noodle soups, leftovers from the day before and drinking cheap coffee.

"Two hundred krónur."

I handed her the money, feeling good in my new sneakers, new jeans and new jacket. My clothes didn't fit in with the other philosophy students anymore. They all wore ripped jeans, thick woollen sweaters and scarves wrapped around their necks. I was becoming like the lawyer guys sitting nearby discussing politics, the state of the nation and the last chick they'd banged. As I was scouting for cute girls I heard a voice calling. It was Júlía.

"May I sit?"

"Sure."

Júlía was a friend from class. She wasn't the most attractive girl, a bit overweight and her face was so round that I always thought of melons when I saw her. But she was funny, plus she smoked weed.

"Are you going to this multicultural thing, the exchange stuff?"

"What's that?" I took a sip of the coffee and continued scouting for girls while she explained.

"It's like, an exhibition, down the road. For exchange students and such."

"Why not? It sounds better than going to class, anyway."

We finished our coffee and went outside. It was freezing as usual, snowing and windy. On our way to the exchange exhibition I saw Fjóla. She was with her friends. She still refused to have any contact with me. I saw her laughing but it was obviously forced, just to assure me she didn't care.

If she only knew. I'd already got a room at a top location, by the pond in downtown Reykjavík. Fjóla and I crossed paths. She didn't even look at me.

I hope she noticed my new clothes.

I followed Júlía into a small hall. Quite a large number of

people were examining brochures and talking to stall holders. Student exchange organizations were attempting to fish out the students wanting to study abroad. There were also many foreign exchange students milling around and the air buzzed with different languages.

Who is that girl?

Júlía and I were still strolling around but I wasn't going to let my new target out of my sight. Júlía stopped walking around to have a chat with a bunch of friends, clearly more connected to this community than I was. I'd never even seen any of the people in this room before.

How come I've never seen that beautiful girl during my ten per cent attendance at uni this winter?

I moved towards a booth promoting a student exchange programme. The target of my lust was talking to another girl.

Wow, that face.

So skinny.

I'd never slept with an Asian girl. I once heard a story at school, of an Icelandic guy who travelled the world with a mission to bang a girl in each country he visited. He mailed postcards to his friends with the flags of each one in which he was successful.

I took up a brochure and pretended to read it, peeping over the top, my attention on the target. Until Júlía arrived. *Oh please don't cock this up for me.*

"See anything you like?"

"No, just looking."

Why don't you go away?

"Hi, Júlía." A guy I didn't know suddenly came up and grabbed Júlía's attention. *Now's my chance.*

Feeling confident in my new clothes and with enough money to drink my feelings away if this failed, I walked up to the two girls at the booth, holding the brochure in my hand.

"Excuse me, I was wondering if you are associated with this organization?"

First time I've used that pick up line, ha-ha.

"No, or in fact yes; I'm not but she is." The Asian girl spoke with a funny British accent.

"Okay, I was just wondering if I could get some help? I'm thinking about going abroad."

"What are you studying?" the other girl asked. She spoke in awkward Icelandic.

"Business," I lied. "I'm just finishing my degree. More looking for business opportunities abroad than being a student."

Why, Böddi?

"I'm not sure you are at the right place for that. But what country are you mainly thinking of?"

"China. Import, export."

The Asian girl came up with a smile, biting her lips together. *Yes, I guessed right!*

"Are you from China?" I asked, pretending innocence.

"Yes."

"Which part?"

"Kunming."

"That's exactly the city I'm aiming for!"

Where the fuck is Kunming?

Júlía arrived by my side, now saving me from spinning some stupid lie such as that I was a prince from Iceland who had just saved the world from a nuclear disaster. I walked to one side with Júlía and asked her to wait. Reaching back towards the booth, I grabbed a pen and wrote down my phone number on the back of the brochure. Then I went back to the girls.

"Here's my number. I'd love to hear more about Kunming. How much longer are you in Iceland for?"

"I leave in one week." The girl bit her lower lip slightly and her mystical-looking eyes glanced shyly to one side.

"Well. I'll see you soon, if not in Iceland, then in Kunming."

Why not, hey? I always planned to travel eventually, that was why I did that teaching English course.

It's not like I'm doing anything important in Iceland.

I might as well use all that money to have some adventures.

Kafli 19 - Laos, 2011.

Meeting Marissa

THE ELECTRIC FAN is blowing in my face. I can't believe I've been at Max's for three days already. I constantly observe my body for signs, wondering how I can reach the greater state of being that Max described to me yesterday.

I need to get rid of the crap I'm wrapped in.

The only palpable thing is my anxiety. Anxiety has been present my whole life and before I thought it was just part of the deal of being a human being. I now have expectations of getting rid of it. That scares me.

What if I fail?

It was hard to blame anything but myself. I was lying alone in a peaceful room in Laos, yet anxiety was still my companion, that racing heartbeat; the heat under my skin. I grasped at things to accuse but part of me didn't want to do that anymore. I got up and dressed quickly, then made my way across the living room to the kitchen. Max was preparing breakfast.

"Good morning, Böddi."

"Morning, Max."

"How did you sleep?"

"Okay, I guess."

I ought to cheer up a bit since I was a guest in his house. Max eyed me perceptively.

"I told you that the Energy in the house is very powerful," he said. "You will go through all kinds of feelings while you're staying here. Help me with breakfast. Please put some plates on the table for us."

"Okay." My voice was dull, like I used to reply to Mom when she asked me to do things.

"How are you?" Max was stirring a pot.

"I'm all right." I wanted to eat before talking.

We sat down at the table, Max in his natural happy state. I was heavy, low on energy and feeling depressed.

"Stop it." Max used a level voice. He drew the knife across the bread.

"Stop what?"

"Stop feeling the way you are feeling. You are ruining my breakfast."

I looked down at my food.

"Stop it," he said again, reaching for the butter.

"What the fuck are you talking about?"

A short silence while we bit into our food and swallowed. Then Max looked up.

"Stop it," he repeated, more gently.

"What the fuck, Max? Stop what?"

Then, fearing a fight, I raised both hands in a surrendering gesture.

Max stood up. He walked slowly around the table and placed his hand on my shoulder. He leant down so he could look into my eyes. I held my breath. In the way I was becoming used to, he emanated calm.

"Listen, Böddi. Now listen carefully. This is not a game. This is serious. You have no idea how lucky you are to sit in this chair. If you see this as a game then you better start playing it wisely. People on this planet play different games all the time. Some people play the money game, living to get more money. Some people play the family game, they live to have more children. Some people play the career game, those ones live to achieve success." He maintained eye contact with me while he was speaking though it was the hardest thing for me to stick with. I fought the urge to stand up and leave.

"If you want to look at this as a game, Böddi, then this is the master-game you are playing right now. You are on the fast track to burning all your karma. If you choose to leave, then go, I won't stop you. But if you want to stay you will have to start to listen and learn. Understand? Are you willing to stay on track?"

I have never finished anything in my life.

I can't leave now, I made a promise to myself: to trust The Experience.

I lowered my head and closed my eyes, started shaking. I was on the verge of crying, like a kid.

I am so small.

Forcing myself to look at Max again; the man who had the wide-open smile of a child, I told him, "I do want to stay. Tell me what I should stop? What was I doing wrong?"

Max knelt on the floor in front of me. He laid his hand on top of mine.

"Stop suffering, Böddi. This is not only your personal matter. You are affecting my house, the environment and me with your suffering, with your ups and downs. The fact that you are staying in this house and being in this house means that your healing has begun. You are in the process of healing. You're becoming cleansed of all the shit you've carried on your shoulders since birth, even from past lives."

His breathing is so steady, it helps me breathe.

"I am aware of the process you're going through but you have to know that living on the spiritual path is the most difficult task a man can attempt. This is not about seeing ghosts; talking to spirits or believing in an unknown identity. This is serious and very real. Your suffering is real. The effect of your suffering is real. Your job is to make sure you don't suffer and to take care of me. Understand?"

"Okay. How do I stop suffering? How do I stop the ups and downs?"

I used the hem of my t-shirt to wipe under my eyes.

"It's deeply cultural and generally accepted that life is full of ups and downs. This is bullshit, Böddi. The path you are embarking on, it only goes up. How to do it? Just do it. Or in your case, just do it or I'll throw you out."

I checked Max's face: he was laughing again. "Now," he added. "Take the stuff off the table, wash the dishes and please don't look so serious. It's going to be a good day, so shift your perception."

While I cleaned the table I felt small, like a young boy; even the furniture seemed bigger.

This is all real. Max is real, I am real. I am playing the Master-game.

I have to burn my karma. Whatever that means.

The spiritual path was not going to be easy.

"Max?"

"Yes?"

"Why am I here? Why me? Why am I the lucky one sitting in this seat?"

"This talk is nonsense. Your good karma brought you here. Simple."

I was learning that Max's responses were always down-to-earth.

"What is karma?" I asked, still feeling like a kid.

"Karma means actions of body, speech and mind."

"Hmm. Okay. But, Max. I'm afraid. I am afraid of failure. I have always been suffering and I'm afraid of not being able to stop it."

He dried his hands on a worn towel and draped the towel over a hook.

"Don't be afraid. As I said before, you are on the fast track to burning all your karma. It may be the fast track but there's still plenty of room for mistakes. We should always give people space to make mistakes. Enjoy the ride."

It was calming to learn that the pain was a part of the path of burning all my karma, though I didn't fully understand the meaning.

"So, what's my assignment today, Max?"

"I already gave you one." He turned at the kitchen doorway. "The assignment is to stop suffering."

That didn't seem as boring as cleaning the stones, but it was overwhelming to try to understand, so I decided not to. I figured I'd stay inside since Max had mentioned the healing energy inside the house.

Max didn't seem to be around. So I made myself some tea, grabbed a random book from the bookshelf and settled myself on the living room sofa. On the cover was a picture of a wheel, it looked like a ship's wheel. After a couple of hours of reading, with an intention to learn more about karma, I must have fallen asleep.

"Hello? Max. Are you here? I'm back." It was a female voice. From the direction of the sounds, the owner of it was entering the house by the front door.

My cheek felt numb from lying on my hand. I pushed myself up into a fully sitting position and turned around to see who it was. A girl was standing in the entrance, holding a scooter helmet in one hand and a big bag in the other. She was wearing a yellow dress and her pale blonde hair covered half of her face. I could just see the kink in her hair from the helmet. But it was her eyes that first struck me, large, wide open and intensely blue. The moment seemed to hover while I slowly inspected the rest of her. She stood in such a way as to show off her trim body, one hip thrust forward. She had brown, slim legs and a small waist which I could see in silhouette through her thin dress and her full breasts, angled towards me. Or was it simply my lust suggesting they were? After categorizing her in the 'most beautiful' of my personal rating system, I stood up to greet her, making sure my t-shirt was pulled down over the front of my shorts, relieved the sofa was between us.

She walked forward, dumping her bag and helmet by the door.

"Hi." I made my voice deliberately low.

"Hi," she said lightly. "Who are you? Where is Max?"

"I think he went outside, but I'm not sure. I'm Böddi, Max's friend. Who are you, if I may ask?"

"Oh sorry." She stretched forward to shake my hand.

Those breasts in that sundress ...

That faint scent of perspiration and sun-warmed skin ...

Pay attention to what she's saying, Böddi ...

"I'm Marissa. I'm also Max's friend."

That smile.

"No worries." I managed a smile back, though my mouth felt rubbery. My whole energy was changing, as usually happened when a pretty girl was around.

"So how do you know Max?" Marissa asked.

Where should I begin? "Long story. How do you know him?"

"Long story also."

I love the way she laughs.

Say something.

"What are you doing in Laos?"

"I work at an orphanage in Vientiane. I teach English and take care of the children. It's a beautiful job and I love my kids. What are you doing in Laos? Are you staying here with Max?"

She had a strong Australian accent. I felt the beat of time.

How I behaved now could change everything. Was I going to be real or not? I met her eyes.

Those big blue eyes.

Be real.

"I guess I'm exploring myself. Trying to figure out what this whole universe is all about. Trying to grow, maybe. Yeah, I'm staying here with Max, don't know for how long though."

She can probably see right through me. I hadn't done a very good job of hiding my nervousness at telling the truth.

Her eyes softened. "Wow, that's great. You are in the right place. This house is very special and Max is a great shaman."

Shaman?

"He is a wonderful man, you should consider yourself lucky."

I nodded.

"Would you like ... ?" I was making an awkward inviting gesture towards the sofa.

Smiling, she moved around it and we both sat down. She sat surprisingly close but I wasn't complaining. The atmosphere was getting more comfortable by the second. *And uncomfortable at the same time.* I shifted.

"So. A shaman? What does that mean?"

She smiled and rested her hand on my arm. It caused a tingle under my skin. I pulled a cushion onto my lap and planted my elbows in it, laying my chin in my hands as I listened to her.

"A shaman is a spiritual healer. Shamans believe in the universal web of power that supports all life. For them, everything is alive, even stones, clouds and any other stuff. They live in harmony with nature and they say that everything is interconnected. They don't belong to any dogma or religion."

"How do you know all this?"

"I used to work with indigenous people in Australia. After working with them, my journey to seek the truth began. Working with those people had a great effect on my life. Some of them were much wounded by how we treated them. We ruined their way of life by imposing our ideology on them. The levels of trauma they had are only found in people who go through war or have been tortured, or they could have witnessed genocide and other horrible things."

"So, how is this connected to shamans?"

"I met a shaman on my journey," Marissa said. "The man changed my life. I realised that there are people in this world who live in the realms of spirits. Their souls can travel long distances. I had some experiences in meditation; drumming, singing, with this shaman. He was the most compassionate man I've known, similar to Max. His energy was amazing. He had healing energy. When I first met Max, I knew *he* was a shaman too. I could feel it."

"Wow." I was mesmerised, both by her voice and the things she was telling me. By listening to Marissa I had taken yet another step on the path. When I heard new things about spirituality, hundreds more questions burst into my mind.

"Yeah. One time I asked the indigenous shaman what he thought about science. He explained to me that the truth has stayed the same for thousands of years, but science keeps changing every year. When I told him that people have landed on the moon, he hadn't even heard of that."

"What was his reaction?"

"He said, so what? I go there all the time."

Marissa laughed. When she stopped I wanted to hear it again. We sat quietly for a moment and then my thoughts went back to Max.

"Wow. Max a shaman. That's fascinating."

Marissa looked at her watch. Don't go.

"I have to leave, my lunch break is almost over. I have to go teach a class. It was really nice talking to you. Just tell Max I said hi and tell him that the bag is next to the kitchen table. Yeah?"

I felt like the small boy again. "Okay."

As she was leaving I followed her to the door. "One more question, Marissa. Do you believe in the shamanic way of living, then?"

She gave me an engaging grin.

"No. I'm open to anything. Now I'm studying Tantra."

"All right ..."

"So glad to meet you, Böddi. Don't you just love meeting interesting people in interesting places?"

"Yeah, I guess." My mouth stretched in a smile.

"You know what they say." She nudged me gently with her elbow.

Uh-oh.

"If you go to bars you meet people who go to bars, if you go to a temple you meet people who go to a temple and so on and so forth. And now we both live at Max's place. Bye, bye."

She was out the door, jamming the helmet over that blonde hair of hers. She left an ache in my belly as I stood in the doorway, watching this beautiful girl named Marissa leaving on her scooter. I remembered a TV show that was on air in Iceland when I was a teenager. It was about couples practicing Tantric sex. I remembered how incredibly awkward the show was and how people used to make fun of it. These couples were openly talking about their sexual experiences using the Tantra method. I always felt bad for those people, since Iceland is a place where everybody knows everybody. Those people on the show: everybody would know what his or her sex life was like. Was Marissa talking about the same kind of Tantra?

***

Max arrived home.

"Böddi, what happened here? Can you please open some windows?" He was chuckling.

"What do you mean?" I could feel his gaze on my back as I walked over to the window to open it.

"Were you thinking about sex, Böddi? Were you thinking about porn or something?"

How the fuck could he know that? I kept my back to him, opening the window. It was hard to make myself turn and face him. *Did he see us? How does he know?*

My face burned.

"What, can you read my mind now?" I tried to sound nonchalant.

"Yes, I can read your mind, Böddi." Max's lips curled up in a teasing smile.

"Did you see her?"

"See who?"

"Marissa."

"Ooohhhh," he said. "That explains it. No I didn't see her. You should try to control this lust of yours. It's all over the house. You must have liked her. You are like a dog, Böddi. You should try and talk to her with your heart and head instead of with your penis." He was laughing but it felt serious. Again, I felt like that clueless kid.

"Can you really see the energy?"

"I can see."

"Are you a shaman?"

Max let out a sharp burst of laughter. "You have been talking to Marissa. That's her image of me. She always calls me her shaman. People have many images of me and therefore I have many names. If people want to call me 'Shaman', that's fine with me. I call Marissa 'Perulata'."

"What's Perulata?"

"An Australian insect, sometimes called the white drummer. You will see why."

Do I really fill the room with my sexual energy? I couldn't deny that I had mused on the subject of Tantra. I'd stared at Marissa's breasts and got turned on the moment I saw her, let alone when she laid her hand on my arm. How amazing that Max could perceive all this.

My energy is a palpable force. Every minute I was learning something new in this house.

Max was in the kitchen going through the stuff Marissa had brought.

"She's beautiful," I said in a low voice, not really expecting him to hear.

"What?"

I bet he can even hear my thoughts.

"She's nice. And she's ...beautiful."

When Max returned to the living room, he was holding something wrapped in paper. He stood in the middle of the living room.

"I know, Böddi. She is. She is a wonderful girl. She's your sister. Next time you meet her, try to treat her as your sister and not as a beautiful girl. Try to see an old woman in this young girl's face. Try to see things as they are and as they will become. We are all subject to ageing, even though I look so fabulous for my age." A flash of his cheeky grin again. "No, really, Böddi, she deserves more than to have you suffocating her with your sexual desires."

My whole being protested. "Does having a girlfriend stop you from growing spiritually?"

Please say no.

Max looked at me with loving eyes, slowly unwrapping the outer paper. "Not necessarily, but in your case, yes. You have other things to think about and are way too vulnerable and fragile right now."

I swallowed. *I need to trust Max on this.* Max came towards me. He peeled off the outer layer of paper and inside there was more transparent paper folded into a bowl shape, containing loads of peanuts. I took a handful.

"Okay. You are right." I shut myself off from thoughts of Marissa. "I was supposed to stop suffering. That's my assignment. I understand. When are you going to take the letter to James?"

That was what I came here for.

"I'm not going to"

"What?"

You can't move the goalposts now.

"You will give him the letter yourself. We are going to Phon-thong prison together, tomorrow."

Kafli 20 - Laos.

Trip to the Phonthong Prison

A MOSQUITO. That sound. It's early in the morning of my fourth day here at Max's. I'm listening to the breeze making music with the trees outside the window. The sound is intoxicatingly peaceful, with the occasional buzz from the mosquito to disturb it. My anxiety level is low. I'm pushing all thoughts of the anxiety away because I don't want to create it. What will happen today?

Itching on my legs from mosquito bites. I was trying to understand the meaning of this only being itching. There was only the *presence* of itching and my reactions to it depended totally on my way of thinking. I decided to try not to be attached to the *feeling* of itching.

As I lay there the enemy zoomed in ever-decreasing circles around the bed. The mosquito was preparing another attack. I followed the creature with my eyes and it constantly appeared and disappeared in front of me in the sun's rays through the window. I could feel my body getting more defensive, and I was gathering myself to counter-attack.

Smack. I opened my palms and there it was, a crushed mosquito inside my left hand. There was a small amount of blood on my hand. A routine thought came to my mind: had the mosquito shed my blood or was it someone else's, there on my palm?

I continued to look at the dead mosquito and something didn't feel right. The action of killing the mosquito didn't feel right. I'd been a vegetarian since The Experience, telling myself I was doing it for the welfare of animals but now I had killed a mosquito without even thinking about it.

Is the killing justified because the mosquito was planning to attack me?

I wonder if we all have this killer instinct. Isn't this exactly what governments do if their country is threatened in some way, they kill?

"Böddi. Get out of bed, we are leaving."

Max was calling from the living room.

It was an important day. The reason I came to Max's place to begin with. I was going to give the letter to James. I hurried through my morning ablutions and went to eat breakfast.

"Are you ready to go to Phonthong today?" Max asked. "I

had to go through a lot of processes in the last two days to get you in, just so you know."

He was putting food on the table as he spoke. My ingratitude hit me. I hadn't even thought about how Max had managed to get me into the prison. This visit to the prison would be an experience of the feeling of gratitude.

"Thank you so much, Max," I said. "I hope someday I will be able to pay you back somehow. How did you get me in?"

"I have my ways."

We both sat down. I should have made breakfast. Max had talked about me taking care of him, not the other way round. I promised myself that tomorrow I'd make the breakfast. I wouldn't apologise now but rather I would let my future actions speak for themselves.

"Max?"

"Yes, Böddi. How are you feeling today? Your energy is lighter. Some changes are occurring for you?"

"Yes, I feel lighter. I feel less anxious. My mind is somehow clearer."

"Good. It's a part of the process. Just remember that things have a tendency to rise and fall. Enjoy it while it lasts." This was accompanied by his loving smile.

"Max?"

"Yes?"

"I was thinking about violence. I killed a mosquito this

morning. It felt weird. I have never felt bad about killing an insect before. It made me think about violence in the world."

"Go on."

"Well, I wondered why people are violent. For example, the people in Phonthong prison. There must be murderers, rapists and all kinds of bad people in there. Why are they violent?"

Max was chewing his food. I noticed he never rushed his food, unlike me, who gobbled it down. When he had swallowed he said, "I'm glad you asked this question. But it's a stupid question. The people in prisons: criminals; politicians and others, are not the only people who are violent. Everybody is violent. *Everybody.* You are violent, as you could see when you killed that mosquito. I am violent as well. The difference between you and me is that I am aware of it. I don't suppress it nor do I run away from the fact. When people say they are non-violent it is an absurd statement. They are only not violent within the framework their society gives them in order to stay outside the prison walls."

"How do you become aware of it?"

"I just mentioned the rise and fall of your anxiety. It's the same with violence. Next time you see a mosquito, try to observe your violent thoughts. You could even talk to the mosquito. Tell the mosquito that you are going to kill it and watch how the thoughts of violence slowly go away when you become aware. They vanish into thin air and you will think twice before killing. The result will be that when the thoughts of violence rise again you will be more aware of them."

"Sounds like a plan for my next mosquito war. Now, let me clear the table while you get ready."

Hopefully he will notice that I am taking care of him.

***

The drive to the Phonthong prison took about forty minutes. We drove through bare land with scattered trees pointing high into the air. My excitement at seeing James increased as Max indicated we were getting closer but I was also disturbed by the sights and smells around us.

The scenery was now more like a third-world country than an exotic holiday location. The stink of burning trash entered the car and I bunched up the hem of my t-shirt and stuffed it over my mouth and nose. Maybe it was the fact we were driving to a prison that had shifted my perception of the landscape. It didn't matter if you were in Paradise when you were locked up in a hellhole.

Max and I had our most talkative drive together yet. Even the silence in our conversations had meanings. Usually Max was silent until I asked a question. I sometimes hoped he would just talk and explain everything he knew, but that wasn't how he operated. It didn't matter what the question was, whether it was chit-chatting about the weather or figuring out the puzzle of life, he was there to answer. In my head, thoughts were cooking all the time, forming the next questions to be asked. It was like Max needed to know where my mind was at to form his answer instead of spouting out his wisdom. His way made sense and I accepted it.

Suddenly we were driving on a dirt road and the car started jumping up and down. Max said we were approaching Phon-thong prison. A simple, cheap-looking concrete complex was revealed through the dust of bare land. The light brown dirt road surrounded the prison. The prison was encapsulated within grey walls which were around three metres high with barbed wire layered on top. I could see a couple of guard towers in the middle of the compound. In each corner there were security floodlights, about five metres above the ground. Max was now driving at walking pace.

"Don't talk to anyone unless I say so," he said urgently. "No quick moves, Böddi, and don't make any eye contact, is that clear?"

"Yes." My muscles stiffened up. There was a pain in my neck.

He slowed down even more. We were approaching a gate with two guards standing either side of it.

"Give me the letter, quickly."

"Okay. Why?" Heat radiated through my chest.

"Because they won't let anyone bring stuff to the inmates. The guards will take the letter, read it and probably toss it afterwards. So it's better that I take it."

He stuffed the letter between his belly and his underwear. Max had never asked about the letter, not one question.

Why is he smuggling the letter to James for me?

Why is he paying the guards and the prison authorities just to get me in, without asking a single question about the letter's content or for anything in return?

Max stopped the car. The guards approached and I could feel my heart pumping faster. The guards were stone-faced, wearing uniform and carrying guns. Sweat prickled under my hair. Max and the guards exchanged words in Lao. I sat silently as Max had instructed me.

"Get out," Max said. His smile was gone.

We both stepped out of the car, my legs shaking so much I wondered if I would actually be able to stand up. The guards looked nervous and pointed at me while they spoke to each other in Lao. Then they grabbed us and pushed us up against the car.

"Turn around, they are going to search us."

I can't breathe.

Max took the letter out of his pocket and handed it to one of the guards.

We're busted.

We're screwed.

I can't believe he's just done that.

The guards pushed me this way and that, made me hold up my arms and keep my legs apart while they searched me. One guard frisked my shaking body with both hands, from head to ankle.

Frozen. Powerless.

Don't touch me ...

My blood pounded so hard I couldn't hear anything else. Once they had let me be and taken a few steps away I saw Max turning around to face them. I did the same without asking Max, my whole body vibrating with fear.

One of the guards opened the letter right in front of us. I looked at Max. He said nothing and gave me a glance that implied I should shut up and wait.

Two long minutes or so while the guard read the letter. I wondered if he could really read English. I suppressed an urge to talk to the guard and explain that it was my stupid idea and Max was just trying to help me.

Keep your mouth shut and wait.

The guard folded the letter, walked towards Max and handed him the letter. They exchanged a few words in Lao and then Max told me to get in the car.

"What was that? Are we in trouble?" *What if I've ruined everything for Max?*

"No. I gave him the letter I got from the prison manager, in response to the one in which I explained that there was a special guest coming with me. That's you. I had to pay a lot of money to get you in. I've earned trust and respect here through the years, but it's the first time someone came with me. I have always been alone." Even Max's hand was shaking as he reached up to adjust his hat. "The guards had no idea, so I had to show them a note from the authorities."

He started the truck and drove on until we stopped outside another gate. I was trying to name the feeling I had but I couldn't. It was a mixture of nervousness, excitement and fear. I was also claustrophobic, and felt relieved when Max told me to get out of the car.

There were two guards waiting for us at what seemed to be the main gate. The guards recognised Max, but looked at me suspiciously. Again, Max showed the guards the letter from the prison manager and this time it was easier as we had already passed the first gate.

We were ushered through the main gate, followed by the two guards. We walked on muddy soil. I noticed a small fishpond on my left side and a pitiful-looking vegetable garden on my right. There were four small houses in the whole area and I couldn't believe people would actually stay there for years. I couldn't have imagined a worse shithole to spend the rest of my life in. I thought about Max's son. How terrible it must have been, knowing he had suffered here for years. Max started explaining the area while we stood in the centre of the prison complex.

"Böddi, look there. These are the two prison blocks. Each has ten cells in it. There are five to six people in each cell, sleeping side by side and head to toe."

"Ten cells? There can't be, it's too small. How can anyone live there?"

"It's not by their choice, my friend. The cells are small, as I told you before. They have no lights inside, but there's a fluorescent light outside them. There are no beds inside the cells and mattresses are forbidden."

We progressed into the garden.

"What's this?"

"This is their cooking place. They have no access to electricity so they rely on wood. But they have to pay for that and not all of them have money to buy wood. They eat the same food three hundred and sixty-five days a year. The only thing they get to eat is pig fat soup, sticky rice and fish paste. The weird thing is that the fish harvested from these small ponds around the garden is sold outside of the prison walls, and not fed to inmates."

Oh my God.

I could never have imagined this.

"What do they do? They just let them rot in their cells? How can people treat other people like that?"

But I'm still not feeling the gratitude I should for my own freedom. What's wrong with me?

"Follow me," was all Max said.

We passed the two cell blocks and came across a smaller building. A guard opened the door, eyeing me suspiciously. Inside was an empty room; raw, dirty and smelling like an old warehouse. Not how I imagined a meditation room to be.

Max told me to wait in the room while he talked to the guards. Every molecule in my body felt uncomfortable. The energy in this room was very different from Max's house. I hadn't previously comprehended that the energy in Max's house was different from a normal house but now I knew. I had something to compare it with.

Max returned. He told me to sit down and wait for the others. We sat together with crossed legs on the stone floor. My body was locked with tension.

What a bizarre place to try meditation for the first time.

One of the guards stood by the door and I guessed the other had gone to get the prisoners. Finally they started marching into the room, one by one. The inmates were handcuffed on both their hands and feet.

Max's first student was a black woman who had an obvious swell to her belly; she must have been seven or eight months pregnant. The second was an Asian male in his forties. Next to come in was a white man with long hair and a beard. He looked like he hadn't had any food for months, his face colourless, inanimate. The fourth inmate to walk in the door was another young Westerner, his head jerking from side to side, looking all around him, eyes wide with fear. His body was in slightly better shape than the other guy but just to look at him I suspected he was on the edge of a nervous breakdown. After that came another Asian male; rough-looking, shirtless and tattooed all over his body. The sixth student was a tall black man, wearing a torn shirt. I noticed scars wherever his flesh showed.

Lastly, a man came in who I somehow recognised. I'd never seen a picture of James but I was sure it was him. His physical appearance was awful. He looked weak, he had a full, unkempt beard and he walked as if he was in pain. But there was something about his face. Even though his whole appearance was terrible, his face was calm, focussed and relaxed. *James.*

Max started the class with his calming, loving voice.

"Good morning, dear students. Today we have a guest joining us in the meditation and I want you to welcome him by opening your hearts to him. Today we will meditate in silence, in the emptiness. In there, you'll find the truth. I would like everybody to get rid of his or her old ideas about your past and the future. The only thing that's real is right now. Everything else is an illusion of the mind.

Remember that there is no method we use and there is no control. There is no measure. There is no 'how to meditate'. The mind will not become free through a method. Meditation is not conflict, therefore there is no control.

Let's rise above. Let's rise above the fear. Rise above the pride, images, pain, ambition, vanity, greed and so on. The mind will only go further into illusion if we hold on to these things.

As always, the goal of today's meditation is the ending of suffering; underneath the suffering there's a chance to understand, to love, to reach wisdom and peace.

Now, I want everybody to take a deep breath, close his or her eyes and get into the silence. Find the state of quietness. Find the state above the obstacles. Rise above the obstacles of doubt; the doubt of the end of suffering; the greed within you; the aversion within you. Rise above laziness and restlessness.

Let's rise above."

I closed my eyes.

This is weird.

How will I get the letter to James?

Oh, the silence, I forgot.

I can't believe I'm here.

Is this real?

Oh, the silence. I think too much. Remember, no control. Think about The Experience.

✻

My knees hurt. The floor is hard.
Who is the black woman? Why is she pregnant?
Oh, back to the silence.
The room is silent. Am I the only one thinking so much? Think about The Experience.

✻

My left side is calmer than the right side. Is it because Max is on my left side?
The floor is too hard. But I have to relax. I have to be silent.
How can I be silent? Am I forcing it now?

✻

Okay, I surrender to the silence.

✻

Just keep thinking about The Experience.

✻

I wonder what Mom would say if she knew I was here.

How did all this happen, me ending up here in prison?

Can Max read my thoughts now? If I think about porn, can he feel it?

Silence, please be silent.

*

Are all these people bad people?

What makes them bad? What are they in for?

Should I open my eyes?

Go to the silence. The Experience.

*

Is now the only real thing?

Are all our thoughts about the past and the future just bullshit? Just something we make up?

Go back.

*

What's this vast blackness?

What's this face?

A face.

*

Silence.

*

The feelings in my body have changed. There's heat in my head. There's a feeling of electricity in my body. Is that because we are all energy? Do the others feel that too? This is exhausting.
I can't find the silence.
This is boring. How long is he going to meditate?
Try not to think.

*

I loved football. I never play here in Asia. I should find a team. Go back.

*

This is too long, when will this be over?

*

"Now slowly open your eyes," Max's soft voice broke through.

I opened my eyes. The room seemed different. My body felt numb, my head calmer and I had a strange feeling like I was inside a movie. I looked over the room. Everybody seemed calm except the student who had been the third one to enter, the weakest-looking Western male. He was crying.

Max unravelled his long legs, stood up and walked towards him. James was sitting next to the weak guy, watching what was going on. Max knelt down, put his arms around the man, gave him a hug and whispered something. At this point the guard at the door noticed Max's proximity to a prisoner. He shouted something in Lao. The whole room suffered a shock, like a grenade had been thrown into a room full of sleeping babies.

Max stood up again and quickly moved over to the guard, speaking in Lao. Tension cut the air and made it hard to breathe. The guard watched suspiciously while Max resumed his seat. We were not allowed to communicate directly with the prisoners. I looked towards Max and whispered,

"What did you say to him?"

"I was helping him to cry."

The moment the guard shouted at Max I had felt the whole energy in the room change. It was like I'd been thrown back into reality, and judging from the faces of others I assumed they felt the same.

Max continued guiding us with talk about spirituality. For

the final ten minutes of the session, the prisoners were allowed to ask questions under surveillance from the guards.

***

In silence, we walked to the car. I still didn't feel grateful at all after seeing the prisoners in their conditions. I was in state of shock. I didn't know what to think, say or do. So I stayed quiet. Max was quiet as well.

When we'd been escorted back through both the gates we finally arrived at the car. We got in and Max inserted the keys. But all he did then was tilt his head backwards and close his eyes.

I knew how he felt. I was numb sitting next to him, staring at the dusty steering wheel, hoping he would say something soon.

"How was your meditation?" he eventually asked.

"Intense," was all I managed to mumble.

"Tell me." Max started the car.

"I don't know where to begin. It was intense." I had a crazy feeling I was about to cry.

"Tell me, while it's fresh." Max's voice was empathetic.

"My mind couldn't stop thinking. It was impossible to stop my thoughts in those conditions."

"Think about what the prisoners go through. If it's tough for you, imagine how it is for them. What else?"

"Wow." I rubbed my face. "I almost don't remember. It's like I was in a blackout. Like I was in a movie or something. It was so unreal. I remember I thought about the pregnant black woman. Who is she?"

"She was arrested for smuggling drugs," Max said. "She got the death penalty. She's from Nigeria and her name is Atikah, which means 'pure' or 'clear'. Atikah was not pregnant when they put her in jail. She has been there for four years."

The rumble of the engine washed over me and the jolting of the car on the rutted track shook away some of the nervousness. I spread my fingers in front of me to check I was real.

"The story says she was raped by one of the guards. The law in Laos forbids execution of pregnant women and mothers, so she is now serving life imprisonment."

It dawned on me. *Getting pregnant by rape, that's what saved her life.*

"Who is the guy who cried?" I asked, after giving the woman another moment's thought.

"He's a journalist. His name is Vincent and he's a political prisoner. He was working on a story that was not in favour of the government. Vincent has been there for five long years."

Five years and counting, in that hellhole.

"Who was the guy sitting next to Vincent?" My heartbeat accelerated. "The white guy, the last one to come in?"

"That was James." Max allowed a smile at last.

"I knew that was James. What about the letter? We totally forgot about the letter!"

"Relax. It's with James."

Relief.

But I don't remember Max being out of my sight after the prisoners came in.

"But how? We couldn't talk to them. How did you ..?"

"Remember when I hugged Vincent? I slipped the letter into James's pocket then. So the letter has arrived. No worries."

"Wow." I looked out the window, watched the trees at the side of the road galloping past, my mind spinning.

"Max?"

"Yes?" Max kept on looking at the road ahead.

"How did you get me in there? How much money did you have to pay? I want to pay you back," I said. "How do you actually make money, Max? Do you sell carved stones?"

"Questions, questions," said Max. "No. I was an unhappy, ungrateful and selfish millionaire in New Zealand before I moved here. So I had some money set aside. But yes, you will pay me back; there will come a time when you'll pay me back. Go on, anyway. What else happened in there? What did you experience?"

Max changed gear and the car speeded up now we were off the dirt road. I took a deep breath of relief. Safe. The trees on the side seemed to be reaching out for me with their leafy branches for a hug.

"Nothing special in the meditation," I said.

But I was hiding one thing that had popped up frequently towards the end of the meditation. "I did notice one thing about James," I said to distract myself.

"What?"

"His face. It was different from the others. It was calm, peaceful. It was like I was watching the body and his soul was somewhere else. I can't explain it. It was just different."

I couldn't come up with the right words to describe what I'd observed.

Max smiled, turning the steering wheel hand over hand. "What you saw in James's face was acceptance, Böddi. You saw peace."

Kafli 21 - Laos.

The Incident comes out

6:15.

WHAT AN INSANE experience that was yesterday. The prison. Now a mere memory. And all the feelings, all that fear and anxiety I had inside the prison gone. I'm starting to get glimpses into Max's teachings about impermanence and the present moment. I see that there are infinite things happening in each moment. Makes it seem pitiful to get stuck in worrying about small things. Maybe this is gratitude? I still don't feel it though. Well, the sun is shining and I'm determined to try and cherish the day.

It was time to make Max some breakfast. I took fruits and vegetables out of the fridge and began making a salad. I also prepared a tofu soup with carrots and cabbage, the way I'd seen him do. Max arrived in the kitchen just as I was finishing my preparations. He sat down at the table.

"Good morning."

"Good morning."

I smiled, feeling proud of the breakfast I'd made. Max silently began eating the salad and bread. I leaned my cheek on my hand, watching him.

"So, Max, you like the salad?"

"It's good." Max showed little interest.

"How's the soup?"

"It's good, but tell me, Böddi, why did you make breakfast?" He was wearing a disappointed expression.

I frowned. "To take care of you, why? Don't you like the food?"

He already said he does, why am I asking him again?

"The food is good," he repeated. "It's not about the food. I'm not impressed with you."

"What? Why?"

"You should take care without expectations. You should take care of me as a plant, not asking anything in return. When you water the plant, do you ask it whether the water was good?"

"What do you mean?"

"Well," said Max, with a softer expression now. "How do you take care of a plant?"

"You water it, I guess."

"Yes. That's exactly what you just did to me. You just watered me. But then you asked for something in return. You did not take care of me just for the sake of it. When you take care of a plant you give it water but you should also nourish it, study its needs, find the right soil for it, and look after it with awareness, gentleness and tenderness without asking for anything in return. That's taking care. You are not supposed to take care to fulfil your own desire for compliments."

"But I was only trying to ... I didn't want anything in return, really."

"Yes you did. You were asking for acceptance, praise; approval. You were behaving a certain way just to be liked or whatever it was. That is taking care for selfish reasons. Next time, when you want to take care, think about the plant and don't ask for anything in return. Think of me as a plant. Keep my energy positive, at all times, and you will benefit immensely. This is the truth about all human relationships. Do you understand?"

"I guess."

I could feel my bottom lip wanting to stick out in a child's pout.

"I'm going to town," said Max. "Your job for today is to meditate for thirty minutes and I want you to finish that before I come back. Not twenty minutes, not twenty-five minutes. Do it for thirty minutes. Right? I'll see you in the afternoon."

He pushed his chair away with a scraping sound, stretched, grabbed the car keys from the hook and walked out.

"Okay," I said to his back.

I stood in the kitchen after he'd gone, thinking about taking care. I was sad because I knew what he'd said was right. I prepared breakfast to make him like me more. I wanted to be praised.

I wandered around the living room for a while avoiding my only assignment of the day.

I'm supposed to meditate. My mind battled itself, trying to find any excuse not to meditate.

Do it, Böddi.

I forced myself to sit down on the living room sofa. Closing my eyes, I tried to clear my mind.

I meditated.

***

"Come here and help me, Böddi."

Max was walking through the door. The light had changed, the time felt different.

I opened my eyes. I had fallen asleep while meditating. I jumped off the sofa to give Max a hand with his bags.

I hope he didn't notice I was sleeping

"How long have you been gone, Max?"

"About two hours," Max said.

After dealing with the groceries we sat down for some tea in the living room.

The jungle scent of the tea filled the room and mingled with the scents coming through the open window.

"I sense that your energy is low," Max said. "It's a negative energy and there's a lot of crap in the air. How was the meditation today?"

Emotions boiled inside me. *Where is this anger coming from?*

"I'm not feeling good, Max. I started to meditate when you left and I just saw how the world is fucked up. There is such evil. Wars, starving children, pollution and poverty all over the world. Why are people so mean? I mean, why do people suffer so badly like in the prison yesterday?"

Max waited in silence while I choked on sobs that were bursting out of me like tiny geysers. *What the fuck ... what's happening to me?*

Max waited some more.

"I just feel that there is something wrong with the world," I spluttered. "People are just not good to each other."

Max stood up in silence and walked to the kitchen. I continued sitting in the living room thinking about what I'd just told him. Sniffing. I was sure that what I was saying was correct and honest. It made sense to me.

Up until then I had never thought about anyone or anything

but myself. I had never taken care of another human being before. Now I was seeing the whole world as suffering and I felt a deep understanding towards people and the world as a whole.

I started to wonder how Max would react to this revelation of mine when he came back with fresh tea. Would he reveal some spiritual secret to me? Would he take me to the next level of growth?

Maybe he will show me some shamanic secret that will change my perception of the world forever ...

"So?"

I couldn't wait to hear the secret. Max had settled on his cushion again.

"I think you should take out the trash every day. Since you live here, I think it's fair that we start to share some of the responsibilities in this house."

"Is that all you have to say?"

"These tears are making you look stupid," he offered. "These tears are coming from a place of self-pity. It's destructive and it closes your heart. Your tears are not coming from compassion for humanity. Did you really think that?"

My ears rang.

What?

Is he fucking with me?

A weight lodged in my stomach, pulling down from my chest.

"Now. Let's look deeper into the meditation. Remember, this house pushes you to heal."

Max gave me a level stare.

What did he want me to say?

"I'm suffering, Max."

"You have to be willing to suffer in order to heal. What happened in the meditation?" he asked, yet again.

"What is this that I'm feeling?" I fought to ask in return. "Why is my body so weak? I'm sad and hurt and my energy is so low. I feel like I can't breathe. I feel deeply depressed, worse than ever before. It's like my suffering is laughing right in my face."

I squeezed a few final tears out of my eyes, desperate to make Max understand my suffering.

"Are you hateful? Are you angry?"

"No. I don't think so. No I'm not."

I couldn't be sure I was being honest. Max's blue eyes held their steady gaze.

"You are dealing with hate and anger now. If you can't see this, then it means your anger is being repressed. You ignore it and avoid it. It's not being dealt with. Now is your chance, Böddi. Talk!" Max was speaking in a much louder voice than usual. I shuffled on my seat.

"I don't know." *Just forget about it, it'll go away.* "I can't. It's nothing. It's not ... It's ..."

Scrambling up from the sofa I moved to the window, stood there facing outwards. My heart beat too fast. Sweat was trickling down my forehead. I couldn't breathe properly.

"I'll tell you later." I rushed from the living room.

Don't disturb the beast. Don't look into the face.

"Come back," Max said calmly, as I reached the door of my room.

But I slammed the door on everything. Stood in the room shaking. My body felt numb, but seemed to have a mind of its own with all the trembling.

Slowly I lowered myself onto the bed and buried my face in the pillow.

Frozen. Stop breathing.

I heard the door open and felt the presence of Max.

"Böddi, sit up. You are not getting away from this. Talk. Tell me what happened. Get it out."

My chest hurt. The pain was overwhelming. I couldn't face Max and I couldn't face the world.

"I hate myself."

Leaving a trail of snot all over the rumpled surface of the pillow.

"Go on," Max said gently.

"I hate myself. I'm nothing." I sat up and looked Max in

the eyes. "You don't understand me. I hate myself and I want to die."

Max grabbed me by the shoulders. "If you want to play games, then let's play games. You will lose, Böddi. Self-hatred is bound to make you lose this game. Now. I'm leaving the room. Good luck with fixing yourself. You are losing the game that you are playing. The only opponent is yourself." He made for the door.

"So you are leaving? Ha. Like everybody else in my life. So you are giving up on me." My stomach heaved. All my muscles clenched.

"It's not about me giving up on you. It's about you giving up on yourself, Böddi. Do you understand? Are you taking care of me now? Are you nurturing your plant right now? Do you think it's easy for me watching how tormented you are, in my house? Do you think that's easy? Talk now, Böddi, or get out of the house." He pointed at the door.

Don't send me away.

"It's that face."

My voice was a tiny thing that crept out of me.

"That face?"

I am so cold. Even the heat of Laos can't warm me.

"Tell me, Böddi."

I just stared at him, feeling my eyes fixed open wide. Max approached and put his arm around my shoulders. "What face?

Tell me about the face."

"I saw it in the prison. The face. I saw the face in the prison, in the meditation. I was twelve. I should have fought him." I dragged a breath into my lungs. "I should have killed him, but I couldn't."

My eyes closed themselves.

"What are you feeling now? Tell me quickly. What's in your mind *right* now?" Max's arm felt firm on my shoulder.

"I don't know. I feel like there's energy coming from my stomach."

I kept my eyes closed and clenched my fists.

"Sit down." Max moved me forward with the strength of his arm. My knees gave way and we both sank onto the bed. "Good, this energy is your ego. Go on, tell me. The face. Who is the man behind the face?"

Air rushed around inside my head and my body folded. "He touched me. Sexually. He abused me."

I can't open my eyes. I felt Max's hand on my forehead.

"Sit up straight. I'm here. Please sit up, Böddi."

Slowly, I straightened my back. *Open your eyes.* The light hurt. I was dizzy. I didn't want to look at Max.

"Now listen carefully. It's no problem. I'm here to help you. Listen carefully and your life will begin to change. This might hurt but I say it from a place of deep love for you. You are selfish right now."

Fury now. Not cold anymore, boiling.

"What? You are saying it's my fault?"

"No, it's not your fault that this man violated you. But you have to snap out of this way of being. You need to take responsibility for your part and turn this into a positive experience. You might get the chance to help others one day."

I relaxed a little under the mesmerizing tone of his words. But my body and mind were still aching from shame, guilt and anxiety. So many other feelings I couldn't even recognise.

"But how? He's caused me to suffer for such a long time. How can I change it with my mind?"

I stared at him with blurred vision, hoping for some answers.

"You are killing yourself this way. Now, listen to me. The suffering resulting from the abuse is not that he touched you or violated you."

It is. It is ...

Max looked as if he was reading my stream of consciousness. "The thoughts you have such as 'I hate you, how could you do this to me?' Or, 'I'll never forgive him'; they are the suffering you are experiencing. *Not the fact that he touched you.* That's the past. It's finished. You have chosen to carry this suffering around with you for a long time and you are affecting your surroundings with your negative energy and, therefore, you are selfish."

Can't he see how he is hurting me with these words?

But Max carried on as though he hadn't noticed. "You've hurt a lot of people, Böddi, with your inability to cope with that incident. You hurt people with your ignorance. Are you following me? That was a past life. Every cell in your body has changed since then. Try to see the impermanence. We are constantly being reborn, at every moment. Past life is not some supernatural rebirth thing, at least we don't have to think about that now. What happened to you is past life."

Max moved his head at an angle that forced me to look into his eyes, or squeeze mine shut again.

"Don't drag this around with you," he said firmly. "Deal with it."

"I don't know if I can, Max."

"Relax."

He pressed his hands to his knees and stood up. "I told you that you're on the fast track to burn your karma, Böddi. Now this stuff is all out and you know what? It's no big deal. It's nothing. Understand? It's nothing. Now." He swivelled his body on his hips slightly as if to loosen it. "Let the healing begin. You take it easy for the rest of today. It's been a big day for you, congratulations."

Congratulations?

What does he mean? I have never felt worse in my life and he says congratulations? It doesn't make sense.

But at least someone thought I was doing well.

I spent the following hours lying in bed, reading, eating and taking everything slowly. Max came in from time to time and I felt some relief as late afternoon wore on. Max hadn't abandoned me or judged me.

I thought about the man I had blamed for all my problems. It was a strange feeling. I'd recognised his face when it popped up during the meditation, my stepfather's best friend. I'd never known it was him until then.

Leaves rustled in the faintest of breezes outside my window. Air trailed like fingers over the hairs on my arms and it made me shiver.

Max. He'd forced me to talk about this. He said we have to be ready to suffer if we want to heal. It was comforting to know there was a reason for this terrible day of negative emotions.

I drifted in and out of sleep and when I was awake I dwelt on The Experience. It was leading me through an adventure I would never have dreamt of. *I am on the fast track to burn all my karma.* Max said. I was aware of subtle anxiety crawling under my skin, trying to affect my thinking: "Now I can see you," I said into my pillow, "you can't hurt me anymore." The face had lost some of its power.

Max said the path always goes up. My life has always been ups and downs.

Was he talking about a way out of suffering?

If it's always up, could there actually be an end to suffering?

I started to understand that I always poked at my old wounds to justify my suffering. My routine was to reach out for the *incident* in moments of desperation. *If I can't blame the incident, what will I grasp for then?*

Kafli 22 - Laos.

Date with Marissa

I'VE EMERGED FROM sleep feeling split in half, though I can't pinpoint how or why. I'm lying here quietly, exploring the condition of my body and my thoughts. The room is silent. The silence is different; it's in me now. At least a part of me. I don't know who I am anymore. Everything I ever believed in is slowly fading away in this house. What's next?

I'd slept late and now a sudden energy shot through me. I jumped out of bed and gave myself a quick wash.

"Good morning," said Max as I entered the kitchen. "Your face has changed. Your energy has changed. How are you feeling?"

"I don't know." I patted myself to check I was solid. "I don't feel much. I kinda feel nothing at all. Something about me, about everything really, is different. I'm sorry I didn't make breakfast, I just ..."

"It's all right. Stop saying sorry, Böddi. You are constantly saying sorry so add that to your assignment list today. Stop saying sorry."

"Got it." I opened the fridge and reached for some milk.

Taking a loaf of bread I cut it and spread butter on a slice. As I munched I wondered if I often said sorry unnecessarily, I'd never noticed before. But yeah. Max was right. I was constantly apologizing for everything I did. It was my routine to say *I'm sorry* without even thinking about what I meant.

Why did Max tell me to stop? Isn't it good manners and a positive thing to apologise when you do something wrong?

"Close the fridge, you left it open."

Max was reading the Laos newspaper.

"Oh I'm sorr ... Right. I do say that all the time."

Max laughed and flipped over another page of the paper. The moist smell and chirruping sounds of the jungle permeated the kitchen and the shadows of leaves danced in formation at the shaded window.

I stood by the fridge.

"Max, why do I do that?" I craved an explanation that would change this routine of mine forever.

"Ask yourself that question. That's how you'll find the answer."

Hmm. Try another question.

"What can I do to change it?"

Max put down the paper, chuckling. But he spoke with a serious tone as he gave me that comforting glance from his kind eyes.

"Stop doing things that you are sorry for, is a good start."

"Okay." I was ready for that challenge as well.

What has happened to me this morning?

What has changed?

Calmly, I walked into the living room for my meditation.

After the meditation I wondered what I would do today. Max didn't seem to have any new tasks for me. I counted off my assignments; they were to stop suffering, to stop saying sorry and to take care of him as much as possible. I was feeling good. I just didn't really know what to do right now.

Max entered the living room and joined me on the sofa.

"What now?" I asked.

"Just be. Enjoy just being. The day will take you somewhere if you let it. So now, relax."

Twenty minutes later (which I had spent contemplating the events of yesterday,) I heard the door open. I looked up and saw that there was a girl moving about in the kitchen. My stomach started to tingle.

Is it her?

Max glanced at me and implied with his eyes that I should say good morning. I hoped it was Marissa. She turned around.

It was. Stuff was happening to my body that Max probably wouldn't approve of. I adjusted my position on the sofa.

"Good morning." Marissa placed her hands together, close to her chest.

I mirrored the gesture. "Hi."

The flirty smile I was so used to giving girls felt awkward this time. Max was observing my every action. Marissa turned back to the kitchen.

"So she really lives here," I wondered aloud. Maybe she slept under a stone in the backyard or something.

"Yes, she does, alongside many. People come and go, it's like an airport at times," Max said.

"But where's her room?"

"First of all there are no private rooms in this house, there's no 'my space', 'my room', 'my time', 'my things'. In this house everything is shared. This notion of my space is ridiculous, it's because people can't cope with their mental unease and they need to avoid conflict. In this house there's no conflict."

"But, uhm, where does she sleep?"

"In one of the huts outside, you haven't noticed them?"

Marissa walked into the living room with a tray of tea. I was slightly uncomfortable that she'd noticed we were talking about her. She sat down with us, poured us both a cup and began telling us about her work at the orphanage.

Get your eyes off her, Böddi, she'll think you're a creep.

"I have my day off today, Böddi. Do you want to go for a ride somewhere? Hang out with me." She turned to Max. "I'm taking your student for a ride today, is that cool with you?"

While I sat there like an idiot, I looked for approval from Max as if he was my dad. Max nodded his head slightly and turned back to his newspaper. Did I imagine it or was he holding himself a bit straighter?

I looked at Marissa and smiled. Nothing was going to stop me. "Okay, let's go." My eagerness must have shown in my face because she patted my arm like I was a pet dog.

In the room where I was sleeping (I had to stop thinking of it as mine) I changed my t-shirt, taking a sniff of my armpit to check I had washed properly. I was going to be sitting up close to her on the scooter. I could hear the engine starting up outside. Max didn't look up as I said goodbye, only grunted something from behind his newspaper.

I took the steps down from the porch two at a time and jumped onto the back of the bike, feeling it bounce beneath me, feeling her jolt against me. She laughed and turned round to point out the spare helmet fastened onto the back of my seat. I unhooked it and jammed it on my head. It wasn't usual for a passenger to use a helmet in Laos, so I wondered if she'd already planned for me to come along and thought I might expect a helmet. Marissa raised her feet from the ground as the bike took off, causing her back to curve into my stomach. I melted, like warm water was lapping inside me.

Off down the track we went. This was better than I ever hoped for when Max told me to let the day take control. I was holding Marissa loosely around her stomach, trying to keep my fingers from straying.

She is fit, man.

It'd been a long time since I touched a woman, had my arms around her. Sitting that close was so turning me on.

I had this thought that I was letting Max down by going out with Marissa, I couldn't understand why. But didn't I deserve a day off after being tormented all the day before?

After driving for about twenty minutes along narrow dirt roads, surrounded by trees, we finally came to a stop. I'd spent the whole journey planning what to say to her, how I would act and what pick-up techniques to use. She was so damned hot. I got off the bike and waited until her back was turned, shaking her hair free of the helmet, before quickly adjusting myself and pulling my t-shirt down. Marissa turned to me and grinned. "Shall we?" She indicated a trail winding off into the trees.

Leaving the helmets on the bike we trekked down a narrow path. I was happy to walk behind her, admiring her toned body, her hips swaying slightly underneath the yellow dress and her hair dancing in the breeze. Tension stretched like a thin rope between us, a tightrope loaded with what I was thinking and what she was thinking, neither of us saying much. She wanted to surprise me.

A branch snapped as I grabbed it when the path became steeper and I almost slipped. After about fifteen minutes we came down the hill to the shore of a lake. It was beautiful. A small oasis, I thought, where I could practice my game on her. We settled down under a tree with the lake view before us.

As we started talking I knew what cards I was going to play. I wouldn't ask all the typical questions like where she was from, how her family was. Or what her favourite colour was. Those kinds of questions had never worked so I decided to do what I was good at. Picking up girls.

"So," I began. "Are you more like your father or your mother?" I narrowed my eyes. A girl had once told me I looked sexy when I did that.

"Father," she answered, smiling in a way I interpreted as seductive.

"Do you know what your body language is telling me right now?"

"Does it really matter?"

She laughed and stretched, lying back, looking up at the sky.

"I guess not." I feared I was losing the game when it had only just begun.

"I dated a girl once," I tried next, still sitting stiffly upright. "She gave herself away way too easily with her body language;

it was like having a book read aloud to me instead of discovering it myself."

Maybe this will provoke her competitive side. "That must have been interesting," was all Marissa said. *Why isn't she playing the game?* I tried a few more questions that had never failed me before. I wanted her to get emotional, because I had learned that if you create an emotional reaction from a girl you get closer to her.

Are you scared of anything? You know, a really deep fear? What gives you a naughty thrill? But she moved her head lazily from side to side on the grass, murmuring 'no'.

"Has anyone hurt you?" I tried, hoping my voice wouldn't crack. "You know, by doing something they shouldn't. Someone stronger than you?"

I continued to throw out ever more desperate questions. *Ever had a pet? What colour are your knickers? Have you got a mole or a birthmark anywhere?* All of which she answered with one syllable or less, with little or no interest. All the while she lay back in the long grass looking up at the sky while I held myself rigidly in that sitting position, feeling increasingly awkward but I couldn't stop because that was the only way I knew how to communicate with girls. It was like I was digging my own grave and it got deeper with every question I asked. I started to feel shy; my voice got weaker. Realizing that my game was going down the drain I fell into an awkward silence.

"Have you ever loved someone?" Marissa asked when I had finally shut up.

Huh?

I was not prepared for that question. It wasn't a regular first date question, not in my book. Part of me wanted to jump in the water and swim back to Iceland.

"I don't know."

That was my honest answer. Looking down, I started pulling grass from the ground around the base of the tree.

"I mean, have you ever loved someone and asked nothing in return?"

"I don't know." I thought about it more deeply. "Seriously. I don't think so. I thought I had but after staying with Max I'm not even sure what love is. I'm not sure if anyone has ever really loved me and I don't know if I will ever be able to love anyone."

Marissa glanced sideways at me, her hair brushing my bare arm. Warmth pooled in my belly.

"Same here, I mean, I've never loved anyone, I think. No wonder the world is fucked up, right?"

"Yeah, when you say it like that."

It was a relief that the conversation was finally taking off. I mentally beat myself up because I hadn't started the conversation with being real. No bullshit. The rapport grew between us even though the topic of love was surely on the banned list for first dates.

"So, what do you think love is?" I asked, surprising myself with how comfortable I now felt. Her lips curved up at the corners. She was so good to look at.

"I've read and thought about it a lot. I know it's raw. It's a raw energy. It cannot be manipulated. I think the whole universe is built with love. It's all made of the same raw material. What do you think?"

Wow, this is deep.

"I don't know." I felt my defences go down, one by one. "I don't even know who I am anymore. I just know that I'm hungry for love."

Did I really just confess that to a girl?

What's happening to me? Where's the cool Böddi gone?

"I'm hungry for the feeling of love," this new emerging corny person said. "I want to know what love is." *That sounds like a line from a song.*

Even if it was, Marissa was nodding understandingly. It gave me the courage to continue. "The weird part is that I don't think it comes from another person. I think it's inside us."

Marissa smiled widely. She gave my t-shirt a tug, flicked my arm playfully with her fingers. Finally I relaxed, sliding down in the grass so that I was lying next to her. The energy around us had changed since we started talking about this. The sexual tension was gone. There we were, two people totally vulnerable and lying in the grass looking out over the lake, thinking about love and searching for pictures in the clouds.

"The word love is so polluted, right?" I leaned my head towards her. It struck me that I was copying what Max said earlier.

"Yes. I constantly say that love is like chocolate. I don't know if I would love chocolate if it didn't create such a divine taste in my mouth."

"I constantly say I love my country. If you think about it, people kill for the love of their country. So is love something that can make people kill? Is love dangerous then?"

"Good point. I've been thinking lately about the topic of sex. Some people say God is love, so why do men give up the pleasure of sex for the love of God? Monks, priests and others, they deny themselves sex to please their god. Is having sex not an act of love?"

I wondered if we were heading for a discussion of sex, which was another taboo topic on a first date. Isn't it? This hadn't been a normal date so far, so I decided to trust in the process and go with the flow.

"I think when we are escaping ourselves with the pleasure of sex, then it becomes something that moves us away from God."

It was a surprise to hear those words coming out of my own mouth.

"What do you mean?" She turned her head to look at me while I watched the clouds floating above, feeling her gaze on me like a physical sensation.

"When we have sex," I said slowly, "we forget our inner turmoil for a while. We forget our worries; our self, our problems and how complicated our lives are. We want to escape ourselves. So we constantly seek sex to fill a place of emptiness we carry inside."

Marissa was quiet, but I could still feel her eyes on me. The silence with her was not awkward anymore. It felt natural; a part of our communication. In the silence I was real and I didn't worry over whether she liked me or not. Eventually I turned to her and we made eye contact.

"Well, you must be an expert on the topic of sex since you are into Tantra. Tell me what it is?" I asked.

Marissa made a small sound of exasperation. She sat up, brushing torn-off grass out of her hair.

"Tantra is not about sex, Böddi. The western world has taken Tantra, twisted and turned it and made the whole thing about sex. But the people who practice Tantric sex, which is only tiny aspect of Tantric philosophy, say that it becomes more a meditation than just raw sex. In Tantric sex there is no goal of 'coming'."

Looking into my eyes she placed her hand under her naval, then slowly moved it up to the area above it, continuing to speak in a low, hypnotic voice. "Instead of striving for the one great explosion, it is more about continuous, slow, implosive full body orgasm." She moved her hand again, laying it over her heart, then her throat, then her forehead. I almost stopped breathing. "It's about moving the energy in you up the chakras and activating your spiritual centres." Marissa finished by stretching her hands up in the air above her head.

I lay propped up on my elbow, watching this beautiful girl touching her body and explaining Tantra. My own body tingled in empathy. Imagine if it were her hands on me. I pictured the energy flowing up her body. It was a moment of stillness between us. I closed my eyes, then opened them again, dazzled by the light on water. For a moment there was nothing in the world other than me, Marissa and the lake sparkling in front of us.

"So," I cleared my throat. "Are you experienced in Tantric sex?"

"I have read a lot about it. I have some experience but haven't had many people to practice with."

She laughed softly, holding my eyes. The moment stretched until it broke.

Maybe I should have touched her then.

But I hadn't and it was a relief not to get into more awkwardness. She flopped down onto her stomach beside me again and we continued to lie in the grass, talking about our likes and dislikes, our dreams and disappointments and Max. This was new territory for me; to get to know someone on a deeper level. It was scary but exciting at the same time. There were moments in our talking that were somewhere in between awkwardness and excitement.

Should I kiss her?

Is now the time?

Is it too soon?

In these moments it was like Max was hovering over me, watching me. When we talked about Max the energy changed and I could feel the strings of excitement being stretched to snapping point. After one of those awkward moments I could feel our rapport dying and I had to take action to save it. I got up, put one hand on the tree next to us and gave her my other hand to pull her up. We walked slowly up the little trodden path, now I was in front. We didn't talk, just walked, but I was utterly aware of her presence behind me.

When we both got on the scooter I put my arms tighter around her this time, my hands more firmly on her stomach. I pressed my chest to her back. Her hair blew across my face in the wind and I breathed in the scent of it; sunshine and grass and her own particular essence. The ride back home was different from our ride towards the forest. I was calmer. Right before we took the exit onto the road leading to Max's house I worked out that the only thing that had changed was I didn't see Marissa only as a sexual being but as a human being. I no longer lusted only to sleep with her. This had never happened to me before.

Shit. I'm in trouble, man.

After I peeled off the helmet and fastened it on the back of Marissa's bike I thanked her for the day we spent together. Marissa grinned, shaking out her hair.

"I had a good day too."

She hung around only long enough to gather some stuff from the kitchen before going straight to her hut. I allowed myself one lingering glance as she walked away.

***

"Max," I shouted.

I heard Max outside on the back porch.

"Max."

"Hi there." Max looked at my face like he was searching for answers.

"I'm in trouble, right?" I tried my cheeky smile on him. He turned away and continued to put some carving tools into a big red box.

"Just stay on track. You are not ready for this girl. You are way too fragile and broken. You know what the biggest illusion in human relationships is?"

"No."

"It's the illusion that another person is going to make someone happy. It should be all about bringing happiness to the other person; not about receiving. You are suffering and therefore what you have to offer to other people is suffering. You are not ready, Böddi. She's your sister."

He's just kicked me in the stomach.

I struggled with an urge to fight Max. Without saying anything I walked back inside the house. I wanted to escape. I had already denied myself the pleasure of going on a trip with Anita from the hostel and I hated that Max was now telling me not to get involved with Marissa. How could something as beautiful as our date in the forest be wrong?

I observed my thoughts. They were a battlefield.

What is the right thing to do?

After about twenty minutes Max came back inside.

"Let's go to town. I have to run some errands and you need to get out of your head."

In the car on the way to Vientiane the tension stretched between Max and me. I tried to act like everything was all right but he saw right through me. I couldn't fake it. I wasn't in the mood to go back into a discussion about Marissa so I decided not to talk at all. Max was not very talkative either but when we stopped the car outside a small Laos restaurant in the middle of the city he said what I had been waiting for.

"It's very uncomfortable sitting next to you. You have to let go."

I didn't answer. We walked into the restaurant. It looked pretty decent compared to other places I had been. We ordered food and when it came we sat there for about an hour, barely exchanging words the whole time. I knew it was within my control to change the atmosphere and to take care of him but I couldn't. I felt too sorry for myself that I had to stop thinking about Marissa. After our dinner we drove around town and Max ended up stopping the car outside a building which looked sort of governmental. He told me to wait, in the car if I wanted. He'd be in there for about half an hour. I agreed to wait.

Ten minutes in, I got restless. My mind was wandering around.

Why can't I get involved with Marissa?

Why can't I take care of Max?

Why can't I do anything right?

I looked outside the window. There was a small Internet café across the street. I had been disconnected from the outside world for a few days now. No news, no emails, nothing outside my little bubble in Laos.

How did I end up here?

Am I exactly where The Experience wanted me to be?

I had doubts. Tired of this process, I wanted to distract myself on the Internet. I opened the door of the car and walked towards the café. My energy was low. Something was pulling me in there.

I bought twenty minutes of Internet use and sat down in front of a computer. I checked the Icelandic news, caught up with the football and did my usual surfing of social media. Finally I checked my email, hoping it would not bring up too much reality. I was afraid I might decide everything I was doing here in Laos was just crazy and a normal life awaited me in Iceland.

There were twenty-three emails unopened but one from three days ago from my mother. The subject line was: "I've been trying to reach you. Important." I opened it.

Elsku Böðvar,

I've been trying to reach you. I called your Chinese phone number but it was out of service. Something terrible has happened. Your brother died in London yesterday. He took his own life. I wanted to tell you by phone but I couldn't reach you. I hope to hear from you a.s.a.p. The family needs you. They are transferring his body home today and the funeral will be on Monday. We want you to come home, Böddi, for your brother's funeral.

Contact me as soon as possible. God bless you!

Elska Þig,
Mom

Frozen.

I stared at the screen, completely numb. My heart started beating faster and faster and I could almost hear my mother wailing.

No thoughts.

Frozen in time. Lost.

I walked out of the café feeling nothing. The only sound I heard were my shoes dragging on the dusty street. All else was suspended. I couldn't see anything except the ground below me. Everything in slow motion; the sound, the cars, the bikes and the people passing by. I walked towards the car. I saw Max coming out of the building, started shaking my head, grinding my teeth and clenching my fists.

"Max," I shouted, standing about thirty metres away from him. "Max," I shouted again and again. Max began slowly jogging towards me. My feet gave up. I stopped in the middle of the street and closed my eyes. The world had ceased. Cars were driving around me but I didn't care if I'd be run over. My stomach ached. Max got closer.

"Böddi. Get out of the street, you'll hurt yourself. What's wrong?"

As he reached me his hand touched my back. I stared at the ground and lost all power in my legs. I fell on the street.

"I can't do it."

No.

Not Palli.

No.

The left side of my body scraped along the ground as my hands tried to grasp something, to hold on to something. I scratched the pavement with my fingertips and saw red smearing the dirt. Max put his hands under my armpits and dragged my numb body off the street. My head was spinning and everything continued to take place in slow motion.

"I have to leave." My voice was dry, like there was something in my throat. "I have to leave Laos. He died."

"Who died?"

"My brother. *Palli.* He's gone. He died."

"Get in the car." Max, as always calm and practical.

"No." I pulled myself away from Max. "I'm not coming. This is over. I have to go home, Max. My family needs me."

Tears that felt like scalding water streamed down my cheeks.

Marissa ...

Why?

"No you don't. Now, let's get home and talk. Get in the car, Böddi." Max tried to manhandle me. "There's time for some serious healing here and no rush for decisions in the middle of the street."

"Fuck healing," I shouted in his face, making him wince. "I'm leaving. Are you deaf?"

Somewhere inside me I was ashamed. I knew this was not Max's fault but I couldn't help myself. I walked away from him.

"Böddi," Max called. "Böddi. Come here."

Max wouldn't shout. He once told me that holy men never shouted at another person.

Why isn't he running after me?

Why doesn't he tell me that everything will be all right?

I was tired of failing him. Tired of failing everybody. *Palli. Bróðir minn.* I wanted to disappear from the face of the earth. I continued walking. Max had stopped calling my name.

My brother's life ran through my mind. Memories streamed at the same pace as the tears. Memories of us laughing together, fighting each other, him protecting me, us playing football and him showing me love and care when we were young boys.

Why did he die?

Why didn't I contact him?

Why didn't I prevent this?

I walked further down the street and the hope for a better life faded with every step. I was turning my back on the only hope I had, which was Max teaching me. My feet stopped. Looking up from the ground I saw a dog running down the street towards me. Its barking broke the shield of numb silence I'd had around me. Time stilled. I needed answers in that exact moment.

I couldn't keep on walking any further, again I was in a trap. The dog bounded closer and stopped right in front of me, a big black dog, similar to one of those police dogs you see at airports. He barked at me like he was trying to tell me something. I wasn't afraid. I looked for the owner; there was no-one around. I tried to pass the dog but the dog moved like he was forbidding me to go forward. He continued barking.

"Move away," I shouted.

I tried to go to the left but the dog jumped in front of me again. He kept on barking.

"What do you want?" I was filled with rage, still crying my eyes out. "I'll kick you if you don't move away."

The dog stopped barking and looked into my streaming eyes. His were focussed, calm, and caring. I wasn't sure if it was just my perception. But this dog seemed to be giving me a message. My rage slowly faded as something broke inside me.

I knelt on the street, opened my arms and the dog jumped on my chest. I rolled back on the pavement with the force of his leap, eventually lying still. I lay with my eyes closed while the dog licked my face. Peace came over my body. I felt cared for. While the dog was licking my face I remembered the good times I had with my brother. I surrendered.

Max.

I opened my eyes. Stood up, shakily. The dog was sitting next to me, guarding me while I grieved my dead brother. I walked back to Max's car, not just hoping he was there; knowing he would be. After a little walk I saw the vehicle. I moved around to the front seat window and saw Max sitting inside with his eyes closed, meditating. He sensed my presence and opened them.

"So, are you coming?"

Nobody had ever shown me as much love as Max did, not even my own parents. I couldn't leave him. I got into the front seat and watched the dog sitting outside the car while Max started the engine.

"Can we keep that dog, Max?" I pointed. If I had to look after the dog it would prevent me from leaving.

"This dog probably has an owner already," Max said. "Don't worry, you'll get your animal soon."

I wasn't sure what he meant by this and anyway I was too distracted to ask questions. Max seemed tranquil, in his natural state as we drove out of town. I turned my head only once to look back at my friend who had calmed me. The dog was still sitting there.

I wanted Max to talk. I wanted him to say something that would make me feel better.

"You know I have to go home, Max."

"We have some talking to do when we get back to the house. You don't have to go home, you know this deep inside you. They are just putting his flesh into the ground; your brother has gone somewhere else. If you want to heal and put some healing into your family and into the world, then don't go."

"Max," I said angrily, "Are you going to talk about heaven now? Are you going to tell me he is in heaven, so I won't go home?" The rough road jolted the car and my sentence came out brokenly.

"I did not say he's going to heaven, you said that. You can call it heaven if you want. Heaven is just a word, Böddi. It's just an image in your mind. Try to see the impermanence of things, remember. The impermanence of everything: of your brother, of people, of your feelings right now. *This too shall pass*, that saying makes a lot of sense."

I didn't speak for a few minutes. I was hoping he would feel guilty for being so cold, so raw and heartless.

"I can't stop suffering, Max." It finally came out of my mouth after a resentful silence. "There is no way out of suffering. I will never be able to stop suffering." I knew this would not impress him but I said it anyway.

"Look, Böddi. Listen now, carefully. Suffering is not bad. It just is. You can look at this suffering as a teacher; without suffering, we wouldn't learn anything. Just stay with it. Just accept it. Let it be. Observe it. Then let it go."

Sobs choked their way out of my throat again.

Palli.

"I can't believe he died."

Why?

"This was his journey and his journey continues," Max said. "Try to learn from it."

"Are you referring to reincarnation now? I want proof. I'm tired of living my life trusting in something I can't see or hear or touch. Like The Experience. I want some answers." I rubbed my face, leaving dust on my skin. I didn't care. The thought entered my mind that my brother would probably like the people down in hell better than those in heaven. I wiped snot from my nose with the back of my arm.

"Ask yourself also if you can disprove reincarnation. The human mind is very limited and in an ignorant state. We can't prove everything. Whether reincarnation exists, whether the cosmos is endless, whether heaven exists, doesn't matter. What matters is to realise suffering and that there's an end to suffering. The rest is just speculation, useless words about useless things."

Max pulled the wheel sharply to the left and we turned onto the track leading down to the house. "So, what if you fully knew about reincarnation or heaven, would that stop you from having ill will? Harming others? Being angry?" He slowed the car as a bird flew up from the undergrowth at the foot of the trees beside the track. We narrowly missed it. Max took a breath. "Eradicate these things from your life and you might experience heaven on this earth: heaven as a state of mind."

"You think my brother will reincarnate?"

"Your brother had a choice in this life, everybody has free will. You can either do good karma or bad karma, it's cause and effect. As I said, speculations about past lives or future lives are irrelevant and useless to us."

"Then why do people talk about past lives?"

The car ground to a stop. So much had happened since we got inside it to leave the property.

"What you need to think about," said Max, "is that your past life is something that happened five minutes ago, or five months or five years ago. The rest is merely speculation. Now, get out of the car, let's go inside."

His hand was gently on my back as we climbed the steps to the porch. It didn't seem five minutes ago that I'd said goodbye to Marissa after our date in the forest. My stomach muscles hurt when I thought about it.

All the time I was with her, I didn't know about Palli.

These past few days, I didn't know.

It was hard to take my brother's death as calmly as Max expected me to.

"And rebirth?" I asked hopefully, as he gestured towards the kitchen.

"You are constantly being reborn, every split second you are reborn over and over again. The present moment is the only real moment; the past and the future are in your head. Every moment in our life is like a new scene in a movie. See it as a stream of consciousness, Böddi."

I was pulled into the present, it was the only thing that was real. The rest was merely speculation as Max had pointed out. I couldn't know where my brother had gone or what my family was thinking. I only had my five senses. I was starting to question even those. I sat quietly at the kitchen table watching Max's strong arm as he lifted the kettle.

"Why do we suffer then, when loved ones pass away?"

"Try to link it to impermanence," he suggested. "Try to see birth, ageing, illness and death for all things and all people as impermanence. Your body changes, your cells and your organs, they all change constantly. Did you know that your body is constantly rebuilding itself with new cells? People see impermanent things as permanent and cling to them. This is what suffering really is."

A picture of Palli came into my head. *My brother. Gone.* He was no angel on earth. Could he be reborn as a human or as an animal? What about the dog that stopped me from walking away?

Was the dog a sign?

Is my brother a dog?

Has he been reborn as a dog in Laos?

I was only escaping to fantasy land.

For the rest of the evening Max was quiet.

Why doesn't he talk to me?

I needed him. Anger grew in me like a snake. It crawled from the base of my spine and up through my throat, shedding its skin. My throat ached from constant crying.

Palli.

***

I was still sitting on the sofa, trying to breathe around the snake, when Max walked in and sat next to me. I choked some more of the snake out, wiped away trails of saliva with a corner of a cushion. Max said nothing.

"Max," The saliva made it hard to speak. I tried again. "Am I crying for myself or for my brother?"

His blue eyes looked dimmer than usual. "You never loved your brother, because you don't know how to love."

I do love Palli. He's my brother.

I must have loved him.

You don't really love anyone, do you?

"You should not go home," Max said next. "Try to look at

these things objectively, without sentiment. Look how much spiritual growth you've accomplished since you started your journey."

He pulled a handkerchief from the pocket of his khaki shorts while my eyes wandered to the bare skin of his knees, amongst the forest of hairs on his legs. "Don't let the fear get to you. Just keep on growing." He gave the handkerchief to me, removing the cushion from my hands, which wanted to keep gripping. "There will come a time when you go home as a different man, knowing how to love. Not as a frightened little boy."

He's right, in my heart I know it.

I want to go home.

But I should stay here. He's right.

"Have I made some spiritual progress? How can I measure my spiritual growth?"

I blew my nose.

"I recommend you don't try to measure it," Max said. "But if spiritual growth could be measured, I would think it would be in seeing things as they are, which will result in less suffering."

Kafli 23 - Laos.

Meeting Uppa

THE ENERGY IN my body is neutral this morning. I must have dreamt something positive or maybe the energy in the house has been healing me while I slept.

But now I'm awake I keep thinking about Palli.

How it must have been for him when he died.

He must have been in pain.

My brother.

***

I needed to see Max so I walked out of the bedroom, the wooden floorboards creaking under my bare feet.

I stopped in the kitchen doorway. "Who are you?"

A naked guy stood in the middle of the kitchen, holding the frying pan in one hand.

He made an eloquent gesture towards the pan with the other.

"I'm Uppavasa," he said. "You can call me Uppa. Want some eggs?"

Things are just getting weirder around here.

But I shook the hand he offered me, and resisted wiping mine on my shorts.

He's naked.

"Sure."

Marissa walked in and joined us. She didn't seem bothered by our naked friend. I couldn't help noticing his toned torso as he served us eggs, but I refused to let my eyes stray any lower.

His warm smile seemed stuck on his wide face.

Uppa? What a strange name.

Marissa had greeted him with a hug. They seemed like old friends meeting again after a long time apart as they joked around and finished preparing breakfast together.

Are they a couple?

I wanted to offer my help but couldn't really see myself bringing anything to the situation and anyway I was too busy observing those two.

"Let's consume," Uppa said, laying the final dish on the table.

"Shouldn't we wait for Max?"

It felt like I had woken up in a different house from yesterday. Marissa smiled. "In this house we never wait for anyone with food, not even Max."

"So, you are new in the house? Welcome," Uppa said.

Wasn't he the new one at the house?

I couldn't get it out of my head that underneath the table was more of Uppa's nakedness.

"Hmm. Thanks."

I gave him some details of my arrival there. In the middle of my explanation, Max arrived. Uppa stood up and greeted him with an Indian praying gesture, palms pressed together against his chest. Max patted him on the head and gave his deep chuckle. He sat down at the table.

Uppa and Marissa continued swapping tales and sharing experiences. Max and I stayed silent. It dawned on me that I was living in a community, where people came, lived and practiced spiritual growth.

I am a part of this community. And Max is at the heart of it.

We finished breakfast.

"Don't worry, I'll wash up," I hurried to announce. Even as I did I was uncomfortably aware I was only doing it to show off that I belonged. I mused on this urge to be noticed in groups, this 'look at me, look at me' tendency I had.

While I was washing the dishes Marissa came back in and

said goodbye. She was wearing a white top and her bare shoulders were smooth. There was a tiny tattoo on her back that I hadn't noticed before. She was going to work. Uppa remained in the house, wandering in and out of the kitchen, still naked.

He came in to prepare some tea just as I was wiping down the kitchen. I knew Max was sitting in the living room, probably waiting to drink tea and catch up with Uppa.

"Oh, good karma in washing the dishes," Uppa remarked, reaching across me for some cups.

"I try to help."

"If everybody understood the law of karma, people would be running around doing good deeds all the time." Uppa winked at me.

"How long have you known Max?"

"It's my sixth season here with Max. You have to seriously put in some good karma to be here, man."

"I'm not sure I understand what karma is, but I do hope to understand it one day," I said.

"Karma is actions, of the body, of speech and of mind. Hey, no worries, just stay and you'll fly high."

He wobbled his head to the left and right, a mannerism I'd noticed from Indian people. He must have stayed in India at some time, but Uppa was Caucasian. I guessed he was from Russia or Eastern Europe based on his accent. It didn't really matter, I'd become sick and tired of asking people where they were from. I was more interested in the quality of his mind than any external identity.

"Uppa?"

"Yes?"

"Why are you naked?"

"I'm a nudist. I work for three months a year cutting weed in California in a nudist camp. It was strange in the beginning but now I like being naked whenever possible. Plus, it's just a body. Max tells me it's a wrong livelihood to cut weed, but it pays well and allows me to travel the other nine months a year, so I do it."

Travel for nine months every year? Wow.

From the doorway I watched Uppa sit down with Max. I pretended I was cleaning the kitchen, but I was afraid to join Max and Uppa in the living room.

Why do I always think of myself as a burden? Nobody else here seems to.

I wiped the fridge door down yet again.

"Join us Böddi, don't be shy. It's just Uppa," I heard Max call from the living room, breaking my thoughts about how everything in this house was different from what I'd been brought up to believe. I rinsed the cloth and hung it over the tap, then shuffled into the living room.

Uppa sat cross-legged on the floor, smiling warmly at me. His image reminded me of those old yogis I'd heard of living in the mountains in India. Skinny, composed and concentrated.

"What's cooking in your mind, Böddi?" Max asked.

"Uhm, I don't know."

Be real, Böddi.

I don't feel confident enough to be real.

Yet, I bet Uppa once had similar conversations with Max as I do. Everybody has to learn from someone.

Words started pouring out. Words I'd said so many times already.

"It's too hard, Max. I can't stop suffering. I don't know where it comes from."

Max shifted so he was looking directly into my eyes. "Now listen carefully, Böddi. Your suffering originates from your desires. It's because of your greed and your aversion. Rise above them, take your time and know that the path to purify your mind takes time."

I can see a spider crawling along a crack in the floorboards.

"Böddi?"

"I don't know what to do."

"Böddi. Stop being so special. You are not special. *Everybody* suffers. It's what binds us together. Remember the mosquito you killed. If you had understood that the mosquito you killed also suffers you wouldn't have killed it. You don't know anything about suffering, because if you did you would have taken care of me from day one. If you knew anything about suffering, you wouldn't be feeling sorry for yourself after everything you saw in the prison or after your brother died."

For once Max's words weren't getting through to me. Uppa looked at me sympathetically, like he understood where I was. His eyes showed understanding of me, a beginner in this house of burning karma.

"I don't understand," I told Max. "This is too complicated. I'm weak. I think I hate myself."

"Böddi, remember what I told you."

There, he won't show it but he must be getting pissed off with me by now. I bet he'll ask me to leave, soon.

"How the fuck should I stop suffering? It's impossible."

I looked at Uppa for some answers or at least for his eyes to show more understanding, and he gave me what I took to be another sympathetic look. Max remained quiet.

"I can't do it," I repeated.

"Then get out of my house or show me you are worthy of staying here."

Max pointed at the door.

What, even though my brother has just died?

Have I destroyed my opportunity to heal?

Uppa stayed silent. My bottom lip trembled. I was a child about to bawl his frustration out to parents who have lost their patience.

"You would really do that to me? Let me go just like that?" I made my voice very small.

"You are doing it to yourself. You are just too blind to see it." My head whipped round towards Uppa, who had spoken those words in a soft voice.

I scrambled out of my corner of the sofa and planted myself in middle of the living room. There was pain in my hands and when I looked down I saw how tightly I had clenched them.

This can't be it.

I can't believe this ends here.

It would be like walking away after ten minutes of a football match. The game had just started.

"Come out with me to the porch," Max said evenly. "You have two choices now. Two choices. Do you understand?"

My feet placed themselves one after the other, following him across the floor like a robot. Uppa stayed in the living room, drinking his tea. It was clear that I was at a crossroads. I had failed to stop my suffering and that was my only job in the house, to stop suffering.

Please don't throw me out.

How come Max talks about a slow path but after a few days in the house he threatens to throw me out? It isn't fair.

"Look at that mountain, Böddi. Do you see it?" Max was standing on the back porch pointing into the distance. The mountain was far away, behind the carved stones, behind the

Mekong River, a blue swelling on the horizon.

"Yes," I said, forcing myself to speak.

"You can gather your stuff and leave the house now, or you go to that mountain on your own for three days. If you do that then you can come back to the house and we'll continue with our work."

Insects buzzed in the moist, hot air in the back yard. I fastened my hands around the porch railing and let the heat of the wood permeate my palms. I closed my eyes.

Go to the mountain.

On my own.

What for?

"Why? I mean yes, I will take this trip but why? What should I do there?"

"Find your animal."

"What?"

What he had told me to do made no sense but I couldn't blow this opportunity, not when I'd come so far. I thought of the dog in Vientiane. Max had told me that I'd get the chance to find my own animal.

"Go to the mountain and find your guardian animal. The wildlife in Laos is very diverse. There are monkeys, deer, leopards, reptiles and many kinds of birds. I'm sure you will find yours." Max's deep voice rolled over me.

"But I don't understand, what has that to do with me suffering?"

"Stop asking questions now, it's time to take action. So are you ready, Böddi? I have a tent, you can start preparing for the trip."

Fear trickled through me.

"Now?"

"Why wait?" said Max.

I must do this or go, for good.

If I don't do this I can go home to my family.

But I'm not finished here.

"Do you have a guardian animal, Max?"

Maybe the dog that stopped me from leaving in Laos was Max's guardian animal. "Of course. The Asiatic Black Bear is my guardian animal, now go and get ready or I'll change my mind and kick you out of the house."

Kafli 24 - Laos.

The Mountain

MAX STOOD IN the doorway to wave me off. His mysterious inner smile shone out through his eyes. I had the same feeling as on my first day at school, aged six, when my mom had stood behind me, encouraging me. Now instead of my mom it was Max, and I was going to be taught by a mountain.

"When you realise that you are not your feelings, neither are you your perception nor your body; that you are not your thoughts or even your consciousness; you might have a chance to find your animal." These were Max's words before I walked away. I think my mom had said something like, "Don't come home all covered in dirt."

I turned around to give Max a wave to show I would be all right. I was not scared but neither had I any perception of what was waiting for me on the mountain. This was the ultimate test of being with myself; armed with a backpack containing a spare t-shirt and a blanket, beans, rice, already-cooked tofu and some bottles of water. A tent was strapped on top, my knife was in my belt and I had a lighter in my pocket.

I started marching towards the mountain. Feelings of confidence, independence and freedom grew with each step, along, it seemed, with the weight of my bag.

I can do this assignment. I wasn't sure whether I trusted myself or if I had simply trusted Max.

What animals will I find there?

What animals will find me?

It must be safe otherwise Max wouldn't have sent me ...

I'm being given a second chance.

I shut out thoughts of my brother and my family, I had to believe Max when he said that the time would come when I'd be able to help them.

But I'll never be able to help Palli ...

This is me versus the mountain. I am being led by a force greater than life itself, The Experience.

Have faith in The Experience.

This became my chant as I marched.

***

The scenery seemed to me more and more beautiful as I

approached the mountain. The surrounding landscape was the greenest colour I had ever seen and the trees got taller and taller the further away I was from Max's house. My legs quickly tired from the walk and the weight, bringing to mind my football days when I could run for hours. I regretted wearing the sport shoes, they hadn't been on my feet since I was in Kunming.

It was too hot, too sweaty and my feet were rubbed by the shoes. After a lot of consideration of sharp stones and the possibility of snakes or biting insects, the agony of my ripped heels won the inner argument and I decided to go barefoot. I stopped and tied the shoes to my backpack, making it a little heavier, but my feet were happy with the trade-off. I took a tiny sip of water and wondered if there was any more water on the mountain; if not I would be in trouble.

My slow walk continued, the occasional stone which caused me to stumble and yell out but it was worth it for the warm soil under my feet.

Everywhere I looked I could see the presence of The Experience. It was in the clouds, in the rocks. It was in the animals I heard all around, the whizzing sounds of the jungle. The Experience was in the huge, leafy plants sheltering me like a parasol and the tiniest flower I spotted pushing its way up through a crack in a rock. Even the warm wind that blew in my face was full of The Experience. All around me, so close to me yet so far away. I wanted to connect to it.

The Experience is 'Life'. It must be.

Everything is energy.

Energy is constantly moving so my perception of the surroundings is more alive than I've ever experienced. I too am energy. I am alive.

I mustn't let my thoughts break up my sensual experience of the beauty around me. The more thoughts I allowed in my mind, the less space The Experience had to operate and lead me.

Maybe The Experience will tell me what animal to choose.

My job is to surrender to the process.

Maybe three hours had passed since I left Max's house. I had been off the main road for about thirty minutes and was now much deeper into the jungle but still on a small trodden path. I wondered who had walked here before me. While I still had some energy left I found a spot to peg my tent down, in a small green area, as flat as I could have hoped for, surrounded by large trees.

I could hear water streaming somewhere nearby. It turned out to be a small river that ran down from the mountain. After my enlightening hike into the jungle I started to have doubts about my decisions.

Is this the right spot to camp? Did The Experience tell me to camp here?

Am I deep enough into the jungle?

Is it too early yet to camp, should I have continued on for a while longer?

I hadn't seen any large animals yet, but nevertheless I would camp on that spot. I could always move my tent deeper in the jungle tomorrow. After struggling to move large stones away and clear an area around the tent, I was suddenly filled with self-doubt. I sat down on the trunk of a fallen tree at the edge of my clearing and opened a can of beans.

Am I opening the beans too soon?

I was getting more nervous and knew I had to stop questioning everything. I was blocking the channel for The Experience to lead me. After I finished eating the beans, I stood up.

Hmm, what now?

I walked around in circles; pulling out my phone and checking the time as I had been doing all day: four forty-six PM.

What do I do?

The sun was still shining, beating down into my spot between the trees. I calculated that I would have around four hours of sun in which to start my search for an animal.

Why do I feel so anxious, here on my own?

There's no-one here to blame ...

No Max to rail at now ...

I checked the time again: another three minutes had passed. I sat down in the doorway of my tent, knees to my chest, arms wrapped tightly around my legs. Propping my chin on my knees, I stared into the sky; it had seemed so friendly an hour ago and now felt threatening, like everything else.

What is causing this anxiety?

Only another four minutes had passed since I sat down.

Time has become warped.

I had plenty of time to find my animal but my body was freaking out in my first hour on the mountain. I couldn't seem to let go of myself. "Experience," I begged. "Come on, give me a sign. What should I do? Please tell me."

Loosening my tightly-knotted body enough to sneak another glance at the time, I saw it was still only four fifty-nine.

Ah. Now I know.

My first self-given assignment in the jungle was to get rid of time.

The jungle is timeless. The only one creating time in the jungle was me, by constantly looking at my cell phone. I had to get rid of time and therefore I had to get rid of my cell phone. This trip represented a new beginning and even though throwing the phone away sounded like a stupid idea, I knew I had to do it.

Back I went to the fast-running river, only a few minutes' walk away, pushing through the thick, rubbery leaves. It was almost too small to be called a river, a brook, I thought, but the beauty of seeing the water flow through the jungle and down the mountain was breath-taking.

Breathe, listen. The water flows with or without the notion of time. It is timeless.

I looked over the brook and saw a tree on the opposite bank. It reminded me of a tree I used to climb in my childhood, only bigger. Without analysing my actions I jumped over the narrowest part of the water and climbed the tree. I moved up it as high as I could, almost to the top, grasping the branches above me and placing my bare feet carefully into a safe position each time before I loosened my grip. I was breathless and sweating but I felt exhilarated. There were ants crawling everywhere, on the tree, on the leaves and some on my skin but I ignored them.

The view from the treetop was mostly of more trees. On one side I could see other mountains in the background. There were no clouds in the hot blue sky and looking down I could see the river's path as it flowed on its way. I felt great, like Tarzan. Holding on to a strong branch, I reached into my pocket for the phone.

I have to take the sim card out so I don't lose my numbers, was my thought. I hooked my arm around the strong branch and when I felt steady enough I used both hands to extract the sim card but as soon as I did, my excitement decreased.

Why am I taking out the sim card?

If this is a new beginning then why hold onto something from the past?

Typical me.

I didn't really have any numbers I needed, it was mostly names of strangers I stored because it made me feel popular. I laughed at myself and put the sim card back into the phone. This ceremony was becoming more than just getting rid of the time in the jungle; I was getting rid of unhealthy attachments to people from the past as well. It felt great.

I looked down, watched the small river flowing down the mountain. I had a strong feeling of being in the right place at the right time. Just then I heard a crack in a branch near me. I grabbed the trunk more tightly and watched as a bird rustled through the leaves and took off into the sky.

Bird. I am a human being. In a tree in the jungle.

I wish I could fly like that bird, but as a human being I am limited by my nature as well as by my physicality. I'm not meant to fly but I'm free to do whatever is within my human nature to do. Climbing this tree has been within my nature as human being. It is neither right or wrong, normal or abnormal.

I'd climbed the tree to kill time in the jungle; this had led me to get rid of all unhealthy relationships from the past and understand that I'm free to do whatever is within my nature to do.

I looked up into the sky again, thanking The Experience for the guidance. Then I took a quick look at the phone in my hand, before throwing it high up into the air, watching as it spiralled down through the leaves and crash-landed next to the river.

My first assignment, to get rid of time, was complete.

After I had struggled down from the tree, the ant bites on my arms and legs now beginning to itch, I made my way back to my camping spot. The anxiety of finding the next assignment was slowly returning.

Just let go, I told myself. *Trust in the process.*

Build a fire.

I gathered some fallen wood from the jungle, took out my lighter and spent a while setting up the fire. It was getting darker. By the time night had fully descended, my fire was burning. It lit up the whole area around me. In between the trees dark spaces looked like doors to other worlds or black holes leading into another galaxy. I had always been afraid of the dark.

I lay close to the fire on my blanket, surrounded by sounds from trees, unseen animals and plants. I noticed some flowers growing near one of the trees. The light from the fire made the purple and yellow flowers look alive and appear to be moving. It was like the shadows of the flowers were dancing to the crackling flames. I pressed my finger into the soil around the flowers at the tree root; it was damp. Then I noticed a single flower, isolated from the others. It grew on a different area of soil, where there was not enough water. This one flower was dying, alone and weak.

I looked at this one flower and thought about my brother. It is so important to be around people who are fully alive and on solid ground. People are interconnected with their environment, I realised as I trailed my finger in the dry soil. They are like flowers and if they are not around other flowers on hydrated soil, they will die, alone and suffering. Just like my brother.

Palli, you were connected to everything in the universe as these flowers are but you couldn't see it.

I crawled into the tent, trying to rest my mind. The shadows of the flames danced on my tent walls. Still my mind was busy. Then the fire outside the tent started to fade away, and with each moment I grew more afraid of the dark until I finally fell asleep.

The sun came up early and it was already hot inside the tent. I needed to get outside. Today I felt confident that The Experience would lead me and that I would find my guardian animal.

Intermittently I thought about my family. *Palli, I'm sorry I'm not going home for your funeral ...*

Yet I wasn't suffering from guilt, though a part of me said I should be.

I packed my tent and then ate more beans for breakfast, drinking a bottle of water to wash them down. The water was warm, the beans tasted bad but still, it was nourishment. I crushed the can, pressing the lid inside it so I wouldn't cut my hand next time I delved into the rucksack.

Hoisting the rucksack onto my back I continued trekking up the mountain, through the jungle. The earth was warming beneath the soles of my feet and I seemed to be able to sense where to step. My surroundings were mysterious and beautiful. The contrast between the dark undergrowth and the vivid yellow-greens of the sunlit foliage made my eyes hurt. Insects buzzed and clicked, some flying past my head and others hidden at ground level. Raucous birds called through the trees and I caught glimpses of bright colours and heard beating wings. Once I saw a snake wriggling away, surprisingly I wasn't shocked by it. So much hidden and so much on view. The jungle was full of life, beautiful and exciting if I opened myself up to it. *Beauty is in the eye of the beholder.*

Does that mean I'm in control of how beautiful the forest is?

The jungle just is. It's just itself.

I trekked for two hours, sweaty and tired, all the time getting closer to the top. Flies buzzed around my head and drank sweat from my skin. I let go of the straps of my backpack to swat at them but tried not to kill them.

Every so often I stopped to take a breath and drink some water. My focus was on the top of the mountain.

Why haven't I found my guardian animal yet? What animal lives at the top of a mountain?

I must keep on walking.

My breathing sounds really loud in my head.

The trees are thinning out, more light breaking through.

Tramp, tramp.

Emerging from the trees I saw that I'd reached a plateau. Green. Empty. I looked down on the treetops below.

Now what?

Only me. No animals.

I walked across a stretch of grass and pulled off my backpack, letting it drop to the ground behind me. I settled myself on the edge of a cliff and the view was incredible. Far below, a valley with trees and grassy fields stretched into the distance. A clear blue sky hung above, mountains surrounded the valley … and me.

How can I get rid of myself? I want to merge with all this beauty.

What's creating my sense of self? Maybe there's no self and it's all an illusion?

I've created an illusion about myself: I am my house, my girlfriend, and my clothes. I am my pain. I am my future and my past.

It's all attachments.

Throwing the phone into the river had resulted in losing a phone, but the attachments were still there.

What binds myself then, if there is a 'myself', to all these external and internal things?

I surrendered to the massive scenery of mountains and nature. Seeking distance from my sense of self. I looked out over the graceful mountains, rightly placed on this planet, Earth. Billions of people on it. Mostly in conflict. I closed my eyes, feeling the sun beat down on my face.

Why?

Why do we live in conflict?

I opened my eyes again, getting stiffly to my feet. When I shrugged my backpack back onto my shoulders the weight registered as a physical shock to my body that had all but disappeared from my consciousness a few moments before. Slowly, I began lowering myself down the steep cliff, placing my hands and feet tentatively into its rocky face. I was about halfway down when the fear crept over me.

I must not let fear affect the clear headspace I've achieved. I must stay in the state of oneness.

I looked down, swivelled my head to glance behind me, out over the grassy fields and the long valley.

Then I took another step and lost my footing. A dislodged stone rolled down the cliff. My heart was beating fast. I was holding onto the cliff with both hands, but only one foot had something solid underneath it, the other swung in the air. My backpack seemed to be pulling me backwards. I couldn't go back up and was too afraid to go down so I hung there, my whole body stretched as flat as I could manage against the cliff.

As I breathed fast, the cliff was right in my face, so close I could almost taste it. I closed my eyes.

Calm down, Böddi. It's not helpful to be scared. Slow down. Slow down and keep calm.

I followed you, Experience, and you led me to this situation. If you got me into this, then I trust that you will get me out of this.

I kept my eyes closed.

Fear fading, the feeling of oneness coming back again, I was connected to the cliff, to the whole mountain and to the universe. I had to let go (but not of the stones because then I would die), I had to let go of my inner world and hold on to the physical world. If there was any time to have faith in The Experience, it was now.

A few minutes must have passed. Suddenly I stuck my tongue out. Why, I don't know. My tongue licked the cliff. It tasted salty. It felt a natural thing to do. I stuck my tongue out again, into the air, as I opened my eyes. The tongue flicked out as if independent from my body. I looked around. Something had changed. The cliff was different. It looked different, and it smelled different. My fingers were like rubber gloves and the fear was gone. I was exactly where I was supposed to be.

I began to move slowly and the cliff was now sticking to my body as if there was glue between us. The tongue went out again. I slowly moved my head from one side to the other, observing my surroundings. Everything was different. It was as if someone had recreated the cliff while my eyes were closed.

Or did I shift my perception of it?

Inch by inch I moved to the right, reaching for a protruding stone. I grabbed the stone. My body was suddenly horizontal, still sticking to the cliff. My feet slowly followed and I was vertical again. I looked down.

One foot after the other, take it easy.

I descended the rest of the cliff in slow motion, feeling a deep connection to the mountain.

We aren't enemies.

We are friends.

My tongue flicked out and in again. I reached solid ground on my hands and knees, smiling.

At the base of the cliff I turned my body around and continued crawling slowly down the mountainside, my head facing the fields, my tongue flicking out every minute or so. I was in a different dimension. I was experiencing something new but it was as if I'd always been on this mountain. It was part of me. It was my home.

I approached the fields, still crawling on all fours. My eyes glazed over as I looked into the sun, sticking my tongue out like I was trying to lick its hot surface. I felt the rough grass under me.

My knee hurts.

What am I doing?

What's happening to me? Have I gone crazy?

I had faith that it was The Experience leading the way.

The grass was high and I derived enjoyment from observing all the insects around me. There was a spider high-stepping up a stalk, flies buzzing just above the seed-heads and around my eyes. I saw a worm stretching and contracting in the soil at the base of a thin blade. The grass was full of life. I had never seen so many creatures in one place. It was only my perspective that allowed me to see these things. I had spent two days walking over a whole mountain looking for animals or insects but hadn't noticed any. Now I was shocked to discover all this life in a couple of square metres in the high grass. I crawled further into the field, hoping for new discoveries, despite how sore my knees and hands were getting.

I came to an area of cropped grass. A cow stood on the field not far away from me. The cow slowly turned and examined me, chewing grass.

I am a lizard.

A stinging electricity went through my body while I was frozen in the fight or flight mode. I wasn't sure if it was me who was afraid of the cow or whether I was supposed to be afraid because I was a lizard. I was about to withdraw back into the high grass but instead I moved closer to the cow, still crawling and occasionally sticking my tongue out. I was now only a metre away from the cow.

Fear buzzed through me. I decided to invite it to lunch with me and the cow. I started chewing grass.

The fear clearly accepted my lunch offer because I could feel it everywhere in my body; in my fingers, in my toes, in my stomach. Fear took up residence in my shoulders and in other places I won't mention.

I have become the fear.

Let it wash over me.

I owned that fear. My face twitched and my body started shaking. Fear subsumed me.

"Welcome, Mr. Fear," I croaked. Then I made my voice louder. "Please join me and this beautiful cow for some delicious grass for lunch."

I waited a moment until I could hear a deep voice: "Thanks. I'm delighted to be here."

"So tell me, Mr. Fear. What do you do for a living?" I pulled up some more grass with my teeth.

"I'm a universal emotional response mechanic to an actual or imagined threat," Fear said pompously. I noticed he was handpicking the finest grass on the field for his eating.

"That's interesting. How long have you been doing this?"

"Throughout human history." Fear raised an eyebrow, as if I ought to know this.

"How do I handle you? How do I get rid of you?"

"Well," Fear said after a moment's chewing, (grass is quite tough), "Most people try to run away from me or fight against me. Occasionally people simply freeze."

"Are you real, Fear?" I asked, throwing some extra-green grass to the cow, which looked on placidly.

"Not really. I feed off your delusions, mainly. Depends on how you interpret real, I guess." Fear seemed to be struggling with that particular answer. Then he added, "I prefer it when you address me as 'Mr.'"

I coughed a grass-stem out of my throat and spat it out.

"Sorry," I said. "What kind of delusions?"

"The delusion of attachments."

"Are you the one causing my constant anxiety?"

"No, but Anxiety is a relative of mine. I always need a threat, imagined or not. Uncle Anxiety doesn't need any external threat to thrive." Under his breath I heard him mutter, "That lucky bastard."

"You are evil, Mr. Fear. Why do you want people to be fearful?"

His uncaring attitude made me angry. I was also getting somewhat thirsty from all this eating of grass.

"Hey, don't be rude," Mr. Fear said. "People need me. I am healthy for humans, I'm not perfect, just like any other being, and I do admit that there are unhealthy parts of me as well, of course."

"Explain." I was resistant to the idea that there was a positive side to Mr. Fear.

"Are you afraid of the cow?" he asked.

"A little bit."

"That's an example of unhealthy fear. The cow won't attack you. What about when you were afraid of the dark in the tent?"

"That must be an unhealthy fear because the dark itself can't hurt me."

"Correct, you are a quick learner, my friend."

"Thanks." I hesitated at allowing him to address me as 'friend' but his argument was interesting. "Why am I afraid of the dark then?"

I felt much more relaxed, now. That saying face your fear makes a lot of sense.

Mr. Fear looked at me with sympathy "You learned this at a young age, to fear the dark. I remember your brother used to tease you by locking you inside the closet. It was one of the first fears you learned and that's when we really started our relationship. I am sorry to hear about what happened to your brother." He tore up more grass and munched it ruminatively. "You are afraid of ending up like him. You are afraid that alcohol, drugs and other destructive behaviour will take you down the same path as your brother's. It's a reasonable fear."

"Yes that's true," I allowed. (*But he has no right to delve into the subject of my brother.*)

"There you go, that's the healthy part of me. The fear of alcohol and drugs are a healthy fear so be grateful to me."

Now he is just being arrogant. "What do you know about my brother? I don't want you in my life, Mr. Fear, healthy or unhealthy." The more I thought about it the more annoyed I became. "I don't care if there's a healthy part of you. Fuck that healthy part of you! I want to get rid of you."

"Mr. Fear can't leave you, you have to leave him." A sneaky female voice had spoken.

I whipped my head around, wincing at the crick in my neck. "Who are you?" I searched the sky, glanced at the cow and at Mr. Fear.

"I'm an emotion. You can call me Ms. Anger." She had a low, sexy tone that made me swallow my mouthful of grass a bit too quickly.

"Okay, then please introduce yourself, Ms. Anger, and then you may join us for lunch if you please?"

I threw a cascade of grass into the air, noticing that Mr. Fear was not too happy about me inviting Ms. Anger to the party.

"Well, as I said," Ms. Anger's sultry voice became stronger as she began to materialise in the heat-haze (she was hot in more than one way), "I am an emotion. I have a wide range of intensity. I can take many forms, including everything from irritation to rage. I usually appear when there's a threat to you such as to your identity, to your possessions, or to your self-image. I am the one who increases your heart rate and blood pressure and tightens your muscles but that's just the cost of my protecting you from being hurt."

Mr. Fear was annoyed. "Don't believe her, she is not healthy for you. Ms. Anger leads you into all *kinds* of problems. *I* am the one who protects you from being hurt."

"You are just jealous, Mr. Fear. Every time Böddi allows me to shine, you are jealous. You can't stand it when I take the spotlight."

Ms. Anger had raised her voice. It was no longer quite as sexy.

"Böddi, do you want to know a secret?" Mr. Fear flicked his eyes slyly over Ms. Anger and then me.

"Yes."

"I'll tell you how to get rid of anger. Don't suppress it, don't run away from it or deny it. You just have to practice observing it and acknowledging it, then anger will leave. Nothing can *make* you angry, it all comes from yourself."

He appeared satisfied with himself.

Ms. Anger turned up the tension, beginning to look ugly. "How dare you rat me out, Mr. Fear? Böddi has been in fear for most of his life and just occasionally, he allows me to shine. You're a greedy bastard."

"So," I interrupted, finally straightening up from my all-fours position in the field. Placing my (green) hands into the small of my back I stretched luxuriously. "You two just overlap each other, in constant battle, waiting for me to feed you both with my illusions?" I could see how I'd been used and abused by each of them.

"You have protected us for a long time, Böddi." Mr. Fear stuffed another handful of grass in his mouth and ruminated.

"Yeah, I've been living on constant justifications from you," Ms. Anger added.

"Can I join you all?" a male voice floated above our heads.

"Yeah, sure. It seems like it's an open lunch for everyone." I turned my filthy palms outwards in an inviting gesture. A shadowy form, pale grey in colour, cast a mist over the grass as he materialised in front of me.

"Hi, guys, I'm Mr. Sadness. I'm just another emotional pain, usually associated with loss. Hey, thanks for the invitation." He slipped quietly in between Ms. Anger and me. I stared at him a moment, then glanced down to see that we were now sitting around a table. Mr. Sadness was more comfortable to be around than Mr. Fear and Ms. Anger. He and I gazed at each other while the other two continued to quarrel.

"Welcome," I said softly to Mr. Sadness.

"I recommend you accept those two before you allow me to eliminate them from your life." Mr. Sadness was obviously one for getting straight to the point.

"Sounds pretty good," I answered. "Why don't I spend more time with you, rather than with those two?"

Mr. Sadness nodded in his dove-grey way. When he spoke, I felt his empathy.

"You weren't really allowed to hang out with me when you were younger."

I looked over the lunch table and saw that this was becoming like a family dinner in the old days. Mr. Fear and Ms. Anger were quarrelling and we were talking about them. It reminded me of my dad, my mom, my brother and me. I was becoming more distant from Mr. Fear and Ms. Anger, I could barely hear them talking anymore and my focus was on Mr. Sadness.

"They won't go anywhere. They will always stay with you," Mr. Sadness stated in his dolorous voice. "Just accept them. Let them quarrel and let me stay with you too. I will protect you."

Tears ran down my face as I watched Mr. Fear and Ms. Anger quarrelling while aspects of me held onto them, I didn't want to let them go. But maybe I should have done a long time ago. I should have been more angry than fearful through-out my life. Or I should have been sadder. The cow looked at me as I wiped tears away. The cow's eyes were big and shiny. I looked into them. Mr. Fear, Ms. Anger and Mr. Sadness all stared at me like they were waiting for me to say something. I turned my head away.

Mr. Fear, Ms. Anger and Mr. Sadness lowered theirs and contemplated the grass.

"It's all right, I'm here with you." It was the softest voice I could possibly imagine.

"Who are you? I don't know you."

I felt numb as I gazed into the cow's lovely eyes again, waiting for the speaker to be revealed.

"I am Compassion," she said. "I'm here to bear the pain for you and for the others, and have some of this delicious grass you seem to be enjoying so much."

A lightweight form floated into position between the cow and Ms. Anger. I turned to Mr. Sadness, because he was the one next to me. "I feel for you, Mr. Sadness. You are suffering. I feel your sadness. I'm sorry that you are suffering." I whispered these words into to his ear.

"I brought your understanding to this beautiful gathering we have here," Ms. Compassion said in her mature but sweet voice.

I couldn't deny that there was love around the table. Mr. Fear and Ms. Anger had stopped quarrelling. Mr. Sadness was next to me, vibrating kindness and warmth. Ms. Compassion was sitting quietly with a smile on her face. All of us had become strangely 'one' even though we all appeared as separate entities.

"Congratulations, dear Böddi." Ms. Compassion followed this with a sweet smile.

"For what?" I asked, shifting my glance around the table.

"For loving yourself for the first time. Loving all the parts of you."

A river streamed down a mountain. The contours of the mountain were my face.

These are my tears.

A glacier thawed inside my chest, bursting out through my eyes.

These are tears of love.

No more self-pity. Mr. Fear, Mr. Anger and Mr. Sadness started fading away from the lunch and were sucked into the cow's head. Now there was only me, Cow and Ms. Compassion.

"Are they leaving me? I thought they were part of me. Those are my emotions, aren't they?" I asked Ms. Compassion. The cow shook its head slowly from side to side.

"They are universal. They don't belong to you. They are not you, but they dwell in your mind." Ms. Compassion smiled in a blissful way.

I felt a greater concern for the cow then I'd ever had for anyone in my life. I felt its struggles on the deepest level. I understood the cow. It was a stranger to me but I wanted to release it from its suffering. I stood up, walked to the cow and started stroking its head.

"Please don't leave me, Ms. Compassion," I said over my shoulder.

"I can never leave you, it's only that you can leave me. I am universal, I am eternal and I am with you at all times. I don't function in the delusion of separation, I thrive only in oneness with all beings. I'm here to relieve suffering and bring joy."

"I want joy."

"Everybody wants joy but not everybody knows me. I am the answer to the world's problems. All the world's problems are extremely selfish. I can solve them. I am the one that can protect you, and all living beings." Ms. Compassion laid her hands on her heart.

"Can't you tell people that?"

I mirrored her gesture.

"People believe in science, the same science that built the atomic bomb. Science has long been against spirituality; the same way religions have been against science. I work well with wisdom. If people added me to wisdom, humanity would become free."

Sliding my arm around the cow's neck, I pressed my cheek to her soft, golden hide while understanding whirled around in my head. I could feel the cow's jaw swivelling as she munched on her eternal lunch.

People think they are free but they are not.

To be free is to be free from suffering, like Max said.

I understood then: we are all prisoners, not only James and the others in Phonthong, but the entirety of humanity is in prison.

We are trapped in greed.

We are trapped in aversion.

We are trapped in ignorance.

When I was in Iceland I heard the story of Stockholm syndrome. A girl had been kidnapped for years and she developed a bond with her kidnapper.

Maybe the whole of humanity is suffering from Stockholm syndrome.

Could it be that the path to end suffering is to un-condition ourselves?

"Hello, Joy!"

I let go of the cow, broke out in a crazy dance on the beautiful green grass. Mr. Joy had magically appeared. He sat down at the lunch table. Mr. Joy gave Ms. Compassion a loving hug while they both glowed as divine beings.

"Hello, Böddi. Always a pleasure when we meet. Ha-ha, get it?"

"Oh, Joy," I said, finishing my dance with a flourish and a bow. "We should hang out more often."

"I have a feeling you'll be seeing more of me in the coming years. I am in harmony with awakening, nobody can escape me on the path to awakening." He gave me a wink.

***

I lay down in the grass, digesting a whole lot of the green stuff and the day that just passed.

Now there is only me and the cow.

Lunch had finished. The cow slowly walked away. I watched her tail swishing at flies as she ambled off into the distance. The mission was complete; I'd found my guardian animal.

Kafli 25 - Laos.

Home

WHEN I REACHED the bottom of the track I ran towards Max's house, backpack thumping uncomfortably against my spine. It seemed forever since I had left and all the memories came flooding back.

My brother is still dead. But I have changed.

"Max, Max," I yelled.

He was on the porch reading a book.

"Max?"

"Hi there." He looked up at me calmly.

"I found it. My animal. I found my animal." I leaned forward, panting heavily from all the running. When I could get more words out I said, "So do you know what animal it is?"

"How should I know? I wasn't there." Max's glasses slipped down his nose and he took the opportunity to rub his eyes, pinching the glasses between the thumb and forefinger of his other hand. Then he placed his book on his knees and waited for my story.

"This trip was amazing."

Still panting, I shrugged my backpack to the floor, hearing the clinking of empty tins inside, then went to sit on the chair next to Max. "So, my animal is ..." I found that I was stuttering. I had meant to say the lizard but something was holding me back.

What is it?

I want it to be but I know the lizard is not really my animal.

"So your animal is?" Max sat, patiently waiting.

"Holy cow, it's the cow!" I burst out laughing.

Max hasn't got a clue what I'm talking about.

I'm sure it's the cow though. It must be.

Tell him the story of my time on the mountain.

I launched ahead with my tale, words tumbling out of me, telling him everything.

"You want the truth?" Max fitted his reading glasses back on the tip of his nose and studied me intensely. "There's no guardian animal."

"What? Why did you tell me to find it then?"

"We must strive to see things as they are."

What does that mean?

"There's no guardian animal," he repeated. "No inner child,

no God. There is no unknown force like The Experience you talk about, no higher self; these are all the wrong views to have."

I don't get it. He's turning everything I thought I was learning upside down again.

"In my view," Max continued, "It's a mental disease to trust the universe, to trust an unknown entity. Trust yourself."

"So why did you send me then?"

"We grow through experience."

Sweat was making my t-shirt stick to my skin.

I feel like there are balloons hanging over my head, each one containing a different view, and they're all being popped by Max.

But ...

"It makes sense, what you said." I turned his words over in my inner thought-processing factory. "It's weird though, Max, because two minutes ago I was sure about all of that. Why has my thinking changed so suddenly?"

"It's a normal reaction to hearing the truth based on experience," he stated. "You've just had that experience."

"What about feelings and emotions? Are they wrong also?"

"Emotions are for bleeding women, Böddi, no room for emotions in this house." Max laughed heavily and I felt uncomfortable. He continued espousing his views. "Feeling is either pleasant, neutral or unpleasant. I hope that's simple enough for you?"

"Uhm."

But that means the mountain was just another experience and I am still a beginner on the path.

"So what *am* I then?" I queried. "If I'm not my thoughts, my feelings, my perception or my body? Am I just consciousness?"

I prepared myself for the experience on the mountain to be smashed to pieces by Max.

"You are not consciousness either. There's no self at all. Intellectualizing about these things is useless. What you can be absolutely sure of, is that you have a mind, filled with impurities. Strive towards purifying the mind, free it from greed, aversion and ignorance and then we can talk about self and no self."

"Okay"

"Now, let me finish reading this story. We have meditation class tomorrow morning. You'd better be ready."

Kafli 26 - Laos.

The Prison

WOKE UP FEELING split in half. One side of me was still Böddi, the other side was this unknown, unexplored spaciousness. It's a little scary but I've decided to go with it. A new view of the world was established for me on the mountain, this alongside Max smashing some of the delusions of how I viewed life before. Now I am only left with my impure mind that has to go through purification. No more Experience, just trying to see things as they are.

Max and the others were making breakfast while I lay in bed watching a spider crawling up the curtains. I stayed there a while, trying to ease my mind slowly into the day. It had comforted me to understand that my ultimate assignment was to purify my mind.

Later, in the kitchen, I found Uppa cooking and Marissa

helping out. We all sat down when Max came in. Having a casual chat with Max was not a normal chat about the weather or the daily news. A casual chat with Max was like the kind of talks you usually have a few times a year with friends, when you feel you've touched the deepest depths of conversation.

I sense something flowing amongst us all, as if we've been together for many years. Everybody is understanding of everyone else in this house and I am treated like the baby elephant in the herd. I feel secure in my place as part of this herd.

Later on, Max and I went out to the car. I had an impulse to talk about the flow we were in but I mustn't because that would only ruin it. Max was in a good mood as always. When I was doing well Max was too and when I was feeling anxious he seemed disappointed. I guessed this was his way to teach me to think of others at all times. *Max is my mirror.*

"Max"

"Yes, boy." Max rattled the gear stick because it was stuck in third gear.

"I've noticed that you always seem happy when I am happy and sad when I'm sad. Is this coincidence or are you what we call co-dependent?"

I guess I was hoping for a little compliment for knowing the word co-dependent, I had only heard it in the past when my mom was talking behind people's backs.

Max laughed faintly. "It's not co-dependency but you're on the right track, to say that there's a pattern there."

"So do I affect you when I am not happy? Aren't you supposed to be free and detached from me emotionally?"

There were always so many apparent anomalies in what he taught me.

"You not only affect *me*, Böddi, with your anxiety, depression and other stuff. You affect *all* your surroundings. You affect my home, my plants; my garden. You affect the sky, the planet and the whole universe. The difference is that you can't see it in the plants or in the sky, but you can see it in me. So what you see in me is what is in yourself."

"Wow. So I have to be happy all the time so you will be happy too?"

"Well, if you try it would be nice." Max flashed his witty smile at me. "I have decided to connect to you. What do you feel when you sit next to me and when we talk?"

It came to me slowly. "I feel loved."

"Exactly, boy. I have chosen to give you access to my heart. You will have to take care of that. I am on this ride with you. If you go down you are taking me with you. This will make you see the reality of your actions. I sometimes ask myself why the hell I am doing this for you, but I pass on what I've been given, that's all."

"Wow!"

It's my responsibility to take care of me, to stay spiritually fit, to feel love and to avoid hate, jealousy, envy and suffering.

I saw a girl on the street. It was Marissa. There she was, riding a bicycle on the right side of the road. She was riding the same lane as us, wearing a white dress today and a hat to protect herself from the sun. Seeing her pulled me right out of the flow with Max. Seeing her reminded me of a scene from a Pedro Almodovar movie and I could observe my mind go into fantasy land. I swung from perceiving her as my spiritual friend to the girl that I must have to fulfil my fantasies.

Max slowed down and I opened the car window.

"Hi," I smirked, way too flirtatiously.

"Hi, it's my two favourite people on the planet. Long time, no see," she said, as if we hadn't earlier eaten breakfast together. "Where are you going?" She seemed to be smiling only for me, pulling her hat from her eyes.

"To town. We're running some errands," Max said.

I didn't think people like Max were allowed to lie. In the middle of this thought, Marissa's face caught my attention again. She was like a magnet.

"So, are we gonna go out soon?" She whispered this through the window to me.

Shit, watch out.

She had almost crashed into the car. Now she was holding onto the window frame, steering the bike with one hand.

"Tomorrow?" I said without thinking.

"Bye, then." Marissa pulled away, raising her voice. I was sure Max hadn't heard, so I stayed calm.

***

The vibe between Max and me had completely changed by the time we parked the car at Phonthong Prison. We watched the guard approaching, Max telling me to step out slowly, keep my mouth shut and follow him.

Max's students were already sitting in their meditation posture in the bare room when we got there. The guards stood at their usual place in the doorway. It was quiet and hot and I could almost touch the tension in the air. Max prepared himself for teaching while I sat down in front of the students, next to Max.

It reminded me of a school. The students were all waiting patiently for Max. I was the special kid in the corner, the *súkkulaði*, we used to call kids that were allowed to play but didn't really count, not affected by either winning or losing.

Max began with a talk on friendship and kindness towards all beings. I listened carefully. We started meditating and focusing on our breath.

My mind was quite still and this time I could feel a connection to my fellow students, more companionship than I'd had before. Not the same compassion as for the cow in the field, but now there was something in me, a little empathy. My thoughts wandered in the silence. I discovered that Mr. Fear was there, talking about Marissa and how I had to stop seeing her because of Max. Ms. Anger was also present. She taunted me about Max and my parents. She mentioned my ex-girlfriends and some other people I'd tried to forget. Mr. Sadness occasionally popped by too. I kept going back to my breathing and didn't engage in these conversations. I merely heard them and watched them float away like waves of energy into the vast blackness. I got deeper into the meditation.

Max's energy radiated on my right side. I sank deeper into that loving feeling.

Images of me sitting in school started to emerge from the black vastness. I was one of over a hundred students, listening to my professor lecturing at the University of Iceland. All of us, drinking in his 'knowledge'.

This world has so many universities, so many students, and so much knowledge but still it keeps getting worse and worse. No independent thinking, only imposed discipline. Could it be education that is the source of the world's problems? What happened to the teaching of compassion, wisdom and love?

Back to breathing.

Now I was in a primary school class, gazing at my teacher. I was nine. The teacher was passing down his version of knowledge to us kids. The version he had been given to teach us.

Received knowledge. Diminishing children's chances of being free.

My spontaneous thoughts wafted away in the vastness, I enjoyed allowing them to flow and recede. Being merely an observer.

I continued to maintain awareness of my breathing.

Another image, this time from Sunday school at the age of six. No teacher involved here but a priest and a group of kids. It was a priest from my neighbourhood in Reykjavík.

Who can paint the most beautiful picture of Jesus? The winner gets a special treat from the priest.

I am not good at drawing so I never have a chance to get the treat from the priest.

Back to the breathing.

Teaching old traditions rather than values. Exams. So that a child thinks he's a failure. Why not let them grow naturally rather than prune them to bear the fruit society demands? Little minds are being told to be like Bill Gates, David Beckham or Jesus. Why not themselves?

Back to black vastness and breathing.

A colourful room, filled with toys and pictures of animals on the walls. Children running around, screaming and playing.

A game, under the surveillance of the teacher. Who will win the game?

The strongest will win. The most popular will win. The coolest kid will win.

Now they are grown up and pursuing material gain as they were taught to do, ready to kill for power. All they want is success and money.

Max's voice pierced the blackness. I opened my eyes.

"So-called holy people, who live a good moral life, can have dormant mental tendencies that may pop up under certain conditions."

"Can you give an example?" Vincent asked.

"A fully enlightened being cannot be shaken by the world, he's not dependent on conditions. You could place an enlightened being in the middle of the Iraq War, in a jungle, in a prison or in the middle of a party with celebrities, yet he remains grounded in his same principles. Jesus sacrificed his life on the cross to set an example, to turn the other cheek under any conditions."

I'd noticed from the way Max spoke to different students that he interacted with each one according to their religious beliefs. They all needed an individual approach.

After finishing the talk, the students got ready to leave, folding their blankets and preparing to walk out. They were quiet and the whole atmosphere felt slow and heavy. While the other students were exiting, the black pregnant lady was still folding her blanket. I got to my feet quietly, watching her, wondering if I should help or not. She was about eight months pregnant and pretty big. But Max had told me not to interact directly with the students. The woman finally got her blanket together, standing up slowly, pressing the blanket against her front. Her eyes flicked from side to side, she looked to the guards and then at me. I had this weird impression she had winked at me. Then she started screaming.

"Naam, naam!"

Shock punched me in the stomach. *What?*

"Naam, naam!" She was pointing desperately at her thighs.

Max had taught me that 'naam' meant water in Lao. I ran over the rough floor towards her, glancing quickly at Max, his return expression one of fear. The guards were shouting, taking up their guns. I threw my hands in the air.

"Naam, naam," I shouted back at them.

Just as I reached the pregnant woman, she dropped to her knees on the floor, with her face down. I bent over her to help her.

"Are you all right?"

She stared up at me, eyes wide open. Terror and hope mixed together in them. I saw her hand underneath her chest. She was clutching a small paper. Sweating, I reached for it.

A voice yelled, "Stop."

Quickly, I tucked the paper under my sleeve. The guard shoved my head with the side of his gun. A ringing crack. The pain registered a millisecond later and I fell backwards, stranded on my back, waving my hands in the air.

"Don't shoot, don't shoot!" Was that really me who was screaming?

Adrenaline pumped through me like a drumbeat as I tried to calculate every possible scenario through my confusion. *Am I going to die?*

Shuffling feet and uniforms and chaos. One guard pointed his gun at Max who stood still near the wall. The other dragged the pregnant woman across the floor. She screamed and begged him to stop. At the door he smashed the gun in her face, the sound of metal on bone was sickening. She was knocked unconscious. The woman lay on the floor with her hands spread out on both sides. I was paralysed.

Max had edged over. He grabbed my wrists, helping me up.

We pushed ourselves into the corner until everyone had gone. Remained there, unspeaking, until another guard came to escort both of us back to the gate. My head hurt.

On the way home I opened the letter.

Hi Angel

Word got around about the letter you wrote to James and I wanted to write you a letter. This is my story.

My name is Atikah, I am 25 years old and born in Nigeria. I have been incarcerated here for four years during which I have been sick most of the time, emotionally and physically. I have been beaten, gang-raped and abused so often that I have lost count.

Six months ago I was very sick and after a struggle seeking health-care I finally saw a doctor who told me that my 'illness' was flu or food poisoning and that I should drink more water to flush it out (not to mention that the water we drink is so dirty it's probably the cause of many of the diseases we get). It turned out that I was pregnant, already four months; it's impossible to know by whom. Usually there were four or five guards who took me to the isolation room at nights. At first I fought back which ended in them beating me so badly I lost consciousness.

There was no way of getting an abortion. I thought about killing the baby by harming myself but I was too afraid of God's reaction so I haven't had the guts to try anything. I have prayed every night that I would have a miscarriage but I seem to bear a survivor that won't give up the chance to enter this world. There seemed no options until an Angel entered my life in a form of a human being. This Angel is you.

Some people believe that angels are spirits with no bodies, who serve God with love and devotion. I believed that too until I laid my eyes on you. I believe that you are an Angel manifested in human form. I believe that you were sent by God to adopt and save my baby. I believe.

Yours truly,

Atikah

Kafli 27 - Laos.

Tattoo

THERE ARE FOUR of us in this house: the teacher, the lover, (I wish!) the friend and the 'baby elephant' (that's me). How am I supposed to treat everyone the same?

There is always tension between Marissa and me. Always. At least in my head. Uppa: I'm surprisingly used to seeing him naked by now and it was a bit weird seeing him in clothes for the first time. He was wearing a t-shirt at breakfast but was naked from the waist down. I guess that's even weirder than being totally naked, come to think of it. Max: Well, Max is just Max. I care the most what he thinks about me, then Marissa, then Uppa.

I heard the roar of an engine. !I'm coming! I yelled out to Marissa, seeing through the window that she was waiting for me on a scuffed old Enfield motorbike. It suited her bad-ass personality much better than the scooter, not to mention the bicycle. *But where the fuck does she get all these bikes from?*

As I bent to put my shoes on my heart pumped faster.

Max gave me a pointed look. I ignored him, feeling a weight lift from my shoulders as I emerged into the heat of outdoors. The sun beat down on my uncovered head as I climbed on the back of the bike. There were no helmets today. I thought of how her hair would smother my face as we rode. The engine vibrated through me and I fastened my arms around Marissa's waist, glad the bike's movement would help disguise my excited shivering. We rattled down the drive and out onto the road.

"Where are we going?" I positioned my mouth near Marissa's left ear, swallowing a gulp of warm wind, her hair tickling my lips.

"I'm going to get a tattoo."

"Nice." This time I brushed her ear with my mouth; she wriggled within my arms.

There were no limits to how cool Marissa was. Free-spirited and spontaneous. Her ways of doing things were almost intimidating to my manhood.

The idea of looking at her body all afternoon as it was painted with ink was like all my Christmases had come at once. On the other hand the thought of me getting a tattoo was frightening and I'd always chickened out whenever the suggestion had come up, rationalizing my refusal with "I haven't found the right one yet," or "I don't want to regret it." In reality I was too afraid of other people's opinions. If I wasn't sure that everybody would like the tattoo I wouldn't have it.

But now ...

"I'm getting one too then." I acted like it was no big deal.

"Okay." She didn't seem surprised.

Marissa parked on a crowded street in downtown Vientiane. Scooters, 'tuk-tuks' and SUV's drove around with no worries about traffic rules. There were shops on the sides of the road selling Buddha statues, clothes and fruit. Marissa and I got off the bike and I followed her towards the small fruit market.

"Hungry?" she asked. "Want any fruit?"

"I'll eat some of yours. Sharing is caring, right?"

"Yeah I share everything." She grinned. "Except chocolate. Though, in Max's house we share everything except medicine and I've claimed chocolate to be a medicine for my mood. Hey, I'll have a bag of these squashed ones," she instructed the vendor, pointing at a basket filled with small soggy tomatoes.

"Why won't you buy the fresh ones?"

"I'll take the ones nobody wants, they're equally fresh even though they look bad."

I was probably giving her a goofy look, she was so cute. The old woman at the stall filled a bag for her. Marissa paid, while I pretended to be interested in different kinds of fruits so

I wouldn't give away my feelings for her. She backed off down the street and I followed. I was about four metres away from her when, "Watch out!"

She laughed. She had nearly walked into a scooter which was parked on the pavement. "Want fruit?" She threw a tomato in the air. In the nick of time I jumped to one side and caught it.

"What kind of tattoo are you getting?" I spoke through a mouthful of squishy red fruit. My brother had tattoos but I'd never in my life get the ones he had. Palli had U2 inked on his arm and a boot on his leg, as well as the names of girls. Marissa continued walking backwards down the pavement. I followed, watching people dodge her like a bullet.

"The same tattoo as my friend had. Her name was Lily." She looked up at the sky with a half a smile.

"Was?"

"Yeah. Overdose. I made it in time, she didn't. I can feel her though."

"Wow." It wasn't a big enough word but I couldn't think of one that would show enough empathy.

There she is, flowing backwards through the crowd, my ultimate pleasure. We were looking into each other's eyes and it was like we were caught in a love balloon that surrounded us. Outside life seemed superficial. *We constantly seek this feeling of love, trying to fill ourselves or numb ourselves with pleasures to take us away from the painful present.*

I feel I have everything I need, walking down the pavement with Marissa.

So is she the reason, or am I now able to create contentment without outside sources?

I reached for a tomato and threw it high into the air. Marissa looked up, laughing. She ran three steps backwards and adeptly caught the fruit in her mouth. Then she looked at me surprised, her mouth open and full of tomato. We both burst out laughing, Marissa struggling to hold on to the tomato.

"Oh my God, how did you do that?"

Marissa didn't answer. Instead she walked towards me, leaned into my face and passed the tomato from her mouth to mine. I looked into her eyes and for a split second I didn't see her as a girl, it was a magical second where she had no name, no physical entity and no being. I looked at her without being involved; without fear or wanting. Her eyes were full of life and I peeked into her soul.

Her inner beauty is indescribable.

This moment has no history or future.

I love her.

We were at the point where none of our human flaws had yet intruded into our perfect connection.

Coming down to earth, we arrived at the tattoo studio in downtown Vientiane. The studio had a raw, distinctive style to it. About twelve people hung around inside and only a few appeared to be busy. The crowd seemed to be a family of some sort, or a gang. They were mostly guys around eighteen to twenty-five, covered in tattoos and dressed in hip hop-style baggy shorts, long t-shirts and colourful caps. I got the sense that if you'd fuck with one of them, they'd all come and get you. There was an older woman, I guessed around seventy, lying on the sofa, and two younger women around twenty-five just hanging out. Two kids ran around, playfully lashing out at each other with sticks.

Marissa sidled up to a guy who was sitting behind an old desktop computer. She gave him a hug and plonked herself in his lap. I followed her, walking slowly towards the computer desk. The guy looked short, based on his upper body which was all I could see; covered in tattoos. His arms were sleeved in pictures of women, snakes and symbols. Marissa's arms were still around his neck.

Okay, I thought. Enough already with the hugging. Although it was Marissa who had sat in his lap.

"This is my friend Sid," she told me.

"Hello, Sid."

I arranged myself stiffly in a small chair on the other side of the desk and watched them talking about the tattoo Marissa was going to get. Sid was so confident, I felt vulnerable in his territory.

"Well, let's get some ink on this chick's ass." Sid winked

and gave me a smile. I forced my mouth into a smile back and nodded like I approved of him calling Marissa a chick. He slid her off his lap and they both disappeared behind a curtain. After a minute sitting there alone within a crowd of chattering people, wondering how long I should wait for Marissa getting a tattoo, she stuck her head through the curtains.

"You coming or what?"

Yeah. Marissa lay down in the tattoo chair while Sid prepared the needle.

"So, Sid, what have you been up to? Still at the same bar? Same people?" Marissa was leaning towards me so Sid could operate on her behind.

"The bar closed last weekend for two weeks. There was a shooting." Sid spoke in a gruff voice.

"Again?" Marissa looked at me with her mouth open.

"Yeah, there are a lot people in this town who have too much power." Sid sounded like he knew what he was talking about.

"So this happens frequently? Shootings at bars?" I asked.

"Yes. It happens. I was at the bar that night. Probably twenty bullets went off. There was some unfinished business between two powerful men."

"Wow. It's crazy, huh?" Marissa said after a pause.

"You know what they say, Laotian people are nice but Laotian people who have power, are not so nice."

I felt my Icelandic-ness again but not as much as before, because I'd now been in the prison and come so close to real horror. This story struck me though, maybe because I'd only been in touch with criminals inside the prison. I hadn't caught on until now that this was not so unusual all around me. I saw that I was involved in three different worlds: the spiritual world in Max's house, James's hellish life in prison and now Sid's real life in Vientiane.

Sid was charming and streetwise. Listening to him talk about the violence that could suddenly spring up in his neighbourhood was entertaining as well as shocking. My eye wandered to the walls. The pictures pinned up there suggested he was a talented artist. Also, his whole being emanated 'identity' with its inked coils of snakes and women. *What kind of man would Sid be if he was placed in a different environment?* My mind wandered while he concentrated on his work. *Dining with the Queen of England. In the audience at a ballet. In a war zone. What person lies beneath the mask of his external identity?*

Then I started feeling a bit sorry for myself. *I feel so naked in comparison to him. Am I losing my identity through the spiritual process I'm undertaking?*

Sid leaned right over Marissa and applied the needle to her skin. Her exposed body hurt to look at. His face was close to her hip. *Does he have to be that close?* Relentless suspicions in my brain. Persistent images of the two of them together buzzing around my brain like a plague of flies. *I feel raw next to Sid. What's my identity?*

"Been doing this for long, Mr. Sid?" I eventually asked.

"Twelve years," Sid glanced at me and then moved even closer to Marissa's hip. *His crotch is pressing against her thigh. Surely that's not necessary?* How long did I have to sit here, enduring this torture?

"We're done, sugar." Sid gave Marissa a soft slap on the ass. She didn't seem bothered.

But I am.

I stalked outside, leaving them together. Marissa had to pay for the tattoo yet and I couldn't be around the two of them anymore. As I hit the bright sunshine of the street I considered letting go of Marissa. For a second it made me feel comfortingly free.

I can't get caught in another emotional roller coaster. Maybe Max was right.

Standing outside the tattoo studio, watching the slow-paced life of Vientiane, someone tapped me on the back. It was Marissa. Any thoughts of emotional freedom dissipated when I looked in her eyes.

"Let's do something special. Help me remember the day I got this tattoo." She pouted her full lips at me.

"Of course, it's your day. What do you want to do?"

Too late I remembered that men should take the lead. Women liked that. *Act quickly*, I thought.

"Okay, come on, I'll choose. Let's go." Before she could answer, I grabbed her arm, pulling her towards the motorcycle.

***

Now it was me driving. Testosterone exploded in my body. I was the man and I had taken the lead. Though I had no more idea than Marissa as to where I was heading, it didn't matter, because every moment with Marissa felt like the height of all my expectations and I could walk away a happy man, grateful I had known her.

We drove out of town on a quiet road. I could feel my hair, longer than it had been in a while, blowing out behind me. I enjoyed thinking of it brushing Marissa's face as hers had brushed mine. I was also intensely aware of her arms, locked around my waist. I could've gone on like this forever.

Marissa was whispering in my ear.

"Take a left."

I took a left turn without questioning it.

"Next right," again that soft voice in my ear, somehow easy to hear despite the stutter of the bike.

Soon, we came to a closed-off park. There was nobody around, only Marissa and me. Marissa told me to pull in. When the bike had puttered to a stop I waited for her to get off, wondering why she was moving so carefully, then I remembered.

"Ow!" She pressed the flat of her hand gingerly over where the tattoo was. "Ow, it hurts. That bumpy road." But she was still smiling.

I kicked the stand down and disembarked. I felt the motion of the bike still rumbling through me. I was exhilarated from the ride and the notion that Marissa had been in my care. She'd already taken off. Trying to control the happy grin on my face, I ran to catch up. We had to jump a fence to enter the small park, which she did admirably despite wearing a dress and having a sore ass. I tried not to peek under her skirt, but she knew what effect she was having on me, I was sure. In the middle of the sun-dried grass there was a big Banyan tree, its roots spreading over a huge area. We sat down on stony ground under its branches. In distance I could see sculptures that looked like giant mushrooms.

"I wish I was a mermaid."

"Why?"

"They seem so carefree," Marissa said. "Just floating around and looking good."

She laughed softly.

"Yeah, mermaids are sexy, I guess." We gave each other a look. "Are you happy with the tattoo?"

"I like the meaning behind it. I want to remember my

friend. I want to be happy." Marissa trailed her hand through the grass. "She'd like that, me to be happy. I know she would. At first I felt guilty for being happy soon after she died. It took me some time to accept it was okay to be happy and free of guilt."

"Where do you think the guilt comes from?"

"I think we are taught that death is something to be sad about, and if we are happy then the big guy in the sky will punish us."

In these feelings of love I'd completely forgotten about Palli. A weight lodged temporarily in my chest. If I wasn't engaging with Max and Marissa, then I would be occupied with thoughts about my brother's death. I looked directly at Marissa.

"I like you."

Did I just say that?

"I like you too," Marissa smiled. "But we will never be together, buddy. Our relationship must be built on friendship, that's how it works in Max's house."

Kafli 28 - Laos.

No Permanence

FRIENDSHIP: What's the difference between friendship and love? I can't stop thinking of Marissa in a 'love' kind of way. Is this wrong, and if it is, why?

"Any news about Atikah?" I asked Max as I stuffed bread down my throat.

"Yes. Rumours say she lost her baby."

Max said it so calmly, I was shocked. And I felt ashamed. While I was in the 'love ball' with Marissa, Atikah had lost her baby, the one she asked me to save.

I am a selfish bastard.

"That's terrible.." Anger rose as if to attack me, because she had lost her baby.

"Nothing is permanent," Max said quietly.

"That's a harsh thing to say."

I wanted to know what was in Max's eyes but I couldn't interpret the look I found there.

"No, that's the truth. Thinking anything else is ignorance." He stood up from the table and walked out of the kitchen.

I reflected on Max's words later while I was making tea to take to him in the living room. Nothing is permanent. This truth felt vast. My head started expanding on the topic.

I'm not permanent. This house is not permanent. Countries are not permanent. The planet. The cosmos. Nothing is permanent. Everything moves. Everything changes. There's no stagnant point in the universe.

"Is there no stagnant point in the universe?" I asked, walking in with the tray.

"No."

"What's the purpose in this world if nothing is permanent, if everything dies and disappears one day?"

"The purpose is to serve people."

Max had a talent of knowing where my mind was at. I hadn't told him about the letter from Atikah. I wasn't serving Atikah. My mind was focussed on my intoxication with Marissa, not on Atikah.

I don't possess a serving mind. Selfishness is so ingrained in me that even a dying pregnant woman didn't evoke serving thoughts.

I was disgusted with myself but simultaneously delighted by my new awareness.

"Max. Am I ignorant?"

Max burst out laughing. "Realizing one's own ignorance is the first step to spiritual growth. How are you going to spill water into a cup that's already filled with crap?" Max continued chuckling to himself.

"What is ignorance? Is it different from stupidity?"

"Yes. It's mistaking the transient as eternal. Mistaking the pure for impure. Mistaking misery for happiness. Mistaking what is the not the self, to be the self."

"So, I'm ignorant. Is there a way out?" *I must write down his answer in my notebook.*

"Of course there is. Many people have led the way. The spiritual path is in travelling from ignorance to wisdom. Until you reach wisdom, you are ignorant. You can't be half-wise or half-ignorant. It goes, ignorant, ignorant, ignorant, ignorant and finally, wisdom."

"So wisdom is the opposite of ignorance?"

"Wisdom is to be free of suffering. Many people claim to be wise but are still full of anger and aversion. How can that be wise? Wisdom is to know how to end suffering and few have reached that point."

"So people who suffer are just ignorant?"

"Excellent logic, my friend."

There was the smile of his that I loved. It made his blue eyes shine with an enveloping warmth I wanted to bask in. And I got goose-bumps every time Max paid me a compliment.

"What about sick people?"

"A wise man does not suffer. He can physically suffer but a wise man doesn't suffer mentally. He has broken the alliance of karma."

Oh.

"When do we go back to the prison?" I asked next. I had a strong feeling that I had unfinished business there.

"There will be no other time."

My mouth hung open. Max glanced at me, his eyes less warm now.

"I have been informed that there will be no more sessions and that my job there is done."

What about James, the letter I wrote him? What was it all for?

"You seem to take this very lightly." My heart was doing that fast-drumbeat thing again. I could hardly breathe. "That's insane. That's just unacceptable. This is your life, Max. Why aren't you angry?"

"Nothing is permanent."

While I was furious, Max raised his eyebrows as if he pitied my ignorance. I realised I had been way more attached to an expectation of a relationship with James than Max was to his years of service to the inmates.

Kafli 29 - Laos.

Several months later

STRIVING: *I've changed so much in the time I've been here. I've learned that certain conditions lead to cessation of suffering. I've developed much healthier mental tendencies. Now I don't have to force myself to meditate every day, I want to. It's not that it's important to meditate to have a good day; rather to have a quality day that results in a good meditation. In these four months, I've developed belief that there's a way out of suffering, based on experience. Never in my life have I suffered so little and now my path is to always be on the up.*

In Max's house we follow a healthy routine. We each strive with diligence to grow at every waking hour.

One thing that hasn't changed is my desire for Marissa, but I've managed to keep it in check. Occasionally we flirt with each other, sometimes the need to touch her and smell the skin of her neck again as I did when on the back of her bike is so strong it hurts.

My family hasn't talked to me in all these months, they're still angry I didn't attend Palli's funeral. I'm sorry about that but I can't help it.

I have a higher goal and that is to grow as much as possible while staying at Max's.

After writing my morning entry in the purple striped notebook that was now almost full, I left my bed to go to the porch for some meditation and breathing exercises. This was my usual routine before Max set up a discourse for me, Marissa and Uppa after breakfast each day. Max would pick a theme for discussion such as wisdom, suffering or ignorance. Or it could be impermanence, ageing or death. During discourse sessions Max told stories, he seemed to have endless stories to make a point or just to make the discourse more lively.

This was a normal day in Max's house. Today Sid was also involved in the discussion. We all sat in the living room with our notebooks and listened to Max. Max spoke about the cessation of suffering. He was first and foremost our teacher but he was also our spiritual friend, seeming to have the capability to switch the teacher-mode on and off and I now felt attuned to whichever mode was on at any particular time.

One of our routines was an Indian talking circle after each

discourse. A wooden stick was passed around and anyone could say what they wanted while they held it. Questions, stories, babbling or tea-toasts were all permissible when you had the wooden stick in your hand, but nobody might interrupt or interfere with your monologue. Max was the first to pick up the stick from the floor next to his chair.

"Toast to the house. Toast for living in harmony. Toast for mental antidotes where we transform ill will into loving kindness and cruelty to compassion." We all raised our cups. "Pass." Max handed the stick to Sid.

Sid arrived at the house for discourses around once a week. I reckoned he was just doing it to get closer to Marissa and I suspected Max to have invited him to provoke me, to test my devotion to the path. In my mind Sid was only a spectator, while I, Marissa and Uppa were in this to be free from suffering. Sid took his time before speaking.

"Well," he said. "Cruelty is hard to deal with. I have cruel thoughts towards people who ruined my childhood. When I was around twelve years old, I stepped on some kid's toe by mistake. It resulted in him gathering three older kids who bullied me and beat me up. I think this incident resulted in me going off-track in my life. Pass." He handed the stick to me.

I looked at Max in surprise. Here was this rough-looking tattooed guy, talking about a broken childhood due to once being bullied by older kids. I instantly felt shy speaking next, because each talking circle had a theme. Max started, and usually we all linked our talks somehow to his words. Now I had a problem. Max looked at me, with his eyes wide open and a slight smile.

Don't say it, Max ...

"So, Böddi, you gonna share your childhood stuff as well?" Max nodded encouragingly.

Panic.

"I think everybody has some incident in their life that has shaped them into who they are," I gabbled. "It doesn't seem to matter the size or seriousness of these incidents, we can all be so special when it comes to suffering." *I am grasping the stick tightly, it digs into my palm.* "The thing is," I hurried on, not looking at anyone. "Everybody suffers. It's just how you deal with it, I guess. You can transform any experience in life in order to help others."

I bit my lips together. Max smiled at Sid, pitying him with his soft gaze and communicating to him to get over this small incident of my rebellion.

"May I speak now please?" It was Marissa.

I need to let go of the stick.

"Böddi? Pass me the stick."

My palm had marks on the inside as I loosened the stick, red welts slowly transforming through white back to the normal colour of my skin. Now pass it to Marissa.

"Every season I spend here in Max's house," Marissa started, giving me a concerned look. Then she turned away and looked directly ahead. "I learn something new. Each season is pushing me to grow. I'm grateful for the mantra 'it's always up' and even more when you realise that mantra through experience."

She gave her kooky grin and passed the stick to Uppa.

"Oh my friends." Uppa's face opened in a wide smile, like the sun sneaking in through a crack in the curtains. "Here's the story of the pumpkin cutter. I heard this story in India. It's short but effective. Ready?"

I focussed on his shiny bright face and joined in with the others as we all replied,

"Yes," simultaneously.

"There was a man in a small village, a village where people either became holy men or family men. This man was extremely good at cutting pumpkins. He lived in a small cottage, without any family, nor was he excited about going for the holy life. Once a year all the housewives in the village, during certain Indian festivals, wanted only this certain pumpkin cutter to cut their pumpkins. Once a year he was extremely proud. Then he died."

We all laughed. Marissa was still giggling. "So, the moral?"

Uppa said, "Don't waste your life. Don't become a pumpkin cutter. Go for a purified mind or for a family. Don't just waste all your potential in cutting pumpkins."

✻✻✻

Afternoons in Max's house were usually free time. This particular day was no different. I sometimes just wandered around the house or I would read one of the many books on the shelves. Or I would meditate, reflecting on Max's teachings of the day. Sometimes I would also do physical exercises.

I was alone in the house this day. It felt hotter than usual and there was a sheen of moisture on my skin. Something about the shadows of the jungle behind the blinds felt disturbing, so I left the living room.

Too hot to do exercises.

I grabbed a book and went out onto the back porch. But something was bothering me and I couldn't concentrate on reading.

What was that?

I'm sure I heard something.

The hairs on my arms prickled, I definitely heard noises. I peeked over my shoulder to look inside the house, but couldn't see anything.

Where is everyone, anyway?

The stones in the garden seemed like crouching figures, some half-hidden in foliage, ready to pounce. *There, that noise again.* I wasn't sure whether they were animal noises or human. Leaves rustled in a sudden warm breeze. Blowing those odd sounds my way again.

I stood up, put the book aside; planted my bare feet on the plank floor. Grasping the rail, I walked stiffly down the steps. The ground was warm and it was like the life of all the animals living in the earth pulsed up through the soles of my feet. My senses sharpened. Could it be a fox? The sound took me right back to my grandmother's house in Iceland. Max talked fondly of the animals around the house but had never mentioned a fox.

I walked slowly down the long backyard, barefoot, stepping between the stones, grimy now from the months that had passed since I cleaned them. Brushing them with my hands felt like I was being catapulted back in time to those early days at the house. I focussed on my hearing again as the heat underneath my feet tried to distract me.

Again. Guttural sounds coming from the jungle that bounded the garden, the dusty path leading to the huts of Uppa and Marissa.

If not a fox, then what? Human?

No, it can't be ...

Closer to Marissa's cabin. My insides chilled.

Shit, no!

Sid?

Uppa?

Please be a fox.

353

It was like I was being strangled. I hunched over but my feet insisted on taking me forward and then I dropped to my knees; crab-crawled a few metres, my finger and toenails full of earth. My heart pumped out of rhythm, a burning ache blossomed in my chest. I was close to the cabin.

Open window.

The groans, punctuated by the whimpering breath of a woman.

No, Marissa.

It's too much.

I can't ...

I don't want to ...

I'll go back to the house, pretend I didn't hear this. But the questions flooded in. *Is she alone? Is she with Sid? Is she with Uppa? Is she thinking of me?*

The uncertainty blew my chest open like a gaping wound. Trying to picture Marissa pleasing herself while thinking of me wasn't convincing enough to outshine all the other possible scenarios.

I have to find out.

I'd be breaking Max's house rules, spying on someone was unthinkable.

But Max thinks privacy is a ridiculous concept.

I can't bear it if she's with Sid. Why would she break the rules with Sid?

I inched through the long grass outside Marissa's cabin, to the chorus of a woman's cries and the breathing of a man about to crash off a precipice.

No, Marissa.

They are all liars.

A twig cracked under my bare heel but they wouldn't hear it, they were too busy and I didn't care anyway. There was a small window next to the door. I climbed onto the porch, adrenaline shooting through me.

"MAX!"

Max's stark eyes found me at the window. Marissa's whimpering stopped abruptly. She scrambled away from Max and my blurred eyes caught a glimpse of her unbearable beauty before she pulled a sheet over her nakedness.

"Böddi," she cried "Oh, Böddi!"

"What the fuck!" I slammed my hand on the wood. "Are you fucking kidding me!"

Max was busy dragging his clothes on, making calming noises, like he thought I would ever trust him again.

"What is this?" I sobbed like a kid, betrayed by his father. "How could you?"

"Böddi, you were not supposed to see this. You are not ready. We are practicing ..."

"Practicing? You were fucking! You, Max, I trusted you." I refused to let him defend himself with his endless words. "Are you going to hide behind Impermanence? Hide behind your stupid principles? Max?" I was not going to let them say a word. "And you, Marissa. What the fuck!" I stared at the floorboards then, hoping they might swallow me up. "You make me sick, both of you." Forcing my eyes to look at Marissa, one last time.

Max was white, as if his tan had bled away. I stood shaking, not knowing what to say or do. Silence gnawed at us all. I slammed my fist one more time on the side of the cabin and ran. Ran to my room to collect my stuff. Ran out of Max's house. Ran out of Laos.

**

INDIA.

When I took up my passport, ÍSLAND.ICELAND.ISLANDE stared at me, asking "Are you ready for me?"

In leaving Max's I was doing exactly what I'd promised not to do. Escaping. I had two choices, fight or flight and I chose flight. Max had told me that some philosophers said that everybody is a potential killer if put in certain conditions. At that time, in that emotional turmoil, I was a potential killer. I'm not sure if Max was testing me or not, but in India I'm determined to take what Max said also, that everybody is a potential lover, in every condition.

Kafli 30 - Iceland, August 2015.

Böddi and Svenni

I'M SITTING ON the grass at Austurvöllur, a square in downtown Reykjavík. Opposite me is the parliament building and the statue of Jón Sigurðsson stands tall and proud on its plinth in the centre. Outdoor cafés line the square and the tables are full of tourists as well as local regulars all around, drinking lattes and wine and relaxing in the sun. It's the end of the month and the usual drunks are sitting on a bench together, finishing the last sips of alcohol they managed to buy with their social security cheques.

I remember these guys from my childhood, the same crowd but different people. Elsewhere, young people are playing hacky-sack and mothers walk their new-borns in smart prams down the paths between the swathes of grass, saying hello to people they know and to those just curious to get a glimpse of the cute babies in the prams.

This is the best time to be in Iceland, August. It's my third day, and the first time in five years that I have come home to the country of my birth. Sitting with me is my half-brother Svenni, aged twenty-two. We've spent the day together, upon his request to reconnect with me.

It makes me think about how I once looked up to Palli, and that he was not my only brother.

"You are different," Svenni says, moving closer to me.

I smile at him, glad to be in his company. "Different from what? Do you even remember me?"

"Yes. I remember you. You were always in a hurry. That's how I remember you. You seem different. You are calm. Peaceful."

He studies me for a moment. We both have our father's eyes.

"You seem to be settled in yourself and your surroundings." He remembers me as a storming youth in our father's house.

"What do you mean by peaceful?" I ask him after a moment's contemplation.

"I don't know." He rearranges the cap on his head and scratches his ear.

"Well, what if we break it down a bit. What is peace?"

"I don't know. Not war? The absence of disturbance? The absence of evil doings?" He looks rather confused and slightly intimidated. His long black hair underneath the cap lies on his black t-shirt. He's wearing all black apart from white stripes on his sneakers. He probably didn't expect this question. After a few seconds during which I am quiet and he stares into the sky, he continues trying to articulate his thoughts.

"Like this building." He points at the parliament. "Do you think these people advocate peace? Do you think the United Nations advocate peace? Do you think the USA advocates peace?"

I say nothing, let his thoughts run their course.

"They do advocate peace," he carries on. "But with evil things added in. How can any of us talk about peace and yet go into war? How can we talk about peace while we exterminate nature? It's not a good peace. What do you think?"

I gaze at him, for the first time feeling like an older brother. *And I have another young brother, and a sister, too.* I think of myself at Svenni's age doing everything with Palli, imitating him until I was running around changing Krónur into Euros for him, popping pills and snorting coke alongside my big brother.

"I don't know. I was once told that I have to understand how little I understand. Understand my own ignorance before I claim others to be ignorant," I say.

"The people in that government building claim that they are the wise." Svenni is warming up to his theme now. "Wise enough to advocate peace. It's a manipulation of peace. They are not peaceful people. How can someone who is not peaceful, teach peacefulness and tell others to be peaceful?"

All those questions I once asked Max, just in a different form.

He reminds me of myself when I was becoming aware and not knowing how deep the rabbit hole goes.

"So, what do you think a wise man would do in the parliament?"

"I don't know. But what I do know, is that Buddha or Jesus would throw these guys out in a second and send them back to school to learn ethics for beginners." He makes a 'tsk' sound with his tongue and shakes his head.

"Svenni, do you notice any violence in you right now?"

"I don't know. Maybe."

"Do you think that it has something to do with Dad? And that he's a congressman?"

"Maybe ..." I sense he is closing off to this topic. *His father's son. My father, too.*

"You are also different," I say, chuckling. I notice that he is looking over his shoulder to check if anyone has heard our conversation.

A bunch of men and women in suits hurry past the statue and one pauses to point something out, causing the others to slow their steps slightly. I can't make out what they're looking at; something beyond the statue, an upper window on the corrugated roof of one of the buildings surrounding the square.

Maybe it's just a pigeon. A shopper trips and drops a bulging carrier bag, a young woman in a flowing hippy dress, but she doesn't really look like a hippy. A young guy stops to help her cram her purchases back inside the plastic bag. A brief memory of Marissa, so long ago, flashes across my brain. I focus my attention back on my brother.

"Take a look at all these people, Böddi," Svenni says. "They are running around in circles embracing material things. They are not thinking about peace."

I take a short breath, realizing that the boy is waiting for me to talk.

"I think you are right. Most of the world's peacemakers have been outsiders, condemned by society. Peacemakers must think of purity of heart and mind. But ask yourself, Svenni, are you a peacemaker?"

He ducks his head and stares at an insect crawling between the blades of grass. I am refreshingly detached from wanting Svenni to agree with me for the sake of it. I'm happy that we are spending time together and reconnecting. It's a good day to be sitting in sunshine on the grass, watching Reykjavík enjoying its brief summer.

"I'm an ignorant being," I say at last. "I don't see things as they are. I'm blind like the rest of the people around me."

Svenni looks up. "Then the whole world is in darkness, is there a way out of darkness?"

He seems more hunched over than before, bowed by the concerns our talk has awakened in him.

"Yes, I think so."

"You know any?" He raises a hopeful eyebrow.

"No, it's built on faith. I was lucky to be abroad when I stumbled upon my teacher. I love and respect him, though he eventually turned out to be a flawed human being. But there was a great lesson I learned from staying with him. He sparked a fire in me to seek the truth, he directed me onto a path. There's no such thing as a wrong teacher; if you think like that, you'll never find a teacher because you'll never trust anyone."

"What books should I read?"

"Our society teaches us that knowledge is found in books. But, Svenni, the longer you spend on your journey, the more you will find out that we grow through experiences. We grow through trying out different costumes, whether that's shaving our head and singing Hare Krishna songs, going to Mecca on a pilgrimage, or living a simple life in a monastery in Thailand. Look for people with a spark in their eyes and learn from them." I think about the first time I met Max, in the post office in Laos, and feel a smile spreading across my face.

"Talking about eyes." Svenni looks directly into mine. "Have you noticed that even here in Iceland, most people don't look you in the eyes when they talk to you, even the people who are closest to you? There's so much fear going on. Sad, isn't it?"

"Yes." I feel a growing fondness for my brother. "Iceland is like an inversion of the world. It's a wealthy country but spiritually poor. People walk around with their walls around them. There's no less pain and suffering in Iceland than in any developing country, believe me."

"Was it poor in Asia, I mean material poor?"

"Yes."

So far, Svenni has not been away on his travels and he's asked me many questions about mine.

"Have you been poor? Maybe a stupid question," he says, looking awkwardly at me from the corner of his eye.

"There are no stupid questions, Svenni, only stupid answers. I've been poor before. I've lived with no possessions but that's not necessarily poor. I've spent time with men who have nothing at all and I know that they walk and feel like kings of this earth."

"I guess I'm as ignorant as the people in the parliament." Svenni does that funny movement of his eyebrow again.

"That's the start of every man's journey, to realise his own ignorance. You are maybe even one step ahead of those guys."

"Have you found yourself?"

"How can I find something that doesn't exist, ultimately?"

Svenni picks at the grass, seeming confused again. Maybe I said too much. I need to be mindful of my speech and I must guard my ego. The teachers that have affected me the most throughout my journey are not those who merely talk, but those who live according to their teachings.

I ruffle my brother's hair and he pulls away from me, laughing. We'll have lots of time together. Talking is easy, living on the path is the part that is hard.

Kafli 31 - Iceland.

The Face

I AM STANDING in the stairway of an apartment block in Árbær, Reykjavík. The door I am looking for is on the fourth floor. I take the last few steps up onto the landing and see it straight away. The name Bjarni Óskarsson is written on a plate next to the door.

Bjarni Óskarsson. Seeing the name stirs up powerful emotions, but in a far-away sense. Still, as I stand here it wells up in my chest. The process of purifying is clearly not yet finished. I swallow hard, and blink back the tears which are no good to anyone. Especially not that twelve-year-old boy I once was.

Now. It's time to face him now. I knock on the door, two sharp raps.

"Hello." It's a rough, whiskey-ruined voice coming from behind the thick wood. Shuffling footsteps approaching.

"Hi," I say when the door is pulled open, creaking on its hinge.

Old man. A dirty-looking man of around sixty, standing in front of me. I'm taller than him and he needs to look up to see me properly. He glares suspiciously.

"What do you want?"

"I want to talk to you."

He is wearing light brown pants pulled up high on his overweight belly. He has on a grubby blue shirt, which is open at the neck and rolled up at the sleeves, showing off fading tattoos on his upper chest and arms, where the skin sags. His eyes express sadness, a whole life of misery. The smell of alcohol escapes into the stairway.

"What do you want?" he asks again.

I repeat, "I want to talk to you." Peering into those half-dead eyes.

"Are you one of these guys coming to sell me God? If that's so, I have nothing to talk to you about." The old man starts to close the door on me.

"No," I say softly. "I'm not going to sell you God. God has been sold out for quite a while now." I take a closer look at him. "Why is your finger bleeding?"

He ignores my question. "So, you are saying God is dead?"

"No. I just said God is sold out." I manage to smile. I don't know how we got into this conversation at the door. "Why are you bleeding?"

"I cut myself earlier, opening a can of beans." There's a moment of silence while he screws up his eyes, inspecting me.

"Can I come in?" Best to be blunt.

"You'd better explain why you are here then." He pulls the door fully open again.

The apartment is small, messy and sad. Beer bottles, dead plants and dusty furniture.

"Wanna beer?" the old man asks, shuffling across the room to a kitchen.

"No thanks." I feel unexpectedly calm and at ease. Light, almost as if I'm floating.

He comes back into the living room holding a beer and a cigarette in the same hand, moving towards a record player. I watch while he takes up a vinyl in his left hand, delicately, like he is holding a baby, like he is holding something that is dear to him. He puts the record on and lifts the arm, lowering the needle carefully. Then he lights up his cigarette and smiles, a crack in his weather-beaten old face.

"You like them?"

"Pink Floyd? Yeah they are good." My own mouth returns his smile while he positions himself opposite me in a tattered wooden armchair.

The intro to Wish You Were Here is playing and I stand up and move into the kitchen. What is this strange connection between us? There is no fear even though he's a total stranger to me as well as my most intimate nightmare. In the kitchen I rifle through objects on the work surface until I unearth kitchen tissues and a vodka bottle. I walk back into the living room, towards Bjarni. He's away with the music.

"Give me your hand." I pour vodka onto a sheet of tissue.

He lifts his left hand lethargically. I kneel beside him and start cleaning the wound. He is silent, surprised that a young man is in his apartment cleaning the blood from his hand. I untie one of my shoelaces and withdraw it from my shoe, use it to tie the homemade bandage around his hand. He gapes at me and I smell his breath, rank with alcohol and poor diet.

"Why are you doing this? Why are you here?"

I spend a moment gazing at him, the face that has haunted me for decades. This is the face I blamed for all my problems. This is the face that caused every ounce of pain I suffered. I take a deep breath, determined not to turn away.

"I'm here to serve you. I'm here because I love you."

He isn't sure how to react. It has probably been a long time since he heard these words.

"Love me? Are you one of those gays? Why do you love me?" The old man takes a nervous sip of his beer, dribbling down his chin and into the grubby folds of his neck.

"Because I don't judge you." I sit back on my heels while he takes more gulps of his beer, breathing noisily between. He stares at me warily while I go on. "I'm choosing love. Love is there and I'm going after it."

As I continue to watch 'the face', his eyes become wet, his lips tremble and his breathing pattern changes. I look into his eyes and at that moment I see God for the first time. God is inside this old man, clouded by the impurities of his mind. We are a part of the same thing, we've travelled together, this old man and me, but we have travelled different paths.

He remains silent for a few more moments, then begins weeping like a small child. I am grateful, for him being there and giving me opportunity to serve. I have the opportunity to purify my mind and for that I am full of thanks. I don't need anything from the face, not applause, not appreciation. I need to help this poor old man who has failed his whole life to realise his own ignorance.

"You are one of those God people aren't you?" he finally gets out, wiping his eyes. "Speaking in riddles and puzzles to sell me the idea to find myself through religion."

"How can you find yourself if you don't exist?" I ask, tidying the cleaning stuff away.

"I don't exist?"

"Ultimately, no."

"I'll tell you this, son. I hate religion. I got treated badly in my childhood through people claiming they know God, and I've avoided them ever since. They beat me and did things to me that I've never talked about and I won't talk about, now or ever. I hate religion and also God." He raises his querulous voice on the last words.

"You said you liked Pink Floyd, right? What does that mean to you?"

"What the hell has that got to do with it?"

"Just answer my question."

"Well," he thinks for a minute, his eyes screwed up. "I like their music."

"And?"

"I like the era they represent, not this new pop music crap you see on TV. Today's music culture is rubbish. The old seventies music, that's the real thing."

"Well, culture and religion are the same, you know?"

"That's crazy talk. It's not the same, religion is rubbish and culture is culture."

"You just said the music culture today was rubbish too," I say, smiling. I get up from my knees, glancing around the apartment before meeting his eyes again.

"And?"

"What makes me Icelandic? I go to Kringlan shopping mall, I celebrate the seventeenth of June for Independence Day, I eat fish with boiled potatoes; I know the Sagas and so on. What makes us Christians? We go to church on Christmas, we celebrate Christmas; we give our kids birth ceremonies and confirmation and send them to Sunday school and so on. Culture and religion is the same, it's all how we identify ourselves with ideas. I am Icelandic. I am Christian. I am this and I am that. It's all man-made ideas. God has nothing to do with it. Can you see that?" I search for a bin in which to drop the tissues and find an overflowing carrier bag hooked on the door-handle.

"This is crazy talk. Let me get another beer while I think of an answer." He stands up from his chair, pushing past me into the kitchen.

I observe this old man, how fuming with anger he seems and how ready to get into a debate with me. It isn't my purpose to change him and I'm not here to impose my views. I'm here to serve. I feel sympathy for him. He has never had the opportunity to come across the teachings as I have. He shuffles back into the living room and lowers himself into the chair again.

"Men kill in the name of religion!" He is clearly still in a debate mood, and not a friendly one.

"Also, in the name of culture." I add my part, sensing it is time to stop because he's becoming frustrated. "It's time for me to leave," I say. "I'm very happy that we got the chance to meet and exchange our views, you've taught me a lot in my life and I want to thank you for that."

"Taught you a lot?"

I don't answer. Instead I head towards the door. He remains in the living room, just an angry and confused old man.

About the Author

DAVÍÐ KRISTJÁNSSON was born in 1982 in a small town called Akureyri in the north of Iceland. He grew up in Reykjavík, the capital city. In his early twenties Davíd became intrigued with the Buddhist understanding of human nature, including traditional Yoga and Eastern Philosophy.

He studied law at Akureyri University and continued his studies in China. Just as the financial crisis hit Iceland in 2007, Davíd went to the USA to live with his first spiritual teacher, whom he had met in a bookshop in Iceland.

He then lived in Beijing where he was involved in a community of spiritual and creative people. At this time he started writing his novel, Burning Karma. He continued to move to different places and add to his study of spiritual matters, spending time in Cambodia and then in an Ashram in India.

Davíd believes that knowledge comes from experience. Burning Karma is inspired by many people he met on his travels and his own experiences with spiritual growth. His gratitude towards the people in his life and their inspiration has pushed him to write this book, in hopes of inspiring others.

Davíd lives in Reykjavík with his girlfriend. He is currently attending film school in Berlin. '

Lightning Source UK Ltd.
Milton Keynes UK
UKOW04f1338110316

270034UK00002B/14/P